Billy Pinto's War

AMERICAN LEGENDS COLLECTION,
BOOK 6

Billy Pinto's War

Michael Zimmer

FIVE STAR
A part of Gale, Cengage Learning

Farmington Hills, Mich • San Francisco • New York • Waterville, Maine
Meriden, Conn • Mason, Ohio • Chicago

Five Star™ Publishing, a part of Cengage Learning, Inc.

LIBRARY OF CONGRESS CATALOGING-IN-PUBLICATION DATA

Names: Zimmer, Michael, 1955– author.
Title: Billy Pintos war / Michael Zimmer.
Description: First edition. | Waterville, Maine : Five Star Publishing, [2017] | Series: American Legends Collection ; book 6
Identifiers: LCCN 2016041929| ISBN 9781432832285 (hardcover) | ISBN 143283228X (hardcover)
Subjects: LCSH: Indians—Mixed descent—Fiction. | Shoshoni Indians—Fiction. | Kidnapping—Fiction. | Revenge—Fiction. | BISAC: FICTION / Historical. | FICTION / Westerns. | GSAFD: Western stories.
Classification: LCC PS3576.I467 B55 2017 | DDC 813/.54—dc23
LC record available at https://lccn.loc.gov/2016041929

First Edition. First Printing: April 2017
Find us on Facebook– https://www.facebook.com/FiveStarCengage
Visit our website– http://www.gale.cengage.com/fivestar/
Contact Five Star™ Publishing at FiveStar@cengage.com

Printed in the United States of America
1 2 3 4 5 6 7 21 20 19 18 17

FOREWORD: THE AMERICAN LEGENDS COLLECTIONS

During the Great Depression of the 1930s, nearly one quarter of the American workforce was unemployed. Facing the possibility of economic and government collapse, President Franklin Roosevelt initiated the New Deal program, a desperate bid to get the country back on its feet.

The largest of these programs was the Works Progress Administration (WPA), which focused primarily on manual labor with the construction of bridges, highways, schools, and parks across the country. But the WPA also included a provision for the nation's unemployed artists, called the Federal Arts Project, and within its umbrella, the Federal Writers Project (FWP). At its peak, the FWP put to work approximately 6,500 men and women.

During the FWP's earliest years, the focus was on a series of state guidebooks, but in the late 1930s, the project created what has been called a "hidden legacy" of America's past—more than 10,000 life stories gleaned from men and women across the nation.

Although these life histories, a part of the Folklore Project within the FWP, were meant to eventually be published in a series of anthologies, that goal was effectively halted by the United States' entry into World War II. Most of these histories are currently located within the Library of Congress in Washington, DC.

As the Federal Writers Project was an arm of the larger Arts Project, so too was the Folklore Project a subsidiary of the FWP. An even lesser-known branch of the Folklore Project was the American Legends Collection (ALC), created in 1936, and managed from 1936 to 1941 by a small staff from the University of Indiana. The ALC was officially closed in early 1942, another casualty of the war effort.

While the Folklore Project's goal was to capture everyday life in America, the ALC's purpose was the acquisition of as many "incidental" histories from our nation's past as possible. Unfortunately, the bulk of the American Legends Collection was lost due to manpower shortages caused by the war.

The only remaining interviews known to exist from the ALC are those located within the A. C. Thorpe Papers at the Bryerton Library in Indiana. These are carbons only, as the original transcripts were turned in to the offices of the FWP in November 1941.

Andrew Charles Thorpe was unique among those scribes put into employment by the FWP-ALC in that he recorded his interviews with an Edison Dictaphone. These discs, a precursor to the LP records of a later generation, were found sealed in a vault shortly after Thorpe's death in 2006. Of the eighty-some interviews discovered therein, most were conducted between the years 1936 and 1939. They offer an unparalleled view of both a time (1864 to 1916) and place (Florida to Nevada, Montana to Texas) within the United States' singular history.

The editor of this volume is grateful to the current executor of the A. C. Thorpe Estate for his assistance in reviewing these papers, and to the descendants of Mr. Thorpe for their cooperation in allowing these transcripts to be brought into public view.

An explanation should be made at this point that, although minor additions to the text were made to enhance its readability, no facts were altered. Any mistakes or misrepresentations resulting from these changes are solely the responsibility of the editor.

Leon Michaels
August 25, 2015

Session One
Hudson Pratt Interview
Stockton, California
26 January 1936
Begin Transcript

I've been thinking about our conversation in the car last night after I picked you up at the train station. You called this incident we're going to talk about the Billy Pinto War, and I told you it wasn't.

It seems like ever since that autumn of nineteen aught-four, when all hell broke loose across Wyoming's San Pedro Plateau, I've been telling people that what happened up there wasn't a war. It was just a sixteen-year-old kid who'd been kicked once too often, and finally started kicking back. But after I left you at the hotel, I got to thinking about all the people who were killed, all the lives changed forever by the Pinto affair, and I began to wonder if maybe I'm not the one who's been wrong all this time. Maybe it was a war. I'll say this, though. If it was, it was as lopsided as hell. A Shoshone half-breed who probably didn't weigh more than a hundred and forty pounds soaking wet against what, for a while there, seemed like half of San Pete County.

In my opinion, the deck was stacked against that boy from the beginning, but I don't guess you came all the way to California to record opinions. You want to hear my side of the story, and it looks like you're planning to record it, too. That's all right by me. I reckon you can make up your own mind afterward about whether or not it was an honest-to-God Indian uprising.

This all took place back in September of 1904, when I was

coming to the end of my first full term as the sheriff of San Pedro County, what everyone in those days called San Pete, until the state redrew the lines and the whole damned county up and vanished to suit some politician's fancy. With statewide elections a little over a month away, I've always speculated that politics had a lot more to do with the way the Pinto affair—hell, let's call it a war—was handled in the press than most people realize. For men either seeking office or trying to hang onto the one they had, the prospect of a fresh Indian uprising was a handy stump to climb onto.

As I recall, I was sitting at my desk filling out paperwork on delinquent tax returns on the night all this got started. Tom Schiffer was my deputy at the time. He was a good man, but he had an irritating way of standing in open doors to smoke his cigarettes. That wasn't a problem during the summer months, but it always annoyed me when the outside temperatures started to fall. September had been mild that year, but it cooled off quickly when the sun went down, and I can remember glancing up from time to time that evening and having to nearly bite my tongue to keep from telling him to shut the damned door. You could tell he was as chilled as I was, leaning against the jamb with the light in the street behind him softening toward dusk; he had his free hand thrust deep into the front pocket of his trousers, and his shoulders were hunched. I kept my mouth shut, though. I'd be going home soon, letting Tom take over until the saloons closed around midnight, it being just Wednesday, and pretty quiet compared to most weekends.

Truth be told, I was feeling tired and more than a little cross-eyed from all the filing I'd done that day. I was looking forward to going home, where I knew Angie had a big pot of ham hocks and great northern beans simmering on the stove, and more than likely a pan of cornbread sitting in the warmer to go with it. I'd had a hearty breakfast at sunup, but only a thin slice of huckleberry pie and a cup of coffee for lunch, and my mouth would start to slaver like a drippy spigot every time I thought about the meal Angie had waiting for me.

I was working hard to finish up before full dark when it was as if something in the air all of a sudden changed. I looked up with a puzzled frown. Tom was still at the door, but he'd straightened and taken his hand out of his pocket, and was looking off to the west with uncommon intensity. His words are still carved into my brain.

"Here's trouble, Hud."

I sat back and put down my pen. "What kind of trouble?"

He didn't immediately reply, but kept staring down the street until I finally shoved away from my desk. Flicking his half-smoked cigarette into the street, he said, "Riders coming."

Now, that in itself didn't mean a whole lot. San Pete County was way up high, probably averaging seven thousand feet or more in elevation, but our good grass hadn't escaped the notice of those Platte River ranchers to the north. A lot of them would trail their herds up here during the summer, and a few, like old Judge Henry Lynn—Judge Lynch, we called him, and you'll find out why soon enough—ran cattle on his Broken Cinch ranch the year round, although he had to feed hay through the winter months to keep his stock kicking. But this was still September. The passes were clear and the graze was as tawny and rich as rolled oats. Horsemen coming into town of an early autumn evening, even in the middle of the week, wasn't any kind of a novelty, so maybe that was why I was having trouble making sense of my suddenly twitchy scalp.

"How many?" I asked.

"Looks like five or six of 'em, although they're still out a ways."

I came around the desk and over to the door, and we both stepped onto the boardwalk for a better view. The horsemen were approaching at an easy jog, the dust from their mounts filtering the hazy evening light in a way I've seen artists try to capture, but seldom accomplish. As they drew near I could see there were indeed five of them, and a sense of something ominous approaching the community—*my community*—struck me like a hard jab in the gut.

They'd come a ways, judging from their looks, but appeared to be well-equipped for the journey; bulky bedrolls and swollen saddlebags added heft to their silhouettes, and even from a quarter of a mile away, you could tell they were a rough lot, dressed in old-fashioned wide-brimmed hats and heavy coats of wool and fur. Rifles jutted from scabbards, and when they got closer I could make out heavy cartridge belts and holstered revolvers strapped around their waists. Then Tom grunted sharp-like, as if he'd also been belly poked.

"Hell, ain't that Early Jennings on that blue roan?" he said.

"I believe it is," I replied, then walked back to my desk to begin riffling through the wooden in-box that sat overflowing on the corner. I'd been out of town more than I'd been in the last couple of weeks, either collecting overdue taxes or delivering delinquent notices to homesteaders and some of the outlying ranchers, and I'd been lax about keeping up with my administration duties. Sure enough, about halfway through the stack I came across a telegram from the prison in Rawlins, informing me that Early Jennings was being released on the fifteenth, after having served just four and a half years of a ten-year sentence for murder. I swore softly at whatever authority was behind this mockery of justice, then unfairly took out some of my frustration on Tom.

"Damnit, you should've caught this," I said after telling him what I'd found.

"How?" he replied with a look like he'd been snapped at by a dog he'd thought of as friendly.

"By keeping an eye on what comes in. You're in charge when I'm not here."

"The hell I am. The only authority I've got is to throw some drunk in the puke tank until he's dried out. Anything else, and I'm told to leave it be until you get back."

I kind of bit my lower lip at that, since he had a point. I kept telling him that when I was out making my rounds through the county that he should just keep a lid on things until I got back. Every once in a while, my words will come back and bite me on the ass. They sure did that night.

I went back outside and stood there watching as Jennings and his boys trotted their horses into Echo City. There wouldn't have been much I could've done even if I had seen the Rawlins telegram beforehand. Early Jennings's release appeared official, and he had as much right to be there as anyone. I'll admit it was making me edgy, though. I'd been both the arresting officer and a key witness at his trial, and he hadn't taken my involvement kindly. I was wondering how far into town he intended to come, and was considering going back inside to fetch a shotgun, when the whole outfit swung in at the rails in front of the Yellowstone Saloon and dismounted.

"You recognize any of the others?" Tom asked as Jennings's crew looped reins to rails.

"I can't say that I do, although I'd wager they're cut from the same hide as Jennings."

Stopping on the boardwalk in front of the saloon, Jennings jutted his chin toward Tom and me, then spoke to the others. There was a general response from his men that I could see but not hear, and a couple of them spat on the walk. Then they all tramped inside, letting the saloon's batwing doors swing back and forth behind them. There was a law in Echo City against spitting in public, but neither Tom nor I mentioned it. We let a silence grow between us for a few minutes, then Tom asked if I wanted him to go down to the Yellowstone and keep an eye on things.

"I don't suppose that'd hurt," I said. "Don't crowd 'em or give 'em cause to start trouble. If we're lucky, they might ride on after a couple of drinks."

Tom gave me a funny look, and I knew what he was thinking.

"It's worth keeping our fingers crossed for," I told him.

"What are you going to do?"

I thought briefly about the delinquent tax forms that still needed to be completed, but already knew that was a chore that was going to have to be put aside for a while. "I think I'll talk to Red Gifford, ask him to look in on Molly Spotted Horse," I replied.

Molly, in case you ain't aware of it, was Billy Pinto's ma. I guess that should have made Billy's last name Spotted Horse, as well, although for as long as I'd known him, he'd always been called Billy Pinto.

What you might not know about Molly is that for a while, she'd been married to Early Jennings. At least in the fashion of the country at that time. It wasn't anything registered in a courthouse or presided over by judge or clergy, but it was known throughout San Pete County and accepted as binding, if not proper or one-hundred-percent legal. A lot of folks over the years have said that Early was Billy's pa, but others, and Red Gifford was one of them, claimed he wasn't. Red said Billy's pa was a Wind River fur trader named Williams, which was how Billy got his name. I couldn't say how accurate that is, but I reckon Red knew Molly and Billy better than anyone else in Echo City, and I've always sided toward his version of the boy's ancestry.

After Tom left, I went back inside long enough to grab my hat and coat and to turn off the electric light above my desk, although I left the gas lamps along the walls burning. Most nights we'd have a prisoner or two in the cells at the rear of the building, but I remember the jail was empty that night, and in my mind I can still hear the sound of my heels on the hardwood floor as I returned to the front door and let myself out.

The Yellowstone sat on the west side of town. I went east along Front Street as far as Fourth Avenue, then south toward Gifford's hardware store. Maybe before we get too far along, I ought to tell you a little about the layout of the town and its history. It might help later on.

There's not much left of Echo City today. The town faded real quick after United Lumber went bankrupt in '17. The larger brick buildings were torn down and hauled away after the county was dissolved, and the wooden structures that weren't moved or salvaged for lumber were in sad shape the last time I went through there. That was by train, and it didn't even stop, since the depot was long gone.

Winters can be brutal that close to the Continental Divide. By January the snow is measured in feet rather than inches, and if buildings aren't heavily reinforced, or if the snow isn't removed regularly, it ain't long before roofs start to sag or collapse. After that, it's only a matter of time before the rest of the structure comes down. But when I was the sheriff of San Pete County, Echo City was a thriving little burg. The main business district ran along Front Street, just south of and parallel to the Union Pacific railroad tracks. Fourth Avenue teed with Front Street, then ran south in an almost straight line toward Nathan Mosby and Ted Clark's United Lumber Company, way off at the foot of the San Pedro Plateau. There were other streets, of course. Grant and McKinley were aligned with Front Street, running east and west—my own house sat near the sunset end of McKinley—and First through Ninth avenues flanked Fourth, going north and south, but it was Front and Fourth that encompassed probably ninety percent of Echo City's businesses.

The county courthouse sat on the southeast corner of Front and Fourth, with Phillip Bailey's State Bank on the southwest corner; the jail was right next door to that. In fact, the jail and the bank shared a solid brick wall, the opinion at the time being that it might make thieves think twice before attempting to break into the bank with the sheriff's office so close by.

There was a lot more to the town than that, of course, but nothing really pertinent to the Billy Pinto story. Well, maybe Spill Street, but I'll get to that later on. I should probably also add that there weren't any businesses north of the tracks, and very few homes. There were some pens east of town—downwind—with chutes for loading cattle and sheep into boxcars to be shipped to Eastern slaughterhouses, but most of that land north of the tracks was covered with lumber from Mosby and Clark. They probably had twenty acres covered with peeled logs, slab wood, railroad crossties, and plank lumber, all of it harvested from those canyons that fingered down off the Plateau like ragged claw marks. In fact, if it weren't for Mosby and Clark and their logging operations, I doubt if Echo City would have ever amounted to more than a whistle-stop along the U.P., and San Pete County probably never would have existed at all. But it did. The pines that covered the San Pedro Plateau's flanks and its various gorges grew tall and straight, and were relatively easy to get to if you didn't count that long haul between the mill and the railroad.

Angie and I moved to Echo City in '99, when I was offered the deputy sheriff's position under my old commander from the war. [*Editor's Note:* Pratt is referring here to Captain James V. Nelson, and the Spanish-American War in Cuba; Pratt was a sergeant under Nelson in the First United States Volunteer Cavalry, later known as the Rough Riders, and was a participant in the battles of Las Guasimas and San Juan. James Nelson was elected sheriff of San Pedro County in 1896, took a leave of absence to serve in the military during the war in 1898, then returned to Echo City in January of 1899. He died on June 5, 1900, of complications of yellow fever, contracted during his service in Cuba. Pratt was appointed temporary sheriff of the county in his stead; his position was formalized in the county election in November of that same year.]

Although the sun was down, it was still light when I walked into Gifford's store. Red was standing behind the counter talking with Frank Brady, so I busied myself poking around. Although Gifford sold a variety of goods, his emphasis was on tools and the merchandise needed to make them work—nails for hammers, bits for drills, punches and copper rivets and steel rods. I was examining a selection of ax handles when Brady left with a brown paper bag tucked under one arm. Red shoved the cash drawer home with a hearty ring and came over.

"Needing a new handle, Sheriff?"

"No, just a few minutes of your time." I slid the handle back into its display box. "I wanted to talk to you about Molly Spotted Horse. Is Billy around?"

"Not today. He went up on the Plateau to do some hunting with Jess Harding. He should be back by tomorrow or the next day, though. He knows I've got some supplies going out to United Lumber that I want him to deliver." Red's brows wiggled with concern. "Is Billy in trouble, Hud?"

"No, I just wondered where he was. It's Molly I'm worried about."

"Now, I *know* Molly isn't in trouble. There's not a kinder, more easygoing woman around, your Angie and my Elizabeth notwithstanding."

"Red, Early Jennings just rode into town. He's—"

"Jennings!" Red's face . . . well, it reddened noticeably. "I don't know what kind of hold that man has over Molly, but they aren't married, and I know for a fact she doesn't want anything to do with him."

"I don't doubt that, but Early's back, and Molly needs to know about it."

"And you want me to tell her?"

"I don't know her as well as you do."

"No, you don't, do you?" His expression had turned as stiff as one of Nathan Mosby's pine planks. "No one does. She's only that Indian woman who cleans houses and takes in laundry."

That struck me wrong, and I said, "Damnit, Red, there's a lot of people around San Pete County that I don't know. It ain't nothing personal against her or her boy."

"Billy."

"Don't try to rake me with your spurs, I won't stand for it. We both know Molly'll listen to you better than she would me. She'll take your advice, and not be worried you're fishing around for something else."

Red sighed and shook his head. "All right, fair enough. But it sticks in my craw the way people treat her sometimes."

"Some people."

"*Most* people." His gaze slipped out the window to where Frank Brady was stowing his purchases under the seat of a dilapidated buggy, and his lips thinned in scorn. "I'll talk to her. What do you want me to say?"

"Tell her that Early's back, and that she ought to stay out of town until he leaves."

"What if he doesn't leave?"

"He'll leave. The way folks around here feel about him, he'll have to."

"And that seems fair to you, that an honest woman and her son should have to hide because a convicted killer has decided to come to town? How did he get out, anyway? I thought he was supposed to be in Rawlins for several more years."

"It was an early release, that's all I know. I can write to the warden and ask, if you're really interested."

"What I'd rather know is why aren't you running him out of town tonight?"

"He hasn't done anything to give me cause."

"But you want Molly to stay out of sight?"

"Molly can do what she wants," I replied, my aggravation growing. "I'm just making the suggestion for her own safety. Talk to her, make sure she understands what's going on, and that I think she'd be wise to stay out of town until Jennings and his boys are gone."

"His boys!" Red's head reared back in surprise. "How many men does he have with him?"

"I counted five, including Early. I'm guessing they're in town for the night, and there's nothing I can do about it. If we're lucky, they'll move on in the morning."

Red glanced over my shoulder to the street, where Frank Brady was climbing into his rig. We both watched as he backed the buggy away from the rail, then shook his lines along the mare's back and took off for home. I couldn't tell you what Red was thinking, but I had a pretty good idea. Frank's wife had been abducted by a Cheyenne war party way back in '72, and he'd never gotten over it. His feelings toward all Indians was well-known in Echo City, and that included Molly Spotted Horse and her son. Red would tell me some years later that he thought the only reason Frank came into his store so often was in hope of spying Billy in one of its aisles, where he could give the boy a shove or a curse, depending on how far away Red was at the time.

"It's not fair, Hud," Red said quietly, and I didn't have an answer for him that wouldn't have sounded as shallow as a puddle of rain water.

"Talk to Molly, will you?"

"Sure, as soon as I close up." He glanced at the clock on the wall, just a few minutes shy of six o'clock. "Soon."

I nodded my thanks and left. The light had faded noticeably in the twenty or so minutes that I'd been inside. Although I gave some thought to returning to the jail, of maybe even going down to the Yellowstone to see for myself what was going on, I opted to head for home instead. A lot of people have criticized me for not facing down Jennings and his crew as soon as they rode into town, but I believed at the time, and still do, that in the end it wouldn't have made a damned bit of difference. Events none of us could have foreseen had been set into motion the minute the Jennings gang rode into town, and trying to second-guess anyone's decisions now is a waste of time.

It was four blocks from the hardware store to my little six-room house on McKinley Street. Angie already had lamps burning in the kitchen and parlor, and from the outside it gave the place a sense of warm welcome. I stomped my boots on the porch before entering, as much to let Angie know I was there as to shake loose whatever dust I'd collected on my walk home. Being a sheriff's wife ain't easy, and stamping my feet before entering was my way of letting her know it was me at the door, and not bad news. That would have been especially true that night if she'd heard about Early Jennings's return, but I could tell as soon as I walked in that she hadn't.

She was standing at the stove with her back to the door, a wooden spoon in one hand and the lid to the old night-blue graniteware pot in the other. Her hair is gray now, but it was as dark as pitch back then, worn high off her neck most of the time, as was the fashion in those years. She's still slim and willowy, though, and she's still got that sparkle in her deep green eyes when she sees me coming that gladdens my heart even today.

Smiling, she tapped her spoon against the pot's lip before

setting it aside and replacing the lid over the simmering beans and ham hocks, cutting off the view but doing nothing to rope in the aroma. I took off my coat and hat and hung them on the metal rack screwed into the wall, then unbuckled my gun belt and set that on top of the hutch, out of reach of the kids. Angie met me halfway across the kitchen with a hug and a quick kiss. Then she stepped back and her smile faded.

"What's wrong?" she asked.

"Nothing's wrong. Where are the cubs?"

"They're in the other room." She continued searching my face. "What is it, Hud? What happened?"

No matter how hard I tried, I never could keep anything from her. Rubbing my hand over the small mound of her stomach, I said, "Two of them are in the other room."

She placed both of her hands over mine. "I think it's going to be a boy. It kicks like a boy."

"I'll have a talk with him about that," I said. "He needs to respect his mama." Then I stepped around her and went to the stove. "That smells awfully good, and I'm about half starved."

"The children have already eaten. Sit down and I'll fix you a plate."

"In a second." I went into the other room where Lily was sitting on the floor, engrossed in conversation with Missus Bee Jax about behaving herself when company came over later that evening; the porcelain-faced doll with the wide blue eyes and shock of yellow hair painted across its forehead stared back intently from beneath its bonnet. Lily was four that year. Missus Bee Jax was a little younger, being a gift from Angie's parents shortly after Lily's birth. And no, I don't have a clue from which distant corner of Lily's mind the name Missus Bee Jax—spelled B-E-E, then J-A-X, once Lily learned how to spell—came from, but I'll tell you this. That doll was as much a part of our family in those early years as any of the neighborhood kids, cats, or dogs that came and went through our household.

Cory was sitting in the big chair next to the table lamp with his shoes off, his stockinged feet tucked under him. He had the cleaning kit we'd given him for Christmas laid out beside him, and was oiling his little .22 single-shot Winchester with all the intensity of a buffalo hunter swabbing out the bore of his Big Fifty. Cory was eight that year, and if he wasn't in school or doing chores either for his ma or John Moon, who ran the livery down the street from us, he was out somewhere with that rifle of his, hunting rabbits for the pot when he could find them, or plinking empty tin cans and sagebrush trunks when the coneys were scarce.

I won't bore you with our conversation that night—Lily's day and Missus Bee Jax's plans for the evening, or Cory's hunting and how he wanted to borrow my rolling block to go after antelope when the weather turned a little cooler. Cory's desire to hunt bigger game was an ongoing argument between his mother and me. Angie felt he was too young to handle the Remington's hefty .45-70 cartridge, even after I'd subtly remind her that I'd shot my first elk with a .50-70 when only a few years older than Cory was then. In one form or another, I suppose it was an age-old tug-of-war between mothers and fathers, likely going back to the days when the sons of knights begged their pas for permission to slay dragons, while their mamas were all the time saying no, the boy is too young and dragons are too dangerous, he needs to wait until he's a bit older to face such challenges.

I went back into the kitchen where Angie had set out a plate brimming with ham and beans. There was a saucer beside it covered with a hefty slab of cornbread already cut open and thickly buttered. I licked my lips in anticipation as I took my seat. Angie placed a cup of coffee in front of me, then sank into the chair on the other side of the table with a cup of tea. I told her the meal looked good and dug in with gusto, but she wouldn't be put off any longer.

"What happened today, Hud?"

I sighed and gave it up. "It's nothing to fret over, but Early Jennings rode into town tonight."

"Early Jennings." She said it softly, in consideration of the kids in the next room, but didn't try to stop her hand from flying to her lips. "Hud, Early's dangerous, and he swore he'd come back."

"There's a lot of dangerous people out there, honey. You know that as well as anyone. And it makes sense that Early would come back. This is where he lived for years. The question is whether or not he'll stay, and I doubt if he will. After what he did, folks ain't likely to make him feel very welcome. Give him a day or two to strut around and brag how he's not afraid of anyone, and he'll probably fade off like a bad smell."

"What about Molly Spotted Horse?"

"I've already talked to Red Gifford about her. He'll tell her to stay low for a few days. I can't imagine Early caring much about her, anyway. There are gals around town who would be a lot more accommodating than Molly."

Angie didn't reply, but it was clear from her expression what she thought of my "gals around town" remark. Prostitution was a well-known secret in those days, when decent women were outnumbered by doves by a wide margin. The Yellowstone had a couple of jaded whores who hustled drinks and promised wondrous times under dirty sheets upstairs, and the Plateau Parlor House made no bones about the pleasures that could be purchased there. A couple of other saloons around Echo City played host to working girls, but women like my Angie never acknowledged such goings-on in public.

"You're probably right about Molly," she said, keeping her voice low, out of concern for Cory and Lily. "Early Jennings never saw her as anything other than a work mule, someone to take care of him and fix his meals while he was off stealing horses and raiding other people's orchards."

You don't think about that much, do you? About what thieves do when they ain't robbing banks or shooting up stagecoaches. Around San Pete County, it was pretty well accepted that Jennings occupied a large portion of his time in other peoples' pastures, for all that he'd never been caught with enough evidence to pursue criminal charges. What you probably hadn't guessed was that he'd also been spotted in such juvenile acts as raiding melon patches and stealing pies off of kitchen window-sills. I once caught him with his fingers knuckle-deep in a gooseberry pie Bea Johnston swore was hers, but which Early insisted he'd baked himself. He claimed Missus Johnston—Will Johnston's wife—was trying to blame him for her own failings in the kitchen, which everyone in town knew was utter nonsense. The thing is, without any kind of identification on the pie tin, there wasn't a damned thing I could do about it.

Early managed to stay one step ahead of the law for quite a few years, until one night when I caught him slipping out of Dan Palmer's downstairs window with blood on his shoes and Dan's wallet inside his shirt. When Dan didn't answer my knock, I went inside and found him lying dead on the floor in his nightshirt, the back of his head haloed in a pool of blood. Early claimed he'd gone inside only because he'd heard Dan hollering for help, and was only leaving through the rear window because he was afraid nobody would believe his tale of gallantry. Well, he pegged that one square. If it had been up to the town, Early Jennings would have been hung within the week, but Judge Lynn had to recuse himself on account of Dan being both his accountant and a poker buddy; the trial went to Cheyenne, where the prosecutor was afraid to press for a death sentence, since there were no witnesses to the actual crime, and because I couldn't say with certainty that Early's story didn't hold at least a smidgen of truth.

Beyond a shadow of a doubt was the state-appointed defense council's successful argument, which managed to send Early Jennings to Rawlins, instead of the gallows.

Even with that, we figured we were shed of the guy for a good long while. Ain't it funny how quickly time flies? Like a speeding bullet sometimes. Now here it was just a little over four years later and he was back in town, looking as big and mean as ever.

Session Two

Sorry about that. We've had that old dog for thirteen years now. Or maybe it'd be more correct to say he's had Angie and me. Either way, when a dog with a weak bladder tells you he needs to go outside, you open the door quick as you can.

Anyway, right before Humphrey started whining to go out, I was telling you about the night Early Jennings returned to Echo City. Despite the uneasiness my news brought to the supper table, Angie's meal was as good as ever. I cleaned my plate down to the white, then had a second piece of cornbread for dessert. Angie was taking the dishes to the dry sink to wash when the phone rang.

I bet I know what you're thinking, mentioning electric lights earlier and talking about telephones now, when you were probably expecting only cowboys and six-shooters. You've got to remember that this was 1904, though, and what folks in larger cities like Denver and Salt Lake City had been taking for granted for a decade or more was starting to creep into smaller towns all across the nation. San Pete County had electric lights for both its courthouse and the jail, not to mention a number of private businesses along Front Street that had tapped into the system—for a fee, of course.

It was Judge Lynn who'd pushed hardest for a coal-fired dynamo to be installed in the courthouse basement. [*Editor's Note:* Although no further information could be located regarding Echo City's early power sources, dynamo-electric machines capable of converting mechanical power into electricity have been around since the 1830s, and were used in major manufacturing at least as early as the 1870s.]

Judge Lynn was also behind Echo City's rudimentary telephone system. In 1904, the switchboard was located in the Union Pacific's telegraph office, at their depot alongside the tracks. From there, lines ran to various offices, stores, and even a few homes all over town, including to my place on McKinley. The longest telephone line—and I suspect the main reason Lynn wanted a local phone company to begin with—ran from Echo City all the way to the Judge's Broken Cinch ranch, ten miles south of town. The judge claimed he needed a telephone so that he could be, as he put it: *Called in at a moment's notice.* All on the taxpayer's dime, of course.

I'll be honest, I didn't want a phone in my house, and would just as soon not have one today, but the judge had insisted, and I have to admit it made sense, considering my office. Which was why the damned thing started ringing that night, when what I wanted most was an evening without interruption.

The telephone was still a new enough of a diversion that the kids ran into the kitchen as soon as it clanked out its three longs and a short. Angie flinched and the muscles in her face drew taut. I winked to take away some of her worry, but her expression didn't soften. Lily was hanging onto my trouser leg, jumping up and down like it was Christmas morning, as I lifted the earpiece from its cradle. Carl Hennessy was on the other end, which was a relief. Carl was the telegraph operator for the Union Pacific, but he ran the town's switchboard on the side. I figured it was a lot less likely that he'd be calling with bad news than one of my deputies.

"Hud?" His voice came through scratchy and distant. After confirming that he'd reached the right party, he said, "It was Tom asked me to call. Tom Schiffer."

"I know who Tom is."

"Yeah, I guess so. Anyway, he said to tell you them fellas you wanted watched was still down to the Yellerstone, hooraying away."

"Did he say anything else?"

"Said he was gonna make his rounds real quick, then get on back to the Yellerstone. Said he wanted you to know they ain't quietin' down like you'd hoped they might."

"All right, Carl. Thanks."

"Hud, is it true it's Early Jennings and his boys tearin' the place up down there?"

I gritted my teeth and turned my back to Angie and the kids so they wouldn't hear my response, but of course they did. The clarity on those old candlestick models often required having to nearly shout to hold a conversation, not to mention Carl being notoriously hard of hearing. That wasn't a huge problem for a telegraph operator, who can *feel* the keys and the incoming taps and dashes, but it was a real handicap when you had to rely on those early headphones that made even the sweetest voice sound like a bronchitic mule.

"Who told you that?" I asked.

"Told me what?"

"That someone was tearing up the Yellowstone." I glanced over my shoulder and shrugged helplessly. Angie's lips had thinned almost out of sight, and the kids had turned unnaturally still, sensing the tension in the room.

"Hell, if it's Jennings, I just naturally assumed he'd be raisin' hell. Wouldn't you, had you been locked in a cage for four years?"

I cursed under my breath, then told Carl not to believe half of what he heard and even less of what he thought. I think that hurt his feelings, but I didn't care.

"Listen, Hud," he said curtly. "I'm about ready to shut 'er

down for the night. You want me to make you any connections before I go home?"

"No, go on and call it a night. Tell Maggie I said hello."

"Think I'll wander on down to the Yellerstone first, see what's going on."

"There ain't nothing going on there that you need to be concerned about, Carl. Go home, stay out of trouble."

"By damned! Is that an order?"

"Yes, it is," I replied, although I knew he wouldn't pay it any heed. Nor did I have any authority to back it up. I figured, let him do what he wants, and if he gets his nose singed for sticking it where it didn't belong, he'd have no one to blame but himself.

I was slow returning the earpiece to its double-pronged hook, reluctant to face Angie, but she seemed surprisingly calm when I turned around. "Children," she said, "get ready for bed."

Most nights, that kind of a command, especially coming so early in the evening, would have prompted a bucketful of complaints from both kids, but there's a time to argue and a time to do what you're told, and they were both old enough to know the difference. When we were alone, Angie asked what was going on at the Yellowstone.

"Probably nothing," I said, bringing down my Colt and buckling it around my waist.

"What did Carl mean about someone tearing it up?"

"Not a thing. You know Carl, honey. He's the only man I've ever met who could put two and two together and come up with thirteen."

Angie relaxed a little at that. She did know Carl and his propensity for exaggeration. The Pratts and the Hennessys went to the same Methodist church over on Sixth, and we'd sometimes play cards together on Tuesday Night Socials at the Masonic Hall. Carl could be as entertaining as hell, but you'd be wise to take anything he said with a grain of salt.

I pulled my coat on over my revolver, then kissed Angie goodbye. "Don't wait up," I told her. "I could be late."

"Be careful, Hud."

"I will." Then I put on my hat and stepped outside.

It was chilly with all the light drained out of the sky, although not uncomfortably so. I guess you could say my gait was sluggish as I made my way back to the jail. The gaslights were still hissing softly in their wall brackets when I entered, but Tom wasn't around. I thought briefly about waking Jared Caylin, then decided against it. Jared was my number-two deputy, but didn't come on duty until midnight. His primary responsibility was as a turnkey for both the county and the city, keeping an eye on whatever prisoner we might have locked up overnight, but with the jail empty, there wasn't much for him to do. Jared rented an apartment above the barbershop a few doors down, and it wouldn't take long to rouse him if I decided we needed help.

I went back outside and closed the door behind me. The lamps were already lit along Front Street. That was normally the responsibility of the city marshal's office, rather than the county sheriff, but Larry McNichol was in Salt Lake that week visiting with his wife's folks, and I'd told him we'd keep an eye on things until he got back, since Echo City didn't have the budget for a deputy. I knew Tom had taken care of the lights earlier, while making the evening rounds for McNichol.

The horses Early Jennings and his pards had ridden into town on were still hitched to the rails in front of the Yellowstone, and I recall taking a deep breath before heading in that direction. I figured to peek inside and see what the mood was. Like I said earlier, I didn't want too much law hanging around as long as those boys were behaving themselves; no sense provoking trouble.

Echo City had fourteen saloons when I was sheriffing there. Most of them were lined up along Front Street, where passengers disembarking from the Union Pacific could find them without too much effort. There were a few on Fourth Avenue, and a couple of quieter establishments—neighborhood bars—just off of Fourth. Joe's Tavern, on Grant, was where I did my drinking when all I wanted was a quiet beer before heading home on a Friday evening. I even talked Angie into going inside with me a time or two for their chili, although she was always a little self-conscious about being seen in any kind of drinking establishment.

The Yellowstone wasn't anything at all like Joe's. It was bigger and a lot rowdier, with hard-faced girls working their trade and a pianola that could crank out three songs for a penny, although the rolls had to be changed between blocks of music. [*Editor's Note: Pianola* was a contemporary term for a player, or self-playing, piano. No literature could be found for *paying* player pianos during this time period; either Pratt was mistaken in his memory, the machine was manufactured by a less well-known company, or perhaps it had been modified after production.] The Yellowstone's customers were generally a rough lot, mostly single men in off the range or down from the Plateau, smelling either of horse sweat or fresh-cut pine from Mosby and Clark's United Lumber.

I peered in over the top of the batwing doors and spotted Tom right off. He was standing at the bar with a shot glass of whiskey in front of him, although it didn't look like he'd been doing any serious drinking. There were more customers than I would have expected for the middle of the week, and it made me wonder how many of them were there because of Jennings. The threat of violence can bring out the worst, even in good people; when you wear a badge, you see it more often than you'd think.

I had to shift around a little before I spotted Early and his bunch near the back of the room, huddled around a table with a couple of doves. They weren't making any kind of trouble, but you could tell they were aware of Tom's presence, and that they weren't happy with it. Tom hadn't testified at Early's trial, but he'd still been my deputy at the time, and had been in charge of the prisoner during the day. I don't think there was specifically any *bad* blood between them, but men like Early generally didn't approve of the law in any of its guises.

I still didn't want to go inside, especially considering Early's dour expression, but I was wishing I could somehow catch Tom's attention and draw him outside, away from the resentful eyes of the Jennings gang. My chance came a few minutes later when, of all people, Carl Hennessy showed up, well before his usual quitting time. I didn't ask why he'd left work early. I already knew the answer to that, even though the excitement he was hoping for hadn't materialized yet. With a little luck, it wouldn't. Grabbing his arm, I quietly hustled him out of the lamplight.

"What the hell, Hud?" he exclaimed. "You ain't serious gonna arrest me for coming tonight, 'stead of going home, are you?"

"I want you to do something for me. Go in there and tell Tom I want to talk to him." I nodded toward a narrow alley next to the saloon. "I'll be over there."

He gave me a puzzled look. "Why don't you do it?"

"Just do what I say, and don't attract any attention to yourself doing it, either."

Carl shrugged and went inside, and if I'd known then how people were going to take my reluctance to enter the saloon that evening, I'd have gone in anyway, and to hell with how Early took it. But I wasn't thinking about my future at that point. I was thinking about the town, and how I could best preserve the peace.

I remained near the door long enough to be sure Carl was going to do what I'd asked, then retreated to the corner of the building. The horses belonging to Jennings and his boys were standing patiently at the rail in front of the saloon, hip-shot and with their heads lowered. It galled me that they hadn't been cared for yet—saddles and bridles removed and a chance to roll and have some water. Knowing the kind of men they'd carried into town, I suspected it might be a good long time before they did, and there wasn't a damned thing I could do about it, either.

Tom exited the saloon after a couple of minutes and came over to where I was waiting. "They haven't moved away from their table," he announced right off. "Hell, I don't think any of them have even left to visit the privy. As much whiskey as they've been putting away, they've either got hollow legs or they're pissing in their boots."

"Are they causing any trouble?"

"Nope, not a minute's worth. They've just been sitting there drinking like whiskey's going out of style. I'll tell you this, though, they sure didn't like me being there. I could feel them staring daggers into my spine the whole time I was there. I didn't say a word to them, but every time I glanced at their table in the mirror, there was always one or two scowling back at me."

"Scowls don't worry me," I said, relieved. "Let's leave 'em be for a while. Maybe if they start to relax, they'll take a couple of girls upstairs and work some of the mad out of their systems."

Tom chuckled. "They've got Daisy and Mildred with them. I reckon if anyone can whittle down a mad, it'd be those two."

I might have laughed myself under different circumstances. That night I simply jerked my head toward the jail, and off we went. We took our usual seats inside, me behind my big desk and Tom at his smaller one next to the door leading to the cells. Tom stretched his feet out and crossed his ankles, but that didn't last long. We were both as edgy as penned-up cats. After a while I got up and unlocked the gun rack and brought down a couple of ten-gauge Greeners that I took over to my desk. [*Editor's Note:* The firm of W. W. Greener was founded in Newcastle, England, in 1829, and is still in business today. Its shotguns were popular in the nineteenth-century American West.] I kept a box of double-aught buck in my top drawer. After spilling about half its contents across my unfinished paperwork, I lined the shells up side by side where they'd be easy to grab in a hurry. Then I set the shotguns down on either side of the shells, the butt of one of the Greeners pointed in my direction, the other aimed toward my deputy.

"You sure we're doing the right thing, staying away like this?" Tom asked after several minutes.

"I'm not sure of anything, but we can't arrest them if they haven't done anything wrong. Let's just stay close and keep our ears open."

Leaning back in my wooden swivel chair, I rolled a cigarette and thought about what I knew of Early Jennings. He'd come to Echo City some years before Angie and I got there, taking up residence in a little tar-paper shack down along Echo Creek where Molly Spotted Horse still lived. Early was a notorious troublemaker, even back then, and rumors of him beating Molly and the boy were fairly common, although there wasn't anything we could do about it unless she filed a complaint, and she never did.

Molly was a pretty woman when her face wasn't swollen or bruised. You'd see her around town from time to time, going about her business with a quiet dignity very few people I've known before or since could have mustered. Some folks felt sorry for her. Others thought she got what she deserved for thinking she was good enough to leave the reservation and live among whites. Yeah, there was that, even then. But I think the majority of folks didn't really consider her at all, unless it was to wonder why she stayed in Echo City when she could have gone back to her own people. I'm ashamed to admit this, but I was among that latter category. It wasn't until after what happened that night with Early Jennings, and in the weeks that followed, that my opinion on Molly's situation took a big U-turn, but we'll get into that later on. Right now, I hear Humphrey scratching to come back inside. I swear if it wasn't for that dog constantly needing to go either in or out, I wouldn't get any exercise at all.

Session Three

I reckon it was closing in on ten o'clock that night when hell got the chocks kicked out from under it. Tom was dozing and I was probably on my third cigarette since supper—three being about my entire day's quota under normal circumstances, back in those roll-your-own times.

When you wear a badge, the sound of a gun going off somewhere in town can send jolts of apprehension jingling up your spine. When you've got men like Early Jennings and his ilk drinking and brooding down the street, it can all but knock the hat off your head.

Muted though it was, the dull thump of a revolver brought Tom instantly awake. I stood and picked up my shotgun and a handful of shells and shoved two down the breech before closing the gun with that hollow-tubed gulp that anyone who regularly shoots a double-barrel can identify in the dark. Tom loaded up and added a few extra shells to his pocket and we stepped outside just in time to meet Carl Hennessy stumbling up the street like a drunk. I'd known Carl a long time by then, and it's a fact he liked his booze, but I'd never seen him staggering drunk before. I didn't believe he was that night, either.

"He's shot," Tom exclaimed, but when Carl got closer, I realized he was just scared. Bad scared, like I'd seen in others down in Cuba while fighting the Spanish.

"Hud," Carl called while still some distance away. "Tom,

Hud, they shot Fred. Oh, God, they shot him right between the eyes."

Fred Galloway was the Yellowstone's bartender, and there were more than a few people around town who wouldn't have cared much if he had been shot, but being sheriff didn't allow me that luxury.

"Who shot him?" I demanded.

"Early Jennings, one of his men . . . hell, I don't know. Fred was mad 'cause they took a bottle off the back bar without payin'. He went over to the table where Jennings's boys was playing cards and told 'em they had to ante up a buck for the whiskey if they wanted to keep it. That's when Early shot him."

"You said you didn't know who shot him."

"What the hell difference does it make?" Carl nearly shrieked. "He's dead, ain't he?"

I was staring past Hennessy toward the saloon, where several men were standing on the boardwalk, peering in over the tops of the batwings. I put a hand on Carl's shoulder and gave him a push toward the jail. "Wait inside. I might need to talk to you later."

"What are you gonna do?"

"Just get inside," I snapped, and Carl flinched and ducked into the jail and shut the door.

"How do you want to handle this, Hud?" Tom asked.

"I guess we just go in and take the bull by the horns."

Tom and I had been working together for a few years by then, and knew what to expect from one another. I stepped out into the middle of the street where the light from a gibbous moon could strike me fully. Tom remained on the boardwalk, hugging the deeper shadows close to the fronts of the businesses we passed, darting through the occasional patches of lamplight. Although we were watchful, no one came out to meet us, and when we got to the Yellowstone, it seemed quiet enough inside. I climbed the steps to the swinging doors expecting the worse; what I saw wasn't as bad as it could have been, although it wasn't all that good, either. I pushed inside and stepped to the right. Tom was right behind me, and he immediately moved to the left. Fred Galloway was sitting in a chair at Early's table holding a damp, gray dishrag to his forehead. Blood was easing out from between his fingers and his face looked pale, but he was cussing with enough zeal to convince me his health wasn't critical.

The crowd of onlookers noticed Tom and me before Jennings did, and prudently stepped out of the line of fire. I snugged the Greener to my shoulder just as Early looked up. He snarled something to his men that sounded more animal than human. He was leaning over the bartender in a lecturing pose, his revolver drawn but pointed toward the floor. I cocked both of my shotgun's barrels with the same backward sweep of my thumb.

"Don't try anything foolish, Early," I warned.

He hesitated for a moment, then slowly straightened. "I didn't think you'd have the nerve to show yourself tonight, Pratt. I'd heard you were lurking outside like a chicken thief."

"What happened, Fred?"

"Ain't nothing happened . . . ," Early started, but Fred cut him off.

"That skinny little bastard with the white hair slipped behind the bar and poached a bottle of Old Tan off the shelf. When I went to get it back or make him pay, that son of a bitch"—he pointed at Early, his bloody cloth flapping like a battle flag—"took a shot at me."

"Now, that ain't entirely true," Early replied in a strangely calm tone.

Fred jabbed a finger toward the second floor, where a neat round hole had appeared in the smoke-stained white tin ceiling.

"Probably went clean through the roof," he groused.

That was good enough for me. Letting the twin muzzles of my shotgun bob a little to keep their attention, I said, "I want you boys out of town, now."

"In the middle of the night?" the runt with white-blond hair questioned loudly.

"That's right."

He looked at Early. "I thought you said we was going to light here a spell."

Early didn't immediately reply. He was staring at me like he had the power of Satan at his fingertips, and was getting ready to start flinging lightning bolts my way. Then, real slow, he returned his revolver to its holster. "Let's go, boys," he said. "Our welcome here is worn out."

"What about my ceiling?" Fred demanded.

Early paused, glancing disdainfully at the bartender.

"What do you figure it'll cost you to get it fixed?" I asked.

"Last time I had Frank Brady patch a bullet hole, he charged me ten dollars."

"Early?" I said questioningly.

"Where the hell you think I'm gonna get ten dollars, Pratt?"

"Maybe the same place you got the money for your horse and pistol," Tom suggested. "Fact is, I'd like to know where you did get the money for your outfit."

"He got it from friends," the blond man said.

"Where'd you get it?" Tom asked pointedly.

"None of your damned business, law dog."

"You got the ten dollars?" I asked Jennings.

Jennings didn't move for a full thirty seconds. Then he smiled kind of soft-like and said, "Why, surely, hoss."

"That bottle of Old Tan whiskey Whitey took is another dollar," Fred said, then dabbed tenderly at his forehead. "Plus a dollar for trying to bust my skull with a pistol barrel."

"That sounds reasonable," I agreed. "Looks like that's twelve dollars you owe the man, Early. I'll forgo any fines for discharging a firearm inside city limits, assuming we can settle this amicably."

"I expect you will," Early growled. "Else you'd be arresting every worthless rat-shooter in this stinking hole."

What he was talking about was the periodic firing of guns all over town, rats being a major problem in stables and feed bins, haystacks and gardens. But popping a rat in the ass with a .22 was a whole lot different than punching a hole in a saloon ceiling, and whacking the bartender on his head. Not that I had any intention of getting sidetracked on the schematics of local ordinances with a man like Jennings.

"Can you pay him?" I asked bluntly.

"I'll pay him," Whitey said, drawing a wallet from an inside pocket of his vest. He laid out three bills that Fred scooped off the table and into his pocket like it was a sleight-of-hand maneuver.

"Get 'em out of here, Sheriff," the bartender said.

"Let's go," I told them, and the men stood and shuffled forward. They were grumbling and making no effort to hide their feelings, but I didn't care. Stepping farther to the side where they wouldn't pass so close that one of them might be tempted to make a grab for my shotgun, I tipped my head toward the door. From the corner of my eye I saw Tom drift outside first. Early's men saw it, too, and I could tell it bothered them. I guess they didn't like the idea of an armed deputy standing out there in the dark somewhere, covering them with a shotgun.

I followed them outside and stopped on the boardwalk while they loosened their reins and climbed into their saddles. Besides the bottle the man called Whitey had pilfered from Fred's back bar, there had been five empty whiskey bottles on the Yellowstone's table, and the steady way those boys mounted their horses and backed them away from the rails impressed the hell out of me.

Early reined up as his men rode past. I thought for a minute he was going to say something tough-sounding, like telling me I was lucky my deputy was out there in the dark, or that maybe the next time it wouldn't be so easy, but he didn't. Abruptly kicking his horse in the ribs, he rode to the head of the bunch and led them east, down Front Street to Fourth Avenue, then south toward the San Pedro Plateau.

Tom didn't come out of the shadows until they were a couple of blocks away, his shotgun broke and cradled in the elbow of his left arm. [*Editor's Note:* To *break* a shotgun is to open the firearm at the breech so that the shells can be extracted; it's also one of the safer ways to carry any double-barreled weapon that breaks in the middle.] I lowered the Greener's hammers to half cock and let the muzzles dip toward the ground.

"That was a lot easier than I was afraid it would be," Tom admitted quietly, and I could hear the relief in his voice, even above the galloping of my heart.

"We were lucky," I agreed, then nudged his arm. "Let's go."

We hurried down to Fourth, and both of us started to breathe easier when we saw that Early and his boys were still on the road toward the distant mountain. I'd been half afraid they might peel off and try coming back in on one of the side streets.

"You reckon it's over?" Tom asked.

"Let's hope so," I replied, not knowing then how awfully wrong I was going to be.

Excerpts from:

Those Notorious High Country Badmen: A Collection of Brief, Biographical Sketches of Some of the West's More Renowned Outlaws

by

Malcomb Combs

Six Falls Press, 1924

[A] late contender for the title of Old West Bad Man is Early Jennings, whose unusual first name was bestowed upon him by his mother, after a premature birth in the coal- and iron ore-mining community of Rockwood, Tennessee, in July 1871.

Jennings's childhood seems unremarkable. No mention of him can be found until his nineteenth birthday, when he is mentioned in area newspapers as a suspect in the knifing death of Olaf Sunderson, who reportedly accused the younger man of raping his fifteen-year-old daughter. Jennings was a coworker with Sunderson at the Jaspersmith Smelting Company, and was said to be a frequent visitor to the Sunderson household. . . . Jennings fled the state before a warrant for his arrest could be served . . . [he] next turned up in Colorado, where he worked for the Bryers Smelting Company, near Golden.

. . . following an altercation at the Ox Tail Billiards Hall in August of 1892, where Jennings was said to have "lost his temper royally" after a futile evening of six-pocket. [*Editor's Note:* Six-pocket is an antiquated term for billiards, or pool.] Jennings became a prime suspect when the hall was burned to the ground later that night. As in Tennessee, Jennings vanished before an official investigation of the inferno could be completed, although insurance records of the incident strongly suggest arson.

. . . In 1894, Early Jennings was arrested for selling whiskey on the Ute Indian Reservation near Fort Duchesne, Utah Territory . . . [he] was convicted and sentenced to two years in the federal penitentiary at Sugar House. [*Editor's Note:* The Utah Territorial Penitentiary was located in what is now the Salt Lake City neighborhood of Sugar House; the prison was officially opened in 1855; it closed in 1951.]

Upon release, Jennings worked at numerous jobs throughout the Rocky Mountain region, but by the mid-1890s, he seems to have "settled" near the San Pedro Plateau community of Echo City. In 1899 he was arrested for the murder of Daniel Palmer and sentenced to ten years at the state penitentiary in Laramie, Wyoming; he was transferred, along with the rest of the prison population, to the new facility at Rawlins in either 1901 or 1902 . . . [and] released in 1904 . . . by this time [he] was the reputed leader of the "Jennings Gang," with aggregated histories of murder, theft, bank robbery, and cattle rustling. [*Editor's Note:* It is interesting to note that, although Jennings is commonly referred to as the group's leader, there is no official record of his holding that position; most recent historians have concluded that the band was only loosely confederated.]

Jennings returned to Echo City in September of 1904, where he was arrested for the murder . . .

Daniel James Huttleston was born in the North Riding of County Yorkshire, Upper England, in 1857. His father [*Editor's Note:* Milton James Huttleston, 1832–1880] was a cutter in the limestone quarries of the Pennine Mountains

. . . [the elder Huttleston] quit the trade when his brother was crushed by an improperly cut slab that fell "crookedly."

The family migrated to New York City in 1859, then moved farther west to Buffalo the following year. Through family connections, young Daniel was given employment on a Great Lakes steamship at the age of fourteen, but seemed quickly disillusioned by lake-faring life and quit the trade within the month . . . after disembarking in Sandusky, Ohio.

[The younger] Huttleston's first brush with notoriety seems to have occurred in 1873, when he was mentioned in a Kansas City newspaper as having been part of a gang of young ruffians and pickpockets who frequented the riverfront district of that city. [He was] subsequently placed on probation, then evicted from the town. No further record of his whereabouts could be located until he and Aaron "Big Hoss" Benjamin (see page 74, *High Country Badmen*) were indicted in the 1890 robbery of the Teton National Bank, in Grand Teton, Wyoming. Benjamin was sentenced to five years in the state penitentiary near Laramie; for a first offense, Huttleston was imprisoned for two years.

In 1896, Huttleston was again sent to the Laramie penitentiary, where he served eighteen months for the theft of a horse from the Bar-T Cattle Company of San Pedro County. Upon his release, he fell in with Early Jennings (see page 166, *High Country Badmen*), where he renewed his acquaintance with Aaron Benjamin. Although the three men reportedly continued their criminal activities across portions of Southern Wyoming, Northern Colorado, and Northeastern Utah for several years, they seemed to have escaped capture, and official charges were never filed.

In what seems an odd twist for their personalities, both Huttleston and Benjamin enlisted in the United States Army during the Spanish-American War, and served "with distinction" in the Second Battle of Manila, in 1899. [*Editor's Note:* Two notations need to be made here. First, the 1899 engagement near the Philippine capital of Manila was an action of the Philippine-American War (1899–1902), not the Spanish-American War of 1898, as the author alludes to here. Secondly, although often referred to as the "Second Battle of Manila," there were actually numerous conflicts at this location, dating from 1365 to 1945; some purists might argue that the 1899 engagement was actually the eighth major Battle of Manila.]

Huttleston and Benjamin were discharged from the army in June of 1902, and returned to their Southern Wyoming haunts at least as early as March 1903 . . . both were indicted in the autumn of 1904 for the Echo City murder of . . .

Born in San Francisco, California, in 1869, Aaron "Big Hoss" Benjamin was the son of a prostitute and an unnamed father. His first encounter with the law occurred in 1879, when the ten-year-old was charged, but not convicted, with the torture/mutilation deaths of several cats in the downtown area. Although his name appears on area police blotters at least seventeen times between the years 1881 and 1885, no further charges were filed during this period. It wasn't until Benjamin's second charge in 1885, for mugging an elderly woman, that he was sentenced to three years in the state penitentiary at San Quentin.

It was in San Quentin that Benjamin received the tattoo

of an "obviously large stallion," which resulted in his earning the appellation of "Big Hoss." [*Editor's Note:* An Arrest Card from the San Quentin Historical Association archive shows the semipornographic tattoo located on Benjamin's right forearm.]

Although implicated in a series of burglaries in the years following his release from San Quentin, Benjamin was never arrested. He left California for good in either late 1888 or early 1889 . . . [his] name next appears in a Virginia City, Nevada, newspaper, where he was listed as a suspect in the August 1889 murder of Robert Serkis, a local mine inspector. . . . [Benjamin] fled the state before the Serkis investigation was completed.

Benjamin next turns up in Grand Teton, Wyoming, where he and Daniel Huttleston (see page 141, *High Country Badmen*) were convicted of robbing the Teton National Bank of $5,000 in "coin and paper."

[After his] capture, Benjamin was sentenced to five years in the state penitentiary near Laramie . . . released in August of 1895, and soon thereafter began a partnership with Early Jennings (see page 166, *High Country Badmen*), and his old accomplice from the Grand Teton bank robbery, Daniel Huttleston.

Although the three men reportedly committed numerous crimes—most notably the theft of horses and cattle from throughout Southern Wyoming, Northern Colorado, and Northeastern Utah—they were never apprehended.

In a move that seems strangely out of character, both Aaron Benjamin and Daniel Huttleston joined the Army during the Spanish-American War, and served "with distinction" in the Second Battle of Manila, in 1899. [*Editor's Note:* see *Note,* above, for additional information on this engagement.]

Benjamin and Huttleston were honorably discharged in 1902, and were again back in Southern Wyoming in March of 1903. . . . [Both] were indicted in the autumn 1904 murder of an Echo City . . .

By "Badmen" standards, Wiley "Whitey" Bowen was a relative latecomer to the criminal arena . . . his tragic fall from grace could have earned him sympathy, if not for the viciousness of his later years.

[Bowen] was born in Augusta, Georgia, in 1864 . . . his family moved to Texas during the turbulent years following the Civil War, where they engaged in the cattle trade along the Frio River of Uvalde County.

. . . In 1883, Wiley Bowen married Jane Fletcher, the third daughter of Carrizo Springs grocers Gilbert and Yolanda Fletcher . . . the couple had three children by the end of the decade, and lived in Ulvalde City for the first nine years of their marriage.

In 1892, Bowen moved his family to Carrizo Springs, where he took employment as a cattle buyer for distributors from Fort Worth and Houston . . . The family had traveled to Fort Worth in April 1893 to accompany Wiley on a business trip . . . [when] a malfunctioning valve in a gas jet in the [name redacted] Hotel, where the family was residing, resulted in the death by asphyxiation of Jane Bowen and the couple's three children. [*Editor's Note:* Probably carbon monoxide poisoning.]

. . . The family was interred in the Carrizo Springs Cemetery close to her [Jane's] parents. Wiley later sold his home and most of his belongings before returning to Fort Worth, where he shot and killed the proprietor of the [name redacted], the house detective, and a maintenance man . . . before being wounded in a shoot-out with the Fort Worth police . . . Bowen was sentenced to twenty-five years in the state penitentiary at Huntsville . . . [but] that sentence was later commuted to seven years.

Shortly after his release from Huntsville, Bowen and six other men were indicted in the murder of a cattleman by the name of James Francis, from Albuquerque, New Mexico. Although charged and tried for the killing, Bowen escaped additional prison time on a technicality that allowed five of the original seven suspects to be released.

Although Bowen seems to have disappeared for several years after that, it seems doubtful he gave up his life of crime. In 1904 he turned up in Rawlins, Wyoming, where he joined Early Jennings, Daniel Huttleston . . .

Shep Walters's existence before 1902 is largely shrouded in mystery. Although historian George Rudolph Turner writes in his *Rio Tinto: A War for Salt,* that Walters was a participant in the Rio Tinto Salt Wars of Texas in 1880, my own research of the conflict, covered in *Those Notorious Badmen of the Texas Border Country* (Combs, Six Falls Press, 1923), found no mention of a Shep Walters, nor any name resembling it. It should be further noted that a 1903 Arrest Card for Walters lists his age as twenty-six, which would have made him, at three years of age, the youngest gunslinger in the West, if Turner's assertion is correct.*

What is known of Walters comes mostly from newspaper accounts from Southwestern Wyoming, where he is

[*See also *American Legends Collection, Book Three, Rio Tinto,* by Michael Zimmer.]

mentioned in at least three instances as a participant in a surge of cattle rustling against ranchers throughout that region and into the Brown's Hole area of Colorado. In 1903 he was arrested and sentenced to one year in the penitentiary at Rawlins, where he apparently first made contact with Early Jennings (see page 166, *High Country Badmen*); Walters was released shortly before Jennings . . . and [was] with him in Echo City in September of 1904 . . .

Session Four

I told you about Jennings and his men yesterday, before we stopped for the night, and about how Tom and I figured they might be out of our hair for good. I found out early the next day that they were still around. It was the hardware store owner, Red Gifford, who came to me with the news.

"Jennings is down at Molly Spotted Horse's cabin, Hud. What are you going to do?"

I reared back a couple of inches in surprise, not so much from Gifford's news, but from the abrupt way it was delivered. Red was generally an easygoing man, but I'd barely entered my office, hadn't even shucked out of my coat yet, when he came busting through the front door like a gust of icy wind.

"Are you sure it's Jennings?"

"Who else would it be? Damnit, I talked to Molly last night. I told her Jennings was back and that she needed to stay out of sight until he was gone. I even offered her a room at my house until it was safe, but she wouldn't do it. Said she'd be all right, and that Early wouldn't bother her. I went down there this morning to check on her, and saw a bunch of horses hobbled behind the place."

I swore and put my coat back on. "How many horses?"

"Five. A good-looking blue roan, a couple of bays, a sorrel—"

"And a black with a snip on its nose."

Red nodded. "It's them, I'm sure of it."

"Did you see anyone?"

"No, but I didn't want to get too close, either. Figured I'd best tell you and let the law handle it."

"You did right," I agreed.

"There's something else, Hud. There wasn't any smoke coming from Molly's chimney. I've never known her not to have a breakfast going by first light, and the sun was nearly up by the time I got there."

"What about her boy?"

"Billy? I haven't seen him, but I know he went up to Jess Harding's place a few days ago. He's supposed to be back today or tomorrow to help me deliver some supplies to United Lumber."

"All right, Red, thanks. Go on and open your store. I'll check on Molly."

He started toward the door, then swung back. "If you need any help . . ."

"No, I'll be fine."

"Hud, I didn't back away from Molly's because I was afraid. I just didn't want to make her situation any worse. You've got the authority to do something, I don't."

"I know. I'll tell you what, if you want to help, I'd appreciate you going down to Tom's place and telling him I need him at the jail."

"Of course, I'll be glad to. I'll be at the store afterward, if you need me."

I nodded a final thanks, and the storekeeper hurried out. Tom rented a little two-room house over on Ninth, and I knew it was going to take Red a few minutes to get there. While he was doing that, I went to fetch Jared. [*Editor's Note:* Jared Caylin was a part-time deputy sheriff and turnkey for both San Pedro County and Echo City, which shared the same jail facilities; Pratt originally mentions Caylin in Session Two, and states that the deputy "rented an apartment above the barbershop a few doors down" from the jail.]

Jared was young and hard to wake, and when he finally got to the door to let me in, it took even longer to explain what had happened overnight. Once I got it through his skull what was going on, though, he skinned into his clothes double-quick and was right behind me going back to the jail. I tossed him the keys to the gun rack and he brought down both Greeners for Tom and me, and a .30-30 Winchester for himself.

I probably ought to mention that even though I sometimes call these shotguns and rifles "mine," they really belonged to the county; we did furnish our own handguns, though. Mine was a Colt Model of 1892, in .38 caliber. Some people considered the .38 too light for a lawman, but it was the revolver I'd been issued in the Spanish-American War, and that I'd brought home with me afterward. I'd built up an affinity for the gun, not to mention trust in its ability to shoot straight.

Tom arrived just as Jared shoved his last cartridge through the Winchester's gate. I nodded toward the shotgun laid out for him, and Tom picked it up without comment and quickly chambered two rounds. I think we were all expecting trouble at that point; the tension was damn near palpable.

"How do you want to handle this?" Tom asked, pocketing several extra shells.

"It's going to depend on Molly, but if she wants them gone, we're by God going to grab the bull by the horns, and this time we ain't letting go until we're sure that whole bunch has cleared the county."

"Red went back to his store to get his pistol," Tom added. "He's afraid Molly'll be too frightened to talk to us, especially if we're loaded down with guns."

"He might be right," I agreed. "If he's still willing, we'll take him with us."

"What the hell is Red doing with that squaw?" Jared asked. "Hell, he's got a real nice woman at home."

Tom gave him a disgusted look. It seemed like Jared never could get a firm grip on smarts. "He's only trying to help her," Tom said.

Jared snorted. "I think he's trying to help himself, that's what I think."

"You save what you think about Red Gifford and Molly Spotted Horse for someone who wants to hear it," I said, putting an edge to my voice so that he'd know it was time to shut up. I glanced at Tom. "Ready?"

"Let's go."

It was chilly enough that morning that we could see our breath as we marched down Front Street to Fourth, then turned south. Red was waiting for us in front of his store, looking grim enough to sour sugar. He showed me his revolver, a .45 with a three-inch barrel, then slid it inside the pocket of his coat and fell in behind Tom.

Echo Creek ran south to north, before veering east a short distance outside of town to make its ambling way toward the North Platte River. It came out of one of the Plateau's larger canyons that was also the main route into the higher elevations to the south. Because of the railroad's need for gentle grades and flat terrain, Echo City sat up on the north bench above the creek's bend, but there was what some folks around town called a spill-off of buildings down along the creek itself—out of sight and as handy to ignore by city leaders as the town's brothels. Homes along the creek belonged mostly to Mexicans, Negroes, a few Chinese, and a sizable number of down-on-their-luck whites. The majority of those places were nothing more than cobbled-together shacks, made out of logs washed down off the Plateau during the spring runoff, or from scrap lumber shopped for after hours from various buildings sites around town—

meaning it was stolen. Some of the houses were shingled with flattened tin cans or cracked shakes, and damned few had real glass in their windows. Molly's house was covered with tar paper, black as the bottom of a well, but a lot more windproof than most of the structures along what was commonly referred to as Spill Street.

You might envision the folks along Spill Street being dirt-poor and slovenly—drunkards, whores, and drug addicts—but you'd be wrong about half the time. A lot of them had employment in town, and were hard workers, too. It just seemed like what they earned was never quite enough to pull them out of poverty. That was Molly's situation. I think I mentioned earlier that she held down a number of jobs around Echo City, mostly cleaning houses for some of the elderly or wealthier citizens; she'd occasionally take in laundry, too, primarily sheets and such from a couple of the town's sporting houses. She was a fine worker, but like most of the citizens along Spill Street, she never had enough clout to demand better wages.

Molly's place was off the beaten path, which I suspect was her choice rather than a matter of status. It was about as destitute as any of them, although she and her son always kept the weeds down and the property cleared of trash. Red and his wife, Elizabeth, had been inside a few times and said the place was as sparkly as Judge Lynn's dining room. They'd know, I reckon. Like a lot of shop owners, the Giffords would get an occasional invitation to the judge's fancy ranch house, especially around election time. Hell, even Angie and I had been invited to the judge's place a time or two.

South of town, Fourth Avenue turned into the Echo Canyon Road, which took you about anywhere you wanted to go for a good long ways. Mosby and Clark's timber outfit was down there in one of those side canyons, and Judge Lynn's Broken Cinch Ranch hugged the rolling hills and gulches along the base of the San Pedro Range. Homesteaders, smaller ranches, and tie hack communities fanned out in both direction from the larger spreads, and there were still hunters and trappers up top, living among the sprawling forests of aspen and pine that ran south into Colorado. [*Editor's Note:* Tie hacks were individuals who cut cross ties for the railroad; although records indicate that Mosby and Clark's United Lumber Company supplied several tons of cross ties per year, tie hacks were still active in the San Pedro Mountains until well into the 1930s.]

Spill Street was little more than a rutted wagon track hugging the creek's north bank. We followed it upstream, away from the main cluster of shacks, to where Molly's little tarpaper house sat back in the trees. It was cooler here along the creek than in town, and I was surprised by the faintly changing colors. The two apple trees in our backyard were still green, but these were already fading into their autumn dress. The horses Red had told me about were hobbled south of the place, and I noticed the chimney was still without smoke. Red also noticed the idled chimney.

"Something's wrong here, Hud," he said tersely. "I know Molly'd have a fire going by now."

"Maybe she's still in bed," Jared said, his young face twisted in a smirk.

Both Tom and the storekeeper graced him with disdainful looks; neither replied to his crass implication.

"Jared, damnit," I said. "Get around back where you've got a good view of the horses. Don't shoot unless you hear us shooting or someone takes a shot at you. Mostly just try to keep anyone from slipping out the back." I pointed toward a gap in the creek-side trees and he shrugged and took off. To this day, I don't think he fully understood the inappropriateness of his comments.

"Red, I want you to stay close to me," I continued. "If there's any shooting, find a tree and get down behind it. This ain't your fight, and I'm hoping all you'll need to do is reassure Molly that we don't mean her any harm."

Red nodded and put his hand inside the coat pocket where he'd stowed his stubby .45. Jared was already skipping across the rushing waters of the creek on rocks jutting above the surface, as nimble as a cat—or a kid. We gave him enough time to get into position, then started forward along the wagon path. We didn't stop until we were about fifty yards from the front door, though still well back in the trees. I told Red to duck behind a massive stump alongside the path, where he'd have some protection if hell got turned loose with the dogs. Then I moved over beside a towering cottonwood, while Tom stepped behind another nearby tree, and we were set.

"Jennings," I shouted above the chattering creek. "Early Jennings." After a couple of minutes, I called again. Not long after, the door cracked open a few inches.

"What do you want?"

"I want to talk to Molly."

"She's busy."

"Step outside where I can see you," I hollered.

"I'm fine right here, Pratt. Goddamnit, this is my house and Molly's my woman, and you damn well know it. Go on about your business, and leave me to mine."

"It ain't going to work that way, Early. You come on outside with your boys, or else send Molly out here where I can talk to her."

Someone laughed from inside—Whitey, I think. "She's busy, law dog. Wait your turn."

"Sheriff," Red said tautly, half rising from behind his stump.

"You stay where you are," I replied sharply, then raised my voice for the men in the house. "Send her out, Early, or I promise, one way or another, I'll see you back in Rawlins before the week is through."

"The hell you will," he bellowed, and slammed the door closed.

"Hud, we've got to help her."

"Stay where you are," I said, and Red sank back with a stricken look. After a couple of minutes, I tried again. "I ain't going away, Jennings."

"Wait a minute, damnit, I'm thinking."

I knew then that it would only be a matter of time before Jennings either sent Molly out, or exited the building himself. I was hoping for the latter, and that he'd bring his men with him. At that point, all I wanted was to get them onto their horses and out of the county for good.

It took about ten minutes before the door opened and Early Jennings stepped outside. He had his revolver buckled around his waist and was carrying a rifle, but he wasn't making any kind of threatening gesture with it, so I didn't say anything. His men filed out behind him and spread wide to either side. They were also armed to the teeth, but like Jennings, they were keeping their revolvers holstered, their rifle barrels lowered.

"The woman ain't feelin' too good, Sheriff," Early called.

Red poked his head up from behind the stump. "What did you do to her?" he shouted.

Jennings's men shuffled nervously at the storekeeper's abrupt appearance—they'd only seen me up until that point—and I thought a couple of them were going to bring their rifles to bear, but Early said something and they quickly stilled. I'd been optimistic until that moment; suddenly, I was filled with dread.

"What's wrong with her?" I asked.

"She tripped over a piece of firewood and hit her head. She's sleeping it off."

I swore and raised my shotgun. "Drop your guns, boys."

"Now, there ain't no reason to get cantankerous, Sheriff,"

Early countered. "We were getting ready to ride out, anyway. Let us get our horses, and we'll be thirty miles away by sunset."

"Not yet," I said, earring the Greene's hammers back to full cock. "Drop 'em, boys, or I'll . . ."

"The hell," Whitey practically screamed, then jerked his rifle's muzzle up and fired from the hip.

I wasn't expecting that, not as far into the conversation as we'd gotten, but I was primed for trouble, and cut loose with my shotgun before the report of Whitey's rifle could echo back off the buildings in town. Whitey went down hard, and the man next to him hollered and grabbed his thigh. Two others pulled their revolvers and opened fire. Tom dropped one with his shotgun and I sent the other scrambling for cover. Red's bullet smacked into the door even as it slammed closed behind Early and what was left of his gang.

Somebody—either Tom or Red or, hell, it could've been me—shouted *"Sonofabitch!"* as I jumped back behind my tree and reloaded. Then we waited, while those inside talked over their situation. After about five minutes, Jared fired a round from his position across the creek, the solid thump of his bullet striking the side of Molly's shack sounding like a teacher's open palm against a rebellious student's cheek. Jared would tell me later that one of Jennings's men had poked his head out the rear window, and he'd sent a bullet into the wall above the outlaw's head to drive him back inside. A couple of minutes after that, Early shouted that he wanted to palaver.

"There ain't nothing to talk about anymore," I told him. "Throw your guns out and surrender."

After another short pause, that's what they did. Tom and me lined them up against the side of the house and I checked them for hideout guns, then Tom and Jared escorted them back to the San Pedro lockup. Once they were on their way, I went inside to find Red Gifford sitting on a chair beside the fireplace, tears streaming unashamedly down his cheeks. I swore and crossed the room to Molly's side, even though I could tell from the door that she was dead.

Session Five

It took awhile to sort it all out. It always does with a major crime. Doc Freeman did what they call a postmortem, and by midmorning he was able to confirm that Molly had been killed by a series of powerful blows to her midsection. He called it "blunt trauma" in his report, but told me it was probably a fist with a lot of force behind it.

"I'm guessing she was alive while they raped her," he added soberly. "We can only hope she was unconscious. She would have been in a tremendous amount of pain if she wasn't."

It was difficult to listen to. Difficult for all of us, but especially for Red and Elizabeth Gifford. They'd been closer to Molly and Billy than anyone else in town, and Molly's death—I think especially the brutality of it—struck them hard. I've seen Red spend a full twelve-hour shift behind the counter at his store with his face running rivers of perspiration from fever and never complain, but he didn't open up at all on the day Molly was killed, nor the next.

Billy still hadn't showed up by noon, so I sent Tom to the Plateau to talk with Jess Harding. Tom didn't get back until nearly midnight. He told me Jess's cabin was empty, but not deserted.

"If Billy ain't here, I'll bet he's up top somewhere with Jess," Tom stated.

Although Billy needed to be there for his mother's funeral, I've got to admit I was grateful for the reprieve. I wasn't looking forward to telling him what had happened, and Lord knows I had plenty to keep me busy. Besides Early Jennings, we arrested Dan Huttleston and Shep Walters. Huttleston was a pal of Early Jennings from before he was sent away, and Walters had occupied a cell just two down from Jennings in the Rawlins pen. Walters had been released not quite a week before Early got out on the fifteenth; he was also the one who caught my stray buckshot when I returned Whitey's fire—twin pellets less than an inch apart. Doc Freeman extracted both of them with some long tweezers, then wrapped the wounds with cotton bandages.

"He should be in fine health when you're ready to drop a noose over his head," Doc said, glaring at his patient.

Walters wanted to take offense at the remark, but Doc let him know he didn't give a damn what the former convict thought.

"I hope I'm the one who fills out your death certificate, young man. I'll celebrate my signature with a shot of bourbon."

Doc Freeman was in his sixties back then, and as feisty as a terrier with a rat; I liked him, but I know a lot of folks who didn't because of his brusque manner.

The two men killed in the shoot-out were Whitey Bowen and a man known only as Big Hoss, an unusual moniker for someone of only average height and girth. [*Editor's Note:* see the excerpts from *Those Notorious High Country Badmen,* page 43.]

You might be wondering what I thought about killing Whitey, or how Tom felt about the death of Big Hoss, but after seeing what they'd done to Molly, I just flat didn't give a damn. Tom didn't, either. Molly's death haunted me for years, and it still does on occasion, but I seldom think about Whitey Bowen at all.

It would take too long to repeat everything involved in making Jennings and his boys' arrests official—all the paperwork and cataloging of evidence and talking to people who'd talked to the killers, as well as anyone who may have seen Molly on the day before she was killed. I was up until late that night, and had an appointment first thing the next morning with Judge Lynn and Roy Sandler, the San Pete County prosecutor. It didn't take long for me to realize the case wasn't going to turn out well for justice. It was Roy who first tipped me to the direction the court was leaning.

"They were married, weren't they, Hud?"

"It was a common-law marriage," I said.

"But they were still man and wife in the eyes of the people, right?"

"I guess that would depend on an individual's point of view. I think everyone would agree that it was murder, though, plain and simple."

"A smart defense attorney would try to classify it as an accidental death," Judge Lynn interjected.

"I don't think you can *accidentally* rape a woman, can you, Judge?" I kept my voice down, but could feel my ears growing warm, like they always do when I get mad.

"What Henry means is that, as tragic as this woman's death is, it could still be considered a domestic issue," Roy said. "It might not be a case of rape, so much as a husband's rights."

I was sitting at a table in the judge's chambers with Lynn, Sandler, and a court recorder . . . let's see, hell, I can't remember his name offhand, but I know there were just the four of us in there, and when Roy made that argument about a husband's rights, I nearly exploded out of my chair.

"It ain't a husband's goddamn right to abuse his wife, common law or not," I replied, and I may have shouted it, I was so mad.

Roy reared back in his chair, his eyes nearly popping out of their sockets. The recorder jumped, too. Only Lynn remained firmly seated, but I noticed his nostrils flaring, and that his right hand had slipped inside the lapel of his vest where I knew he kept a little over-and-under Derringer.

"Sit down, Sheriff Pratt," the judge said sternly.

I stopped with my knuckles propped on top of the table, my arms trembling. Judge Lynn continued to glare at me until I stepped back and retook my seat. I couldn't stop my hands from shaking, though.

"Control your emotions, Sheriff," Lynn said coldly. "I'll not tolerate another such outburst."

I didn't reply, which was probably a good thing, else I might have ended up in my own jail on a contempt charge.

"Gentlemen, let's not lose sight of our objective," Roy said, his words sounding as wobbly as an old chair.

Trying to keep a cap on my anger, I said, "Molly Spotted Horse was raped and killed, and I want to see the man who did it hanged, and his accomplices put away for a hell of a long time. That's my objective."

"That sounds dangerously close to vigilantism," Judge Lynn replied coolly. "You should know as well as I do, Sheriff, that our courts were not established to condone retaliation. We have a system for justice in place, and, perfect or not, we will follow it. I'll not see anarchy take over in San Pedro County."

"Please, if we could focus on the evidence," Roy pleaded, then looked at me and took a deep breath. "Hud, have you been able to determine who struck the fatal blow?"

I shook my head. Our methods of dealing with criminal suspects was still feeling its way along in those early days, and hadn't yet developed the methods it would adopt after men like John Dillinger and Pretty Boy Floyd started running wild. Or maybe the methods were there, and hadn't yet reached our little high desert burg. The fact is, Tom had locked up all three prisoners while I was still down at Molly's with Red Gifford. Then he'd left them alone to sort out their own defense.

"They're claiming it was Whitey Bowen who killed her," I finally admitted. "Jennings says he and the others were outside, smoking pipes and cigarettes and watching the stars, when Whitey slipped inside and attacked Molly. I have strong doubts that Whitey would have risked angering Jennings, or that he could have assaulted Molly without the others hearing it. From the way the place was torn apart inside, she must have put up a hell of a struggle."

Looking strangely relieved, Roy shrugged his shoulders and raised both hands palms upward. "But unless you can provide *proof,* solid and unequivocal, that the men you arrested were actively involved in the attack, it becomes their word against . . . no one's."

"A woman is dead," I reminded him.

"And so, apparently, is her killer," Lynn added.

"Damnit, Judge, you know that's not true. Whitey Bowen was there, but he didn't act alone."

Lynn glanced at the recorder, then tipped his head toward the door. After the recorder left, the judge leaned confidentially forward in his chair. "I didn't want to have to spell this out, Hud, but you have to understand our position on this matter."

"Aw, hell," I breathed. "Because she's an Indian?"

"This county is not going to hang a white man for the murder of an Indian, no matter how odious the crime. It's not going to happen, and it would be a waste of taxpayer money to pursue it any further than we have to. By all means, we'll hold a trial, and we'll hear whatever evidence you've collected, but you have to understand that neither Early Jennings nor his men will be, *can be,* held accountable for Molly Spotted Horse's death."

"You can send them back to Rawlins."

"No, Hud. It's out of my hands without a conviction, and I doubt if Roy could get that even if Jennings and his men confessed to the crime before a dozen witnesses. That's just the way it is, whether you approve of it or not. Now, for God's sake, man, buck up and get your investigation completed. I want this case closed by the end of next week, and I'd prefer it happened sooner."

Judge Lynn leaned back in his chair, and I knew I'd been dismissed. My hands were still shaking as I walked out the door. My mind reeled, grasping for some argument that could breach the stubborn injustice of the judge's position. Yet even then, I knew Lynn was right. I didn't have enough evidence to put Jennings or his men behind bars for Molly's death, and I doubted if I'd get any, either. I'll tell you what, I left that courthouse with my hat in hand and my mood dragging on the floor behind me.

Tom was at his desk next to the cell-block door when I returned. He didn't say anything as I hung up my hat and coat, then sank back in my chair. Rising, he went to the stove and poured a cup of coffee, then brought it over.

"Fresh brewed," he said, placing the heavy, bone-china mug in front of me.

"Thanks," I murmured, rubbing both eyes with the heels of my palms. It had been a long couple of days, and I was feeling drained. I always did after investigating a murder.

"How'd it go?" Tom asked.

"About what you'd expect." I lowered my hands and related the basics of my conversation with the judge and county prosecutor. I didn't skimp on my opinion of Lynn, either, although Tom already knew how I felt about the man. Sandler, as far as I'm concerned, was just a marionette.

"Judge Lynch," Tom uttered when I'd finished, then shook his head as if that said it all.

Judge Lynch was what a lot of folks around San Pete County called Judge Henry Lynn, but it wasn't because of his willingness to condemn a man to the gallows. Lynn seldom ordered a man hung. I think the appeals process of a death penalty, and especially the extra scrutiny it would entail from outside the county, intimidated him. Mostly the local population mangled the judge's last name in response to his heavy-handed manner in shaping the law to suit his own moods, opinions, even wishes. Like in getting a telephone line strung up between Echo City and his ranch at the county's expense. The term *Lynch* was generally spoken with contempt, but I had it on pretty good authority that Lynn was actually proud of the title.

It shows they know I mean business, is what the attorney who told me about it claimed. Knowing the judge as I did, I never doubted it.

Tom waited until I'd taken a sip of coffee before dropping another hot coal in my lap.

"Billy's back."

I sighed and looked up. "When?"

"Last night. We were right, he was hunting elk with Jess Harding up on the Plateau. Turns out the kid walks up there two or three times a month just to hang around with that old trapper. Trying to learn the skills he sure as hell wouldn't get here or along Spill Street, I guess."

"He walks all that way?"

"That's what Red says." Tom shook his head. "That's got to be what, ten or twelve miles to Jess's cabin?"

"I'd say closer to fifteen."

"Red claims he'll leave home around midnight so he can be there by first light, and doesn't start home again until after dark. I guess he saw me along the road last night, but hid in the sage when I got close."

That didn't surprise me. Most of the residents along Spill Street were wary of the law, whether they'd done anything wrong or not. I always considered their distrust one of the burdens of poverty for both them and me, although I could appreciate their feelings, having witnessed the way Larry McNichol treated them when he was on the prowl for some thief or troublemaker. I think as far as Larry was concerned, just living along Spill Street made you guilty of something, and he considered it his duty as the city marshal to find out what that was. I doubt if Larry had ever been truly poor, but I had, which I guess is why I viewed the situation down there differently than he did.

I took another slow sip of coffee, appreciating its rich taste and especially its warmth on such a chilly morning. I didn't know many men who could brew a better pot of coffee than Tom Schiffer. He'd watch the heat a lot closer than Jared or I would, and move the pot around on top of the stove to control its temperature. I didn't have that kind of patience myself, and I doubt if Jared even knew what Tom was doing when he'd lightly touch his fingers to the side of the pot, then slide it a couple of inches in one direction or another.

Placing an incident report on the desk in front of me, Tom said, "Billy can't read nor write, but I told Red what we needed, and he told Billy. That damn kid is so shy I could barely hear him from ten feet away, but Red wrote down what he said, and we both witnessed it."

"I don't think it's going to do much good," I replied, staring at Red Gifford's neat, tight scroll.

Tom shrugged and returned to his desk. I picked up Billy's statement and read it all the way through. There wasn't anything new or helpful. Hell, the poor kid hadn't even known his mother was dead until he got back early that morning and found Red and Elizabeth sitting at the table in his Spill Street home. I tossed the paper back on top of my desk and took another sip of coffee, but the taste had diminished from earlier, and the aroma wasn't nearly as appealing.

I went home about noon, and Angie and I dressed for Molly's funeral. The service was going to be held in the Giffords' front parlor, rather than at a church or the town's solitary funeral home. I didn't inquire why. They would bury her in a far corner of the cemetery, behind the knoll where most of Echo City's residents were interred. Her closest neighbors in eternity would be the whores, transients, and riffraff who'd had the misfortune of taking their final breath in that high, dry county.

The Giffords thought Molly might have been Catholic, coming from the Wind River Reservation as she had, and having a tin crucifix on the wall above her bed, but neither of them were sure. I guess Billy didn't know, either. Not that a Catholic Mass would have been an option. To my knowledge there wasn't a priest anywhere nearer than Rawlins, and I doubt if he would have come all the way to Echo City for an Indian.

Red took care of the arrangements, while Elizabeth looked after Billy as much as he'd let her. After briefly viewing his mother's body in the plain pine casket Red had purchased from his own pocket, he went back to Echo Creek to wander its banks in solitude. Angie and Elizabeth wanted to go after him, but Red said to let him be.

"The boy needs to be alone," he told the women firmly, and they didn't argue.

I still hadn't talked to Billy, but I figured he was in good hands with the Giffords. There wasn't anything I could have said to ease his pain, anyway.

Graveside services were brief. Reverend Belichick, from the local Methodist church, preformed the liturgy, with the Giffords, Angie and me, and maybe a couple of dozen others forming a crude horseshoe around the foot of the grave. Billy came back for the burial, but stood off to one side by himself, and moved away when Elizabeth tried to coax him closer. I studied his face as best I could under the stiff brim of the new hat Red had bought for him that afternoon, along with a barely used suit of clothes and some store-bought shoes that shined like a polished surrey. I remember there was a breeze coming down off the Plateau that afternoon, bringing with it the sweet smell of evergreens and an occasional boom from the lumber mill that rumbled through the tall sage like thunder.

I don't know if you ran across this in your research, but there used to be a kind of phenomenon associated with Echo Canyon so that, even from eight or ten miles away, if the wind was right you could hear those big trees falling high up the main canyon. Sometimes you could even make out the shrill whining of the huge blades at the mill as they ripped into the timber, whittling them down to whatever dimension the company had contracted for—crossties or planks or roof beams. It was that oddity that gave both the town and creek their names, and even though I barely noticed those distant booms and cries most days, for some reason, I was keenly aware of them as Molly Spotted Horse was laid to rest.

I should probably mention two other recent graves in the cemetery that day, one belonging to Whitey Bowen and the other to the man called Big Hoss. The two outlaws had been buried the evening before, after Doc Freeman completed his examination of the bodies and filled out their death certificates. I'd gone down to observe the burial, although it was strictly an official function, just one more chore ticked off my list. As far as I was concerned, they could have dumped the bodies downwind of the town and forgotten about them.

Reverend Belichick kept the service short. He spoke of Molly's devotion to her work and her son, and the respect she had from the people who knew her. Then he read a few lines from the Bible, the part about no one dying by themselves and everyone belonging to God. [*Editor's Note:* Pratt may be referring here to Romans 14:7–9. "For none of us lives to himself, and none of us dies to himself. For if we live, we live to the Lord, and if we die, we die to the Lord. So then, whether we live or whether we die, we are the Lord's. For to this end Christ died and lived again, that he might be Lord both of the dead and of the living."]

When the reverend was finished, he gently closed his book, then stood silently at the top of the grave while those in attendance filed slowly past. Most of us tossed in a handful of dirt that rattled the casket's lid, and a few murmured quick prayers of their own. Red went over to where Billy was standing by himself and whispered in his ear, but Billy shook his head and started to walk away. I'll tell you, it near about broke my heart to see the stoic way that kid reacted to his mother's passing. It was like he had to hold it all in, else risk destroying himself in letting go.

Afterward, folks congregated back at the Giffords' home for a small lunch and some quiet conversation. Angie went, but I didn't. She told me she could walk the short distance to our house afterward, so I took the rented horse and buggy back to John Moon's livery, then hiked into town without bothering to change into my work clothes. Tom had stayed at the jail with the prisoners while Jared caught some shut-eye, as he'd be taking over at midnight. Tom was looking sulky when I got in. I soon found out why.

"Trial's day after tomorrow," he said bluntly, before I'd even gotten the door closed behind me.

"Saturday? What the hell happened? Lynn told me this morning we had until next week."

"That jackass's daughter came up from Cheyenne on the afternoon train. She stopped in town long enough to say hello to her daddy, then took the kids on out to the ranch. Lynn wants to finish the trial early so he can spend some time with his grandchildren."

"That son of a bitch," I said softly.

"Yeah, ain't he? Said he wants to teach his grandson how to fly-fish."

I think I've already mentioned how my ears get warm when I'm mad. They were about ready to burst into flames at that point. I tossed my coat on the desk and sank into my chair with my jaws clenched like a mechanic's vise.

"I told him we needed more time, but he flat said we couldn't have it. Said it's day after tomorrow at nine a.m., or he'll dismiss the charges for insufficient evidence."

"Shit," I said, and if I hadn't been wearing my good church hat, I swear I would have sent it sailing across the room into the wall. "We're wasting our time, Tom."

"I know."

I sighed and shook my head. "If you want to sit this one out, I won't hold it against you."

"Ain't no way in hell I'm gonna sit this out," Tom growled. "We might be fighting a losing battle, but I say we make that son of a bitch earn his paycheck."

"Let's do it," I agreed, then rolled my chair to my desk and started pulling the papers scattered across its top into a tidy pile to begin sorting through what little evidence we had.

Session Six

Well, Tom and I did what we could, but we both knew it was a lost cause from the beginning. I presented Roy Sandler with motive, opportunity, and physical evidence, but he didn't push the prosecution, and that allowed the defense to make short work of the case against Jennings and his men. The trial lasted two hours. The jury deliberated even less time than that, filing back into the courtroom at eleven forty. No one said a word as the foreman read the not-guilty verdicts aloud, although I had to grit my teeth at what I considered a hypocritical recommendation at the end of the reading, that Early Jennings, Dan Huttleston, and Shep Walters be escorted out of the county for good.

Banished into perpetuity, was how he stated it.

The jury's foreman was Oscar Larnx, who dug wells and relocated privies when the old ones approached full, and you could tell from the careful way he sounded out the words that he'd been coached on the request—the runty little bastard.

Jennings and his boys hooted and laughed and slapped one another on the back. Jennings shouted that he was buying a round on the house at the Yellowstone for anyone man enough to stand at the bar with him. He was starting to add something else when the judge banged his gavel and told him to shut up.

"Mister Jennings, Mister Huttleston, and Mister Walters, you have been acquitted of all charges against you in connection with the Spotted Horse murder, but I support, and will grant, the jury's request for banishment. You three men will gather your belongings and immediately, permanently, remove yourselves from San Pedro County. Do you understand the meaning of the word *permanently*?"

Looking like a child with hurt feelings, Jennings replied, "I ain't no idjit, Judge. It means forever."

"I'll forgo an opinion on your intelligence, Mister Jennings, but I can assure you that it does indeed mean forever. Never, gentlemen, *never* show your faces in San Pedro County again. If you do, you will face my wrath. Is that understood?"

Oh, they shuffled and scowled and mumbled like their kind will when they've been called to heel, but I think they had a pretty fair idea how lucky they were, and it didn't take long before all three of them nodded that they grasped the judge's meaning, and intended to comply.

"Sheriff Pratt." Lynn's gaze settled on me.

"Yes, sir?"

"Have your deputy escort these men back to the jail to collect their belongings. He's to have their horses saddled and brought directly to the jail, so that he can personally supervise their departure. I want them out of town within thirty minutes, and out of San Pedro county by sundown."

I glanced at Tom and he nodded, and I knew it would be taken care of.

"In the meantime, Sheriff, I want to see you and William Pinto in my chambers in fifteen minutes."

"Yes, sir," I acknowledged, then turned to survey the room. Billy was standing in the back corner with his shoulder pressed against the wall as if he wanted to slip behind the paint.

"Your Honor," Red said from behind the spectator's railing.

"Yes, very well, Mister Gifford, you may accompany Sheriff Pratt and Mister Pinto. I want to speak to young William, and I want to be sure he understands my message."

Tom led his charges out of the courtroom. Most of the onlookers—and there were quite a few, it being not only a murder trial, but something of a sexual scandal, as well—followed like ducklings, until the only people left besides Red, Billy, and me were the prosecutor and defense attorney. Red came up to where I waited at the railing gate. He had his hand resting lightly on Billy's shoulder, although I couldn't tell if it was solely a comforting gesture, or if he wanted to be ready to tighten his grip if he had to. Young Billy reminded me of a colt about ready to make a break for tall timber.

"Do you know why Judge Lynn wants to talk to Billy?" Red asked worriedly.

I hadn't a clue, and said as much. I was watching Billy, thinking how young and stiff and vulnerable he looked in the clothes the Giffords had bought him for his mother's funeral. I think I've already mentioned that Billy was small for his age. Maybe five foot six and no more than a hundred and forty pounds, although he looked healthy; wiry as a cat, lean and sleek as a thoroughbred. His hair was black and cut to shoulder length, his complexion dusky, as you'd expect from someone foaled from a woman named Spotted Horse. His eyes were ebony, intelligent even when narrowed in distrust, and I remember thinking that no matter who his father might be—Early Jennings or some Wind River fur trader—his white blood hadn't made much of an indentation in the boy's looks.

"He's scared," Red explained, squeezing Billy's shoulder with gentle affection.

"Have you made any plans for his future?" I asked.

"I'm hoping I can talk him into living with Elizabeth and me, but he says he wants to stay with Jess Harding. I haven't spoken to Jess yet, but we'll take a ride up there as soon as we're done with this nonsense." He made a motion toward the judge's bench. "If Jess is okay with it, I suppose Elizabeth and I will have to be."

"Let me know if I can help," I told him.

"Gentlemen," Judge Lynn called from his chambers.

I pulled the gate back and Red and Billy walked through. I followed them into the small room behind the bench. Lynn had settled himself in a chair behind his desk. He'd removed his robe, and his hair was tousled from running his fingers through it. He looked impatient, eager to be off, and an image of the judge and his grandson standing with fly rods in the icy waters of Echo Creek flashed through my mind. We waited silently as Lynn loosened his tie and the top button of his shirt.

"It gets hot under those robes," he said to no one in particular, then rolled his chair closer to his desk. "Now then, how old are you, son?"

"He's sixteen, Your Honor," Red replied.

Lynn's brows furrowed. "Is the boy incapable of speech, Mister Gifford?"

"No, sir, but he's intimidated by everything that's happened recently."

Lynn pondered that for a moment, then nodded grudgingly. "Very well, I'll trust your judgment of the lad."

I was standing to one side, out of the way but where I could keep an eye on the proceedings. I could tell Billy was aware of my scrutiny. In fact, he seemed aware of everything that was going on around him, wary and on guard, but far from intimidated.

"I'm going to be speaking directly to the boy," the judge said to Red. "If at any time you think he is failing to comprehend what I'm telling him, I want you to stop me. It isn't vital that he understands everything immediately, so long as I can count on you to explain the details to him afterward. Can you do that?"

"Yes, sir," Red replied.

"Very well." Lynn paused to stare thoughtfully into Billy's eyes. I half expected the boy to look away, but he didn't. "First," the judge began, "I want to express my condolences for your loss. My own mother was taken from me by consumption when I was barely thirteen, and I well remember the anguish it caused our family. We mourned her death, William, just as powerfully as I'm sure you mourn the loss of your mother, but the important thing is that we didn't stop living. We didn't stop doing the things we needed to do to in order to endure the pain, and in time to even prosper. We bucked up, son, and that's what I want you to do. It's what I *expect* you to do. It's your turn to buck up, to ignore what you may feel is an injustice and move staunchly forward. You can survive this, William. You may even prosper, in your own way."

Lynn sniffed and leaned back, steepling his fingers above his stomach. Billy hadn't moved or shown the least bit of acknowledgment of the judge's words. He reminded me of other Indians I'd known over the years, their stoicism in the face of authority, the unfathomable depths of their eyes. It was as if a part of him wasn't even there, but I knew he was hearing every word, absorbing both meaning and intent.

"I have visited Indian reservations here and in other states, William," Judge Lynn went on. "I've seen what life can be like under such a trampling environment. It's why I so firmly believe your mother had a purpose in bringing you to Echo City. It was so you could escape the horrible examples of moral capitulation that plague so many of our reservations. Alcohol is not the path, son, nor is sloth the answer. Your mother would—"

Red's eyes had been gradually widening. Now he took a swift step forward, moving to the side as he did to partially shield the boy. "Wait a minute, Judge," Red protested. "You've no call to speak to Billy that way. He's never been anything but a fine young man."

"Mister Gifford." The judge's tone was as sharp as a spike. "You may not be standing before the bench, sir, but you are still in a court of law, and you will conduct yourself in a manner appropriate to your surroundings. Is that understood?"

You could tell Lynn's high-handedness was a spur in the storekeeper's hide. Red looked as mad as a pissed-on hornet. My own ears were thrumming with heat, although I'd been around the judge long enough by then to know better than let those feelings show. Henry Lynn could be a first-class son of a bitch when he was crossed, especially if it happened inside the courthouse, where I guess he figured he was the cock of the walk. Red must have sensed he was treading on thin ice, because although he continued to stutter a protest, he managed to bring his voice down a few notches. I glanced around to see how Billy was taking it, and all of a sudden realized the boy had sloped.

"Hey," I said, making a full circle as if I might have somehow missed him on my first sweep of the room. "He's gone," I added needlessly.

"Where did he go?" Judge Lynn demanded, as if either Red or I might have the vaguest idea.

"He's scared," Red said, although I had my doubts about that, even then. I think Billy had just gotten tired of listening to a windbag blow, and slipped out while Red and the judge were glaring at one another.

"He hasn't been dismissed yet," Lynn yelled as I moved swiftly through the door to the courtroom. Roy Sandler was still there, filling out some paperwork. When I asked if he'd seen Billy, he looked surprised.

"Yes, he just left. Is something wrong?"

I ignored him and turned back to face the judge's ire.

"You should have been watching him, Sheriff," Lynn said, his face mottled with anger.

"I didn't know he was being detained."

"When I'm speaking in this building, all men are detained until I've dismissed them."

Now that, right there, was the Judge *Lynch* I was talking about earlier. As arrogant as a whiskered goat, and democracy be damned.

"Billy hasn't done anything illegal, Judge," I reminded him.

"I'd advise you not to push your luck, Sheriff. I won't—" He stopped and scowled. "Where are you going, Mister Gifford?"

"To look for Billy," Red replied over his shoulder.

"By God, you come back here, sir, or I'll have you locked up!"

Red had already exited the room, but he came back at the judge's threat, his face damn near purple with rage. In a voice as cold as a bucket of ice, he said, "I am not your subordinate, Henry, and I'm not some petty thief or drunkard hauled in here frightened and without means. I won't tolerate abuse, whether it's in your court or my store."

The judge's shaggy brows rose and fell and rose again in astonishment. He lifted a finger as if to begin another lecture, but Red had already left. Lynn turned his smoldering gaze on me. "Find that boy, Pratt, and return him to my chambers immediately. Is that clear?"

"Yes, sir," I said.

Red was waiting for me on the street, his jaws knotted like tiny fists. "I swear, Hud, I'd like to box that old peacock's ears someday, just to hear him squawk."

I couldn't help smiling. "I think you've already done a pretty good job of that. I've never heard anyone speak to him the way you did. I'd say it scraped away some of his bluster."

Red shook his head. He was still upset, but his eyes were roaming. So were mine. Front Street was busier than usual with Saturday traffic, but Billy didn't appear to be a part of the crowd.

"Any idea where he'd go?" I asked.

"My guess would be the mountains, eventually."

"How would he get there?"

"He'd walk."

"Then he should be easy to overtake."

Red gave me a worried look. "Leave him be, Hud. Give him some time to sort out what's happened over the last few days. He'll come back sooner or later, I'm sure of it."

"The judge wants him back today," I replied, making no effort to mask the apology in my words.

"What Lynn wants doesn't interest me. Look for Billy if you have to, just don't find him." He was staring intently, as if willing me to understand. "Billy's been pushed awfully hard lately, Hud. I don't think he's got much more give left in him."

"Are you saying he might be dangerous?"

"Not if you give him time to think things through."

I hesitated before answering, even though I already knew I'd give Red the time he was asking for, the time Billy Pinto needed to come to terms with all the changes occurring in his life. But before I could respond, the jail's front door swung open and Jared stepped outside with his .30-30 held firmly in both hands. Jennings, Huttleston, and Walters followed. Tom brought up the rear, toting one of the Greeners. They filed around the side of the jail to where their horses would be waiting, and I tapped Red lightly on the shoulder.

"I'll talk to you later," I said, then started across the street, the tops of my ears like hot coals.

I've already mentioned how the jail shared its east wall with Scott Bailey's bank, but I don't recall saying anything about the broad alley on the west side of the jail. It was wide enough to accommodate a couple of wagons driven through abreast if the need arose, and led to the rear of Moon's Livery. John Moon had a contract with the county for its equine needs, in this case, the boarding of horses that Jennings and his men had ridden into town on until the fate of the ex-convicts could be determined. A trio of saddled horses were already hitched to iron rings bolted through the jail's brick wall, and Tom and Jared were standing to one side watching as Jennings and his boys booted rifles and checked cinches. Early Jennings looked up as I swung into the alley, a smirk sprouting like daisies along either side of his mouth.

"Well, hell, boys, here comes the mighty sheriff of San Pete County, wanting to wish us a speedy journey. Ain't that . . ." He stopped uncertainly, noticing, I suppose, the look on my face as I moved swiftly toward him. Taking a step back, he said, "You watch yourself, Pratt. I've put up with enough of your—" Then he stopped talking and raised both hands, but he was too slow.

Closing the final few feet between us in a shuffling run, I slammed a right between Jennings's wrists as hard as I could. I was aiming for his nose but got his mouth instead, which worked just about as well. I felt a tooth gouge into my knuckle, drawing blood before the enamel gave way and the tooth either broke or caved in toward his tonsils. Jennings grunted and staggered back against his horse. I jabbed him twice below the ribs with my left until his hands came down, then I hooked a right into his chin that snapped his head back.

Jennings crumpled alongside his horse like any other pile of shit, and I stepped back with my chest heaving. I heard Tom's muted cry, "Holster 'em, boys, or I'll cut you in half," and from the corner of my eye, I saw him standing in a half crouch with his Greener pointed at Dan Huttleston's belly. Huttleston unclenched his right hand and his revolver slid back into its holster.

"Let him come," I said, the words boiling up from my chest like a wolf's rumbling snarl, but Huttleston quickly shook his head and raised both hands. I looked at Walters, but he hadn't moved, and I knew he wouldn't.

I nudged Early Jennings's shoulder with my toe. It might

have been a little more than a nudge, but it wasn't an outright kick. I doubt if it even left much of a bruise. The killer groaned and rolled over, and I told him to get up.

"You son of a bitch," Jennings spat through mashed lips, spraying a light red mist while tears of pain streamed down both cheeks.

"On your feet, Jennings, or I'll give you something to really cry about."

He grabbed a stirrup but the horse shied off and he fell back with a groan. Watching him lie there, whining and writhing, brought back vivid images of Molly Spotted Horse's body as I'd found it inside her house—face puffy and bruised, dried blood in broken trails, an expression of pain rather than fear—burned into my mind forever.

Tom must have seen something in my eyes, because he said, "Easy, Hud."

I looked around, and the roaring in my ears began to fade. Tom gave Walters a shove. "Get your pard and get out of here."

Both men came over, watching me warily as they got their hands under Jennings's arms and hoisted him to his feet. The bloodied outlaw glared woozily in my direction but didn't say anything. Huttleston and Walters got him in his saddle, then mounted their own horses, and the three of them rode slowly out of the alley. Tom, Jared, and I followed as far as the street, then stood watching as they rode west along Front Street, the direction they'd originally come from. When they were out of range, Tom lowered the Greener's hammers to half cock.

"There's a little more trash swept off the street," he said. Then he looked at me and kind of chuckled, though cautiously, as if not quite sure of my mood yet. "I thought you were gonna lift that jackass's head off his shoulders with that last punch."

"Hell, I thought he was gonna kill 'im," Jared added, awe sparkling in his eyes. I'm generally a pretty easygoing guy, and that might have been the first time Jared ever saw me lose my temper that way.

Gently flexing the fingers of my right hand, I said, "How about I buy you boys a beer?"

"You're bleeding," Jared said, nodding toward my knuckles.

"It ain't going to kill me. Come on. I'm thirsty, even if you two aren't."

Normally I did my drinking at Joe's, but the Yellowstone was closer, and we went there instead. Although still early, there were horses at the rails and probably a dozen men inside, enjoying a cool beer in lieu of a noon meal. I ordered rounds for my deputies and myself, then retreated to one of the rear tables where we could talk in private. I told them what had happened inside the judge's chambers, then added what I'd learned from Red Gifford afterward. Tom read it the same way I had.

"Does Red think he could be dangerous?"

Jared's head came up. "Who?"

"Billy Pinto," I replied, keeping my exasperation with my number-two deputy in check. I shook my head to Tom's question. "He doesn't think so, but it was an interesting request."

"Shouldn't we be looking for him, if that's what the judge wants?" Jared asked.

Tom reached out with a finger and slid Jared's mug a few inches to the side, then made a show of peeking behind it. "Nope, he ain't there, but let's give it a couple of minutes and I'll look again."

"You don't half'ta make fun," Jared groused. "Judge Lynch sure as hell ain't gonna be laughin' when he hears we're in here drinking beer instead of looking for that redskin."

"He'll get over it," Tom said, then suddenly laughed.

I laughed, too, and it struck me that, despite the unsavory outcome of the trial, we were all relieved that it was over, and that our lives could get back to normal. Wishful thinking, I suppose. A few minutes later, one of the men at the bar raised his head and looked toward the doors.

"Anybody else hear that?"

I listened, then pushed away from the table. Tom and Jared surged to their feet after me. From way off in the distance, the sound of gunfire drifted over the town.

Session Seven

I have to apologize once more. Humphrey is having some troubles, and . . . well, he's like family. I didn't know a dog could worm its way into a person's heart like he has, although I can't say I regret it. But, back to what we were talking about.

You have to understand that in those days, nearly everyone owned a firearm. Unless they were dirt-poor—like drifters or vagabonds or immigrants just starting out in a new country—most folks owned several. Besides the guns I had access to through the sheriff's office, I personally owned two rifles, a revolver, and a pump-action shotgun I used for birding. Angie had a little .32 Smith and Wesson revolver her father had given her as a wedding present that she could carry in her purse if she wanted, and Cory had that single-shot .22 I've already mentioned.

What I'm saying is, hearing guns go off near town wasn't all that uncommon. But this was different, and we all knew it. For one thing, there was obviously more than one gun being fired; for another, the shots were coming really fast, like in a battle.

I paused on the boardwalk to get my bearings, but it was Tom who first placed the location.

"That's coming from the Point."

I nodded, staring west down the road to where a rise of land hid a ridge the locals called the Point. It was probably three or four miles away, and if Jennings and his boys hadn't dallied along the way, it was about where they'd be by now.

Spotting a seal-brown mare with a Bar-T brand hitched to the rail in front of the saloon, I jumped off the boardwalk and grabbed her reins. [*Editor's Note:* Headquarters for the Bar-T Cattle Company lay about twenty-five miles southeast of Echo City. It was owned by James A. Thedford, who gained some notoriety later in life for his alleged participation in a plot to assassinate President Woodrow Wilson. Although exonerated of the charge, Thedford's business and personal reputations were severely damaged by the accusations, and he was found hanging in the kitchen of a Cheyenne, Wyoming, hotel less than six weeks after his acquittal. Although his death was ruled suicide, there was no note.]

"Hey," a cowboy shouted, shoving through the batwings as I backed the mare away from the rail. "That's my horse."

"I'm gonna borrow her for a minute," I called, then vaulted into the saddle and spun away quick, before he could voice another protest.

That seal-brown was a good horse, like you'd expect from the Bar-T remuda, and she hit full stride almost instantly. A couple of the cowboy's buddies were yelling at me from the saloon, but with the wind in my ears, I couldn't make out what they were saying.

There was a rifle in the scabbard, unusual for a working cowboy but lucky for me, and I had my Colt on my hip. I leaned forward over the saddle horn as we raced through town. The sound of gunfire continued to roll toward us through the sage.

The town of Echo City had been platted on an open, windswept plain above what eventually became known as Echo Creek. [*Editor's Note:* On early maps, Echo Creek is called Porcupine River.] Its location was chosen for the convenience of the railroad, rather than any advantage for the community that came along later, but there were timbered ridges coming down off the Plateau like arthritic fingers, some of them reaching almost to the rail bed. The Point was one such ridge, a smoke-colored wrinkle in the land, with towering ponderosa pines flanking its rocky spine and a shallow notch near the tip where the old wagon road passed through. It was an ideal place for an ambush, and I was certain that was where the shooting was coming from.

It sounded like several guns were keeping up a steady barrage of mostly smaller-caliber firearms, although every once in a while I'd hear this throaty bellow that could have only come from something pushing a hefty powder charge. I'd examined the weapons owned by Jennings and his men shortly after their arrests, and knew they carried only revolvers and pistol-caliber lever guns. Nothing to make the kind of roar I was hearing.

That buffalo gun—and I was certain that's what it was—made me nervous. My first rifle had been a Remington chambered in .44-77, and I knew how accurate and far-reaching that old rolling block could be in the hands of a skilled marksman. It's not the kind of gun a sane man would want to approach across open ground, but there was that old problem again. I was wearing a badge, and there are responsibilities that come with it.

I was still half a mile from the Point when the shooting tapered off, then stopped altogether. Growing wary, I pulled the mare to a stop. Wisps of gun smoke clung to the boulders littering the ridge, and I could see a couple of horses standing off in the sage beside the road. Their heads were thrown high, staring toward a cluster of rocks south of the road. My heart was thumping along at a good clip as I slid the cowboy's rifle from its scabbard and threw the lever. It was an older Winchester in .38-40, more powerful than my Colt or even the .30-30 that Jared used, although I knew it wouldn't offer much defense against a buffalo gun.

Butting the cocked Winchester to my thigh, I gigged the seal-brown forward. Nothing seemed to be stirring. Even the horses remained motionless, at least until they caught sight of me and the seal-brown. Then they snorted and danced a little at this new intrusion, although they didn't bolt, as I was worried they might. Drawing closer, I spotted a couple of men lying in the sage along the road. I recognized Jennings first, flat on his back with his arms spread wide. Shep Walters lay crumpled not too far from Jennings, but it wasn't until I was within a hundred yards of the place that I spied Dan Huttleston, curled up behind a three-foot-tall clump of sage with his legs working slowly, as if trying to walk in his sleep.

I dismounted while still some distance away and wrapped the seal-brown's reins around the trunk of a sagebrush. Then I slowly made my way forward through the low, gray-green forest paralleling the road. I've read that in some parts of the country, sage is a small plant, thin-limbed and generally no taller than a man's hat, but up in that high desert surrounding Echo City, it grew thick and sturdy, and a man could make decent progress without being seen if he kept his head down and didn't mind crawling a little. Dusty knees never bothered me, and I don't think my head rose above the tops of the sage once in that hundred-yard crawl to Huttleston's side.

I've already made my feelings known regarding Early Jennings and his men, and nothing's changed over the years, but you'd have to be a stone-hearted son of a bitch not to feel some sympathy for Huttleston's condition. He'd been just about gutted by a slug across his stomach, and was using both hands to keep his bowels inside. Although conscious, I don't think he was aware of my presence until I was within a dozen feet of him.

"Huttleston," I said in a low voice.

His head turned slowly until he saw me through the sparse,

tan grass. "Oh, God, Pratt, kill me. For God's sake, cash me out."

I shook my head to that. I'd killed enough men in Cuba to last a lifetime, and wasn't about to start adding to those numbers if I didn't have to.

"Who did this?" I asked.

Huttleston moved his head back and forth. "Don't know," he gasped. "From . . . rocks."

"How many were there?"

His head rolled again, but he didn't reply.

Real tentative, I reared up to survey the tumbled boulders south of the road. It was where the outlaws' horses had been staring when I first spotted them, and where I would have set up an ambush if I wanted the odds to be on my side. Naturally, there was no one in sight, and I had to wonder if whoever had bushwhacked Jennings and his men had already fled, or if they were still there, waiting for me to step into the clear.

"Pratt."

Huttleston's voice came as low and drawn out as a rusty hinge on a closing door. I ducked back down and shifted around to face him. "I'm here."

"It was the kid," Huttleston whispered. His legs had stopped their sluggish movements and his hands weren't pressed as firmly to his stomach as they had been only a few seconds before. The flow of blood from his wound had slowed as well, and his lips had taken on a familiar shade of blue. I swore and scuttled closer, having to bend low to hear him above the gentle rustle of the wind in the sage.

"The kid," he repeated in words barely audible.

"Billy?"

He nodded. "From the rocks."

"You saw him?"

Huttleston paused, then shook his head. "It was him."

"How do you know?"

"The Sharps."

"Billy has a Sharps? Who told you that?"

The man's lips moved, but I couldn't make out what he was saying, not even with my ear scant inches away. It wasn't exactly gibberish that he was speaking, but it was obvious he was no longer talking to me, and when I leaned back and looked into his eyes, I could tell he was seeing things I wouldn't see until my own death. I sat there a moment longer, watching the life fade from his body, then I rocked back on my haunches to think. I felt fairly certain by then that whoever had ambushed these men had already moved on, and after a while I cautiously stood to scan the Plateau's bony finger.

"Billy!" I shouted, and my voice echoed back from the trees. "Billy Pinto! Can you hear me?" I gave it a minute without expecting a reply, then tried again. There was still no answer, and I finally gave it up and walked out into the road to have a look at Jennings and Walters. They were both dead, the former with a thumb-sized hole in the middle of his forehead, the latter with a bullet wound in his chest. I didn't have to feel for a pulse from either of them to know they were gone. That's the thing about a buffalo gun, it packs a wallop.

Off to the east I could see a plume of approaching dust, and I started back down the road to where I'd left the seal-brown. By the time I got there, Tom was slowing a team of horses from a run to a trot, the buckboard he was driving bouncing high enough across the rutted track to loosen a man's fillings. I waited until he brought the rig—one of John Moon's rentals—to a halt.

"What happened?" he asked, staring up the road at the two visible corpses.

"Someone shot Early Jennings and his boys. Huttleston's in the sage just off the road. You'll see him when you get up there."

"Jesus," Tom breathed, then looked at me with a question I'd already anticipated.

"Do you know anything about Billy Pinto owning a buffalo rifle?" I asked.

After a moment, Tom nodded. "Yeah, now that you mention it. I remember Red Gifford saying once that he sometimes paid Billy with forty-five-seventy cartridges. He said Billy didn't like going into stores to buy them himself because the storekeepers would either try to overcharge him, or act like he'd stole the rifle. Red said some of 'em would cuss him out if he argued about it."

I sighed and nodded and told him what Dan Huttleston had said. "I asked if he'd actually seen anyone, and he couldn't say that he had, but he sure seemed certain it was Billy."

"Maybe one of the others spotted him and said something."

"It's possible," I allowed, staring toward town where a number of horsemen were approaching at a swift lope. Among them was Oscar Larnx, the jury foreman from that morning, and my own deputy, Jared Caylin, riding alongside Oscar as if they were best buds. It irritated me that Jared could be so damned oblivious at times. He should have been out front, leading like a lawman. Or better yet, he should have told those men with him to stay home and let the law handle it.

I pulled the seal-brown close and returned the rifle to its scabbard. "Have Jared help you get these men in the buckboard, will you, Tom?"

"Sure, I'll take care of it."

"Take them to Doc Freeman and have him fill out the paperwork." I glanced at the sun, judging the time at about an hour past noon. "If Doc ain't busy with a patient, we might be able to get all three of them buried this afternoon."

"Where are you going?"

I nodded toward the ridge. "I want to have a look around,

see what I can find."

"Do you think it was Billy, Hud?"

"Maybe, but I'd like to have more than a hunch and a killer's opinion before I get the kid tagged with a murder warrant."

After the way Billy had acted that morning, I knew Judge Lynn—Judge *Lynch*—wouldn't hesitate to fill out a warrant for the kid's arrest. Likely he'd have to anyway, the way the evidence was shaping up, but it was still possible someone else—someone who'd maybe liked Molly and had been as appalled as I had by the way the trial had shaken out—had taken it upon himself to exact the justice the law had failed to provide.

I stepped into the saddle and reined toward the bony spine of rocks and trees while Tom drove up close to where the bodies were already attracting the attention of a murder of crows and magpies. He'd barely gotten his rig turned around to face town when Jared and the others got there. Everyone started talking at once, but Tom quickly cut through the chatter and got them dismounted to help load the dead men into the buckboard. I rode away, confident the situation was under control.

It didn't take long to find where the ambusher had waited for the outlaws. The imprints of knees, toes, and elbows were drilled into the dust behind a low, vee-shaped gap between a couple of small boulders. The distance to where the three men had been shot was less than one hundred yards, and I could feel my gaze hardening as I stared down on the killing grounds. It would have been like shooting pickles in a barrel for a man who knew what he was doing, and it made me wonder where Billy had learned to shoot—if it had indeed been him behind the buffalo rifle's stock.

My first thought was of the old mountain man up on the Plateau's shoulder. Folks said Jess Harding had been a crack shot in his day, and as lonely as his life must have been, he probably would have taken pleasure in sharing his knowledge with a willing student. Or it could have even been Red Gifford, who was a pretty good shot in his own right. I'd hunted elk with Red a time or two, and he never failed to come back from the mountains without at least a couple of carcasses lashed across his packsaddles.

One other thing I noticed was that there were no empty cartridges lying around, and that fit a pattern, too. Men like Red Gifford and Jess Harding would be adamant about taking your empty brass with you, so that it could be reloaded later on, or turned in at a store for credit the next time you purchased ammunition.

The trail leading away from the site wasn't as easy to follow as where the bushwhacker had laid, and I soon had to dismount and follow along on foot. It was nearly two hundred yards before I came to where the trail left the trees and moved out into the sage. Tracking became even more difficult after that. A less stubborn man might have given up, but Angie will tell you I can be bullheaded at times, and there's no doubt I was stubborn-mad that day, thinking of these men killed just about in my own backyard, and of a good woman—an innocent woman—raped and murdered.

Angry as I was, I nearly missed where the trail veered abruptly to the north. It got puzzling after that, zigzagging back and forth as if whoever I was following had started chasing a rabbit. Then the trail joined the tracks of a shod horse, and it suddenly made sense. I stopped and glanced around, but there was just me and the seal-brown mare. Tom and the others were hidden behind the ridge, along with two of the three mounts the outlaws had been riding when they left Echo City. The third horse, Early Jennings's blue roan, hadn't been in sight, but I had a good idea now what had happened. The horse had probably spooked with the first shot and bolted over the Point. That might be especially true if Jennings was the target. I also figured it likely that the other two horses had been pulled to a stop as soon as the shooting started, then stayed close when their riders left the saddle.

The tracks of the shod horse led south toward the distant Plateau. I remember staring in that direction a long time, thinking: *Well, you've got a horse now. That'll make you harder to catch, but easier to follow.*

It also hadn't escaped me that whoever had done the shooting—and I was fairly convinced by then that it was Billy—was also in possession of the Marlin rifle Jennings had in his scabbard, along with several boxes of .44-40 cartridges.

Seeing no point in continuing pursuit now that the ambusher was mounted, I swung a leg over the seal-brown's saddle and headed back to town.

I knew there'd be a buttload of work waiting for me when I got back. [*Editor's Note:* A *butt* is an archaic term referring to a wooden cask holding approximately 126 US gallons; its origins as a term for a "large amount" seems to be lost in antiquity.] Even so, I kept the seal-brown to a walk. I wanted time not only to mull over the obvious tasks awaiting my return, but the larger challenges I'd soon be facing. And I'll admit I was wondering how a trial would turn out if it was Billy Pinto who'd killed Jennings and his men. No doubt the outcome would be a lot different with an Indian, even a half Indian, in the defendant's chair. Yeah, it was going to be interesting—if it got that far.

I was thinking a lot about Judge Lynn, too. I knew he'd be foaming at the mouth over the killings that were rocking the town, more in the last four days than in the last ten years put together. He'd want Billy arrested immediately. Frankly, so did I. Guilty or not, Billy needed to be brought in until whatever had happened at the Point could be sorted out. Unfortunately, I also didn't have much doubt that a lot of townspeople were already blaming Billy. If not the killings, then at the very least for the disruption to their lives that the killings had caused. In their haste to remind folks of the boy's Indian ancestry, many of them would conveniently forget that it had been Jennings and his men who had started it all with their murder of Billy's mother, then rode away free as birds.

Those were crazy, mixed-up times in a lot of places, but especially so out West. Locally, these kinds of things were often made even worse by old-timers who still remembered the savagery of the Sioux and Cheyenne, and even the Utes, when those tribes had roamed across much of what eventually became San Pedro County. Some of those citizens had lost kin in the Indian Wars, and people like Frank Brady, whose wife had been stolen by Cheyennes and never heard from again, carried a grudge in their gut like a raw ulcer. They had little tolerance for Indians of any nation, and didn't give a damn that Molly Spotted Horse was Shoshone, or that Billy's father was a white man. They painted with a wide brush, and colored anything Indian as the devil's spawn. That's harsh talk on my part, but it's the way it was in those days, the way it probably still is in some of the old folks' homes where those early pioneers are living out what remains of their lives.

Session Eight

Back in town, I reined up in front of the Yellowstone and dismounted. The cowboy whose horse I'd borrowed was sitting on a bench out front. He stared sulkily, but didn't say anything as I looped the mare's reins over the rail.

"Thanks for the loan," I said.

"It wasn't a loan," he reminded me, although he didn't rise or look like he wanted to push the matter, for which I was grateful. He was right about it not being a loan. There's a pretty fine line between borrowing something without permission and stealing it, and I doubt I would have been as forgiving had the boot been on the other foot.

I went to the jail first, but no one was there. My next stop was Doc Freeman's office on Fourth Street, where I found Jared and Tom and the doc sitting in the latter's office. Right off, I noticed a decanter of bourbon and a trio of glasses sitting on the doc's desk; the next thing I observed was the pallid complexion of my number-two deputy. Tom spoke before I could.

"What did you find?"

"Tracks. Just tracks."

"Was it Billy Pinto?"

"No way of knowing." I nodded toward the bourbon. "How bad was that needed?"

"Pretty bad," Jared replied solemnly.

I glanced at the physician.

"Death by gunshot, no doubt about that," Doc said. "Jennings was probably killed instantly. My guess is that Walters lasted longer, although he was clearly injured early on in the attack. I couldn't say if he was able to return fire, but from what I heard from the street when the fighting was taking place, I'd say there were at least three men involved in the fight. As far as Huttleston, he lingered for probably twenty minutes, maybe even half an hour, but you already know that."

"He was still alive when I got there, although he wasn't very coherent. Could you tell what kind of bullet killed them?"

Freeman shook his head. "There wasn't any lead to recover. Passed on through the bodies, I suppose. Based on the entrance wounds, I'd estimate it was a forty-five caliber or larger. Judging from the damage to the tissue where the bullets exited, I'd guess it was a powerful cartridge, too."

"Something like a forty-five-seventy?" I asked.

"I wouldn't be surprised."

"It was pretty gruesome," Tom admitted. "You didn't see the back of Early's skull, where the bullet came out. There wasn't much left inside."

Jared pushed suddenly to his feet and lurched through the door to the street. A second later I could hear him retching dryly in the empty lot beside the doctor's office.

Tom chuckled quietly, although there wasn't any noticeable humor in the sound. "He's been like that ever since we rolled Jennings over. Couple of the other men did some pretty hefty puking, too."

"It takes getting used to," Freeman admitted. He tipped his head toward the decanter of bourbon. "That helps, as long as you don't make a habit of it."

"I won't argue with you," I replied, having resorted to a shot or two of whiskey more than once over the years. "When can we bury them?"

"Right now, if you'd like. I still have some paperwork to fill out, but I've finished the examinations."

"Can you get someone to dig the graves? My deputies and I are going to be busy for a while."

"Sure, I'll have Oscar Larnx do it. Can I tell him the county will pay him?"

"It'll pay you both," I promised.

I've mentioned Oscar more than once now, riding along with Jared out to where Jennings and his men had been shot, and he was the jury foreman that morning, too, but I can't remember if I told you how he made his living. Oscar was a hole digger—wells and privies and such—and would be well-equipped to crank out a trio of graves in an afternoon. You might think less of me for saying this, but it somehow seemed fitting that an outhouse digger would be the one who buried Early Jennings.

I looked at Tom and tipped my head toward the door, and he followed me outside. Jared was standing on the veranda when we got there, leaning against a post. His face looked as pale as a faded pillow case, and there was a sheen of sweat across his brows.

"Go on back to the jail," I told him. "If anyone asks, tell them you don't know anything, but that I'll be there soon."

Jared nodded and stepped off the boardwalk with a loose-kneed gait that might have been comical under different circumstances.

"You figure it was an ambush?" Tom asked.

"I do. Have you had a chance to check their guns?"

I didn't mention this earlier, but I'd noticed while checking the bodies out by the Point that Early Jennings's revolver had still been holstered, as if he hadn't even had a chance to pull it. Walters's revolver had been lying in the dirt at his side; only Huttleston had both his handgun and rifle with him when he died.

"Jennings's revolver had a full cylinder," Tom said, helping confirm my suspicion that he'd been shot first. "Walters had two live rounds left, and four empties. I didn't see any brass on the ground beside him. It looks like Huttleston did most of the fighting. His revolver was shot dry, and there were probably a dozen empty cases scattered around where he was laying, both rifle and pistol. I also noticed the ground behind him was pretty chewed up, probably from that buffalo gun. Huttleston wouldn't have offered much of a target if he kept his head down."

"You're thinking it might have been a lucky shot from whoever killed him," I asked.

He gave me a curious look. "You're not ready to say it was Billy?"

I hesitated, then shrugged. "Looks like it, doesn't it." Then I changed the subject. "Have you seen Judge Lynn yet?"

"For a minute, as I was coming into town. He stopped me in the street and wanted to see who I had in the back of the buckboard. I have a feeling he was getting ready to raise hell until he saw the back of Jennings's skull. After that he just dropped the tarp and told me he wanted to see you as soon as you got back."

"What about Red Gifford?"

"Spoke with him for a minute, too. He came over here to Doc's and asked if it was Billy. I told him we didn't know anything yet, but when I asked him about buffalo rifles, he got a real funny look on his face. He said he'd check."

"So he's got one?"

Tom shrugged. "He didn't say so, but I suspect he does."

I sighed. "All right, go saddle a couple of horses, will you?"

"Sure. Are we going after him?"

"We're going after whoever ambushed Early Jennings and his pards." I glanced at the sun and was surprised at how quickly the afternoon seemed to be slipping away. "Maybe we'll get lucky and catch him before nightfall, but just in case, stop by my house and ask Angie to pack some food to take along. Have her get my bedroll ready, too. I want to talk to Red first, then go see the judge. I'll stop by home before we leave. Meet me there with the horses in an hour."

Tom nodded and took off. I stood there a moment to gather my thoughts, then walked to the next block where Red had his hardware store. It was still closed, which I viewed as a bad sign. His house was on Grant Street, and I went there next, finding him and Elizabeth sitting together on a porch swing. They were holding hands, but they weren't swinging. It didn't look like they'd been doing much talking, either. Both had sad, reddened eyes. I stopped at the foot of the steps and removed my hat.

"Hello, Elizabeth."

"Hello, Hud. How are you holding up?"

"I'm all right. Better than you, I'd suppose."

"It's been trying," she admitted, then rose slowly. "Would you like some coffee, or lemonade?"

"No, ma'am, I'd better not take the time."

"All right. I'll leave then, so that you and Honas can talk." She entered the house at the pace of a woman half again her age, closing the screen door gently behind her.

I looked at Red. "Tom's already mentioned a Sharps."

"Yes, he did."

"And?"

"Billy has one. He used to borrow my rifle until he earned enough money to buy his own."

"How'd he earn that much money?"

"Chores around town."

"A Sharps is a hell of a lot of firewood to chop."

Red shrugged and looked away. "Billy and Jess Harding hunt elk up on the Plateau, then sell the meat and hides to United Lumber. Mosby uses the meat to feed his crews, and the hides to make repairs on his equipment . . . drive belts, things like that."

"There's a law against hunting elk out of season, Red."

"I know, and I've told Billy as much, but men like Jess Harding have been out here so long, they don't necessarily feel that those laws should apply to them. I've always suspected that's why they stay so far away from towns. They don't want anything to do with the kind of life we've brought to their lands." He turned his gaze back on me. "I guess Billy feels the same way, Hud. This land belonged to his people until the white men took it away."

"If he'd been found up here by the Sioux or Cheyenne, they'd have taken his scalp and not worried about a reservation for his children."

"Indians have always been harder on other tribes than the white man ever was, but it's the white man who eventually prevailed. You can't expect a conquered people to look kindly upon their oppressors."

I shrugged and decided not to push it. The Indian question was too complex to discuss on a front porch, and poaching elk wasn't what had brought me there. "Do you know where Billy is now?"

"I don't, Hud, I'm sorry. I went down to Molly's when Tom told me Jennings and his men had been ambushed at the Point, but Billy wasn't there."

"What about his rifle?"

"That's gone, too. He also took his old clothes, most of the blankets, and all the extra food."

"He's making a run for it?"

"That would be my guess, although I don't know where he'd go. Maybe to see Jess. That old man and the Plateau are the only friends Billy has anymore."

"He's got you," I reminded him.

"He does, although I don't know if he realizes it." He smiled sadly. "I don't think he'd consider me a friend anymore, either."

I swore softly. "Are you saying he's turned bronco?" [*Editor's Note: Bronco* is a term common throughout the West, including Mexico and Canada, referring to a feral horse that is hard to capture and usually difficult or impossible to break to the saddle; in the nineteenth and early twentieth centuries, it was often applied to American Indians who broke away from reservations to return to their old ways of life.]

"I suspect he has," Red replied solemnly.

Well, that was a kick in the gut. I looked off into the same distance Red had stared at earlier, contemplating the storekeeper's response, and what it would mean if true.

"Billy has a horse now, too," Red added quietly.

"I know, Jennings's blue roan."

He appeared mildly startled by that, then shook his head. "No, he's got my sorrel, the one I keep at Moon's."

"The hell! When'd he take that?"

"This morning, right after the trial. John didn't say anything to me because he didn't think it was important until the news about what happened at the Point started getting around. He came and asked if I'd sent Billy for the horse, but I hadn't."

"Has he done that before?"

"Taken my horse? Yes, lots of times, when I've needed him to deliver smaller items to one of the outlying ranches, or to United Lumber. He'll either use my saddle horse if there isn't too much gear to pack, or rent a team and wagon in my name for a bigger load. John wouldn't have suspected a thing. In fact, he said he figured I just wanted to get Billy away from town for a while."

I thought about the tracks I'd followed at the Point and wondered if they made any difference in my resolve to bring the boy in. I decided they didn't. Billy Pinto was still my prime suspect. He needed to be found and brought back to Echo City, if for no other reason than to keep him safe until I could determine who did kill Jennings and his men. But if the boy had turned bronco, it was going to put a whole new spin on the ball.

"Let me know if you hear from him," I told Red, then headed back to Front Street. Judge Lynn was next on my agenda, but when I got to his office in the courthouse, he wasn't around. Roy Sandler cornered me in the hall to inquire about the shooting. I told him we were still working on it, then asked about Lynn. Roy said he didn't know where the judge had gotten to, and that was good enough for me.

"Tell him I was here looking for him," I told Roy, kind of tossing the words over my shoulder as I headed for the door.

I paused on the courthouse steps to have a look around. Although I didn't expect to see Billy among the Saturday afternoon throng of cowboys, timbermen, and homesteader families, it would have made my job a lot simpler if I had. I did notice a horseman coming up the Plateau Road at a hard gallop, but I didn't think anything of it at the time. It was getting late, and I put it down to a cowboy eager to begin his weekly hoo-raw at one of the saloons.

I headed for home, cutting through alleys not only because it was quicker, but to avoid the staring eyes and probing questions that had been following me ever since my return from the Point. Tom wasn't around when I got there, for which I was grateful. I wanted a few minutes alone with Angie.

She looked up when I pushed through the door, and I could tell she'd already heard about the shootings west of town. The fact that she was stuffing food inside a small canvas sack told me Tom had already been there and left.

"Hud, how bad is it?"

"It's not good, but it'll work itself out."

"He's so young." Her eyes darted to the hall leading to the

bedrooms, and I knew she was thinking of Cory. He was only eight, but the ways the years fly past . . .

"Billy's had a hard life," I reminded her.

"Was it really that hard?"

I didn't reply, my thoughts sidetracked in wondering how I'd react if I came home to find my family murdered, then be forced to stand silently in a courtroom and watch a biased judge and lazy prosecutor cut the killers loose. Frankly, I'm not sure I wouldn't have done exactly as Billy had, despite the badge pinned to my shirt.

Sensing that I wasn't going to answer, Angie placed the canvas sack on the table beside my bedroll, then went into the back room for the rest of my stuff. While she was doing that, I brought my rifle down from the pronghorn rack on the parlor wall where I kept it.

I mentioned not too long ago about how the county furnished a number of firearms for the sheriff's office, specifically the Greener shotguns Tom and I preferred for close-up work, and the .30-30 Winchester Jared used. Those were the county's weapons, purchased long before I took the deputy's job under the captain. [*Editor's Note:* Pratt is referring here to his former commanding officer during the Spanish-American War, James V. Nelson; a brief description of Nelson is included in the editor's note for Session One.]

I was expected to furnish my own revolver, though, and for a long gun, I favored the Krag I'd brought back from Cuba. [*Editor's Note:* Although Pratt doesn't say, he is most likely referring to the Model 1896 Krag-Jørgensen rifle.]

I'd already retrieved a couple of boxes of .30-40 Krag ammunition from the hutch when Angie came back with a wool scarf, a pair of sturdy leather gloves, and my heavy sheepskin coat. She set everything down on the table, then stood back with a worried expression shading her green eyes. "You'll be careful, won't you?"

"I always am, ain't I?" I glanced into the parlor. "Where are the kids?"

"Lily's playing schoolteacher with Missus Hamilton's chickens, and Cory's hunting out past Spill Street." Noticing my sharp look, she added, "I had no way of knowing, Hud, and surely Billy wouldn't harm a small boy."

"No, probably not," I replied, although without much conviction. "When Cory comes back, tell him to stay close to home until this is over."

"I will," she promised, and I knew she would have done so even without my meddling. She'd be just as worried about Lily, too, and would keep both children in sight until Jennings's killer was brought to bay. It made me smile, and Angie looked puzzled. "What?"

"I was picturing Lily trying to keep the Hamiltons' chickens in line for class."

Angie laughed, then her eyes misted over. A horse nickered from the street and I heard the clop of hooves approaching the house. I'd hoped to have more time with Angie.

"I have to go," I said, then pulled her into my arms and kissed her hard. She hugged me back just as tight, like she always did when I went out after a fugitive, and I swear I could feel the baby inside of her stir against my stomach. I gritted my teeth and took a step back, and was getting ready to tell her good-bye when that damned phone started clattering like rocks in a bucket, causing both of us to flinch. I went over and yanked the receiver from its cradle.

"Yeah?" I said curtly.

"Hud, that you?"

"Who do you think it'd be, Carl?"

"Hell, don't snap at me, son. I'm just a messenger."

I shook my head, for all the good it did with Carl Hennessy

sitting several blocks away at the switchboard in the Union Pacific depot. "What do you need, Carl?"

"I don't need anything. It's the judge told me to call. He says there's trouble out to his ranch, and he wants you there as fast as a good horse can carry you."

"What kind of trouble?"

"He didn't say," Carl replied in that hedging tone I'd come to expect when he wanted to hide the fact that he'd been eavesdropping.

"Carl, what kind of trouble?" I repeated firmly.

"Well, sounded kind'a like Injun trouble."

I gritted my teeth, and my fingers tightened on the receiver until it's a wonder the thing didn't crumble in my hand. Watching, Angie got a frightened look on her face. I turned my back to her, but she stayed close and heard everything I said, and probably most of Carl's end of the conversation, as well, phones being what they were back then.

"It was Burton who called," Carl went on.

Deke Burton was an old Texas cowboy who'd come up the trail more than once in his fifty-plus years as a cattleman. He was foreman at the Broken Cinch, and a good, steady hand by most accounts, though opinionated as hell, like a lot of those old-timers are. Although I didn't care for Burton personally, I figured if he said there was trouble at the ranch, then more than likely there was.

"Hud, is it true what folks is sayin' about Billy Pinto?" Carl asked.

"I don't know what folks are saying, and I don't have time to speculate about it over a telephone."

"They're sayin' he's turned bronco."

"You listen, Carl, we don't know who killed those men at the Point, or what kind of trouble Deke Burton might be having at the Broken Cinch. Until we do, I want you to keep that mouth of yours screwed shut."

"Jesus, Hud, you don't gotta get your dander up. I was only asking. Oscar Larnx was at the Yellerstone a while back sayin' it was Billy, sure enough, and that he scalped Early Jennings while he was still alive, then cut off his—"

I hung up, near about having to bite my tongue to keep a string of curses from spewing from between my lips. I know a lot of men cuss in front of their wives, and I've known more than a few wives—respectable women, too—who could damn near peel the paint off a living room wall when they got up a good head of steam. You don't wear a badge and remain innocent for long, but I've always made an effort to curb my language in front of Angie and Lily; Cory too, until he got older.

"Hud, is that true?"

"Not a bit of it," I replied. "Angie, I was there. Somebody killed those men, and it was probably Billy, but he didn't scalp them. As far as I could tell, he didn't even get close to them."

I don't know how much my words appeased her, but I was real aware of how swiftly the afternoon was getting away from me. I couldn't tarry any longer. Grabbing my rifle, cartridges, and bedroll, I headed for the door. Angie gathered up the rest of my gear and followed me outside. Tom was sitting astride a leggy sorrel with a thin blaze running down her face, holding the reins to the buckskin gelding I usually rode, already saddled and with my scabbard under the off-side fender. He nodded politely to Angie, then looked at me.

"What's got the judge so fired up?"

"Some kind of trouble at the ranch," I replied, booting the Krag. "Why?"

"I saw him leaving town in that motor buggy of his like he was being chased by hornets."

Yeah, you heard right. Electric lights, telephones, even an

automobile; or a motor buggy, as we called it. Echo City was a bustling little town, as long as you didn't get too ambitious with your comparisons. Places like Denver, Salt Lake City, even Cheyenne, had dozens of horseless carriages rambling up and down their streets. Echo City—hell, all of San Pete County—had just the one, a brand-spanking-new 1904 Pope-Hartford, shipped in by train, along with a steady supply of gasoline, oil, and whatever else it took to keep the thing running. [*Editor's Note:* The 1904 Pope-Hartford (Pope Manufacturing Company, Hartford, Connecticut 1903–1914) was available in two designs, the Model A Runabout, with its twin-passenger capacity and open rear, and the four-passenger Model B Tonneau, with front and rear seating and a hinged trunk under the rear bench. As the Model B was a late entry into the 1904 automotive market, Lynn's vehicle was probably the Model A Runabout.]

I paused after sliding my bedroll across the saddle's rear skirting, then told Tom what Carl had told me while I finished strapping everything in place. When I was done, I checked the buckskin's cinch, then turned to Angie and winked. "I'll be fine," I said in an effort to forestall any voiced concerns.

"I know you will. Tom, you keep him out of trouble, you hear?"

"I will, Angie," he promised.

I leaned forward to give her a quick kiss, then swung a leg over the cantle and reined away. I winked again as I turned into the street and she smiled back, but it was a sober gesture. Mine was a dangerous occupation, and we both knew the risks.

Session Nine

We got that old dog after Lily was married. He was a pup then, barely seven weeks old, but he was a handful from the beginning. I swear there wasn't a piece of carpet or hardwood he didn't pee on until we got him trained to take his business outside. Did his fair share of damage to chair legs and sofa cushions, too. I was about ready to sell him for wolf bait more than once, but then he'd give me that puppy-dog look like he hadn't a clue that gnawing on the upstairs bannister wasn't encouraged. Not to mention Angie would have snipped my ears off with garden shears if I'd gotten rid of the damned flea catcher.

Cory and Lily had both moved out of state by then, and Lily's husband is a mining engineer who travels constantly, all over North and South America, and he'll even fly to Africa or Australia if he's needed. Lily usually goes with him, especially if he's going to be away for any length of time, and Cory had already decided on a career in the military, so there was no point in Angie and me thinking about moving to where he and his family might be stationed for the next six months to a year.

I don't know where Angie came up with a moniker like Humphrey. Maybe it's kind of like Missus Bee Jax, just a name plucked out of a notion tree. It's a damned odd one for a basset hound, though. Anyway, Humphrey's settled down for a nap, so we shouldn't be interrupted for a while.

Judge Lynn's Broken Cinch Ranch was about ten miles from

town. It was a pretty fancy spread, the way some of those ranches are if there's outside money to spruce up the facade. The two-story house with its tall cupola and green lawn was surrounded by a couple of dozen tall cottonwood trees, and the stables, hay and equipment sheds, barn, bunkhouse, and various other outbuildings were set out back of the main house by a good one hundred yards; they were all downwind, too, which helped keep odors, barnyard noises, and flies to a minimum.

There was a knot of cowboys gathered in front of the bunkhouse, and Tom and I went there first. The drovers stepped aside as we approached, like curtains being drawn back from a stage. Deke Burton was sitting in a chair next to the front door with his hat on his knee; he might have reminded you of a traveling orator if not for the bandage wrapped around his skull.

"Deke," I greeted, halting in front of the gray-bearded cattleman.

"Sheriff," the foreman replied solemnly. "Deputy."

"Mister Burton," Tom said.

"What happened, Deke?"

"Was that kid, Sheriff. One hunts elk with Jess Harding."

"Billy Pinto?"

"Yep, Molly's boy. Miss Henrietta come in on the train yesterday to visit her daddy, and that Irish gal of hers takes the kids down by the creek." [*Editor's Note:* Henrietta (Lynn) Stokes was the third child and only daughter of Judge Henry and Bertha (Bodine) Lynn. Henrietta Lynn married Geoffrey Stokes in 1888, after meeting the Cheyenne, Wyoming, dentist at a New Year's Eve gala. The Stokes had four children—Susan, Edwin, Abigail, and Clara. Geoffrey Stokes died of injuries sustained in a hiking accident in the mountains west of Cheyenne in 1902; Bertha Lynn succumbed to cancer in 1897. Henrietta remained in Cheyenne, but continued to visit her father's ranch outside of Echo City on a regular basis.]

"They was having a picnic under the cottonwoods," Deke continued. "I was up here helping get the mower ready for next season's haying when I hear the Irish gal scream like somebody'd chopped off a toe. Ran down there real quick, thinking maybe they come on a rattler. Wasn't thinking a bit about redskins, and got caught off guard when that boy come outta the bushes. Whacked me a good one with his rifle butt." He lightly touched the side of his head, as if I might have somehow missed the startling white bandage in the dimming twilight, or the pinkish stain above his left ear.

"Are you sure it was Billy?" I asked.

"I'm sure. Seen him enough, slinking up to Harding's place like a coyote. Like he's planning to steal something, and don't go getting your dander up, either, Pratt. That's the way the boy is, always taking the back way, trying to stay out of sight. You'd see him, you'd think the same as me."

"All right," I said irritably, not wanting to take the time necessary to point out all the bullshit a kid like Billy Pinto had to put up with; it'd be enough to make a grown man skulk, although I doubt if Deke Burton would have cared. "What happened at the creek?" I asked.

"Stole the judge's granddaughter is what happened."

"Stole her! You mean kidnapped?"

"Call it what you want. Got a dozen hands scouring the country for them now, and the judge'll have a dozen more by first light. I'd go myself, but every time I stand up, the world starts to tilt on me."

"Son of a bitch," I said quietly, exchanging a bleak glance with Tom. "Was anyone else hurt?"

"About scared that Irish gal outta her accent, but the only blood spilled was my own. My own damned fault, too. Should've been more watchful."

"The judge has gone after her," one of the hands said.

"Hush, Toby," Deke chided. "True enough, though. Got a bunch of boys to pile into that motor bug of his and took off for the canyons. He can beat Pinto to United's road before dark, he might stop him. The boy gets past there, that motor bug ain't going to do the judge a lick of good."

"That country above where United Lumber has its mill is rough as a cob," Toby added. "I've hunted cows up there."

"What I tell you about butting in?" Deke asked.

"Sorry, boss."

Deke scowled, then looked at Tom and me. "What you got in mind, Sheriff?"

"I've got in mind to go get that girl back," I said.

Deke leaned forward as if thinking about standing, then kind of swooned back with a groan and a curse.

"You ought to go see Doc Freeman about your head," Tom suggested, earning himself a disdainful glance from the old cattleman.

"It's a lump on the head, Deputy, not a bullet in my brisket. Be fine as a ten-dollar fiddle by morning. Wasn't for Suzie, I'd wish they didn't catch that redskin bastard until I got out there myself. Like to have a crack at that boy."

"What's the Irish girl's name?" I asked.

"Irish is what Miss Henrietta calls her. Judge calls her that, too. Far as I know, that's her name. She's over to the house yonder, you want to palaver with her."

We rode away and the cowboys swung back like circling wagons to surround the old foreman. When we were out of earshot, Tom said, "This doesn't sound like Billy Pinto's doing."

"It doesn't," I admitted, but didn't pursue it any further. The truth was, we all had our ideas about what Billy was like, but when you got right down to it, none of us really knew the boy. I'm not even sure how well Red Gifford understood him.

The Irish girl wasn't hard to find. She was sitting on the steps of the back porch, sniffling like someone had told her to shut up before she'd finished bawling. Her eyes widened when she saw Tom and me approaching, and I thought for a minute she might jump up and run away. You could tell she was making an effort to get herself under control.

"Ma'am," I said, drawing rein some yards away and dismounting so as to not overly intimidate her from the back of a horse. I removed my hat as I stepped forward, and even then, made sure I didn't get too close.

"Ye'd be the sheriff, are ye not?" she said. Then, as if remembering her position, she stood and did a little curtsy. When she looked up, tears were flowing anew down her freckled cheeks.

"My name is Sheriff Pratt." I made a motion behind me. "This is my deputy, Tom Schiffer."

She performed another little curtsy toward Tom, gulping back a muffled sob as she did. "And pleased I am to meet ye," she managed. Then, after a pause, she asked timidly: "Are ye here to arrest me, sirs?"

I smiled as amiably as possible under the circumstances. "No, ma'am, we'll not, but I'd like to ask you some questions."

"Why, surely, mister. I'd help ye in any way ye ask, I would."

"Deke Burton says it was an Indian who accosted you along the creek."

"He was, sir, I be certain of that. About scared me out of me shoes, he did."

"Can you describe him?"

"Until the day I die," she replied with such solemnness I almost smiled. Then she went on to describe Billy Pinto, right down to the store-bought suit and stiff new hat that Red Gifford had bought him for his mother's funeral—the same outfit he'd worn that morning in the judge's chambers, and the urge to smile drained right out of me. When she was finished describing the incident along the creek, I asked if she'd seen in which direction Billy had fled. She pointed toward the Plateau. " 'Twas thataway, sir, with Missy Susan hanging on something fierce."

"How many horses did he have?" Tom asked.

"Two, it were. One the color of a cold winter's morn, the other like a fresh copper penny."

I guess that's what clinched it for me. I'd been hoping Billy wasn't too deeply involved in everything that had occurred that day, but whoever had killed Early Jennings and his boys at the Point had also stolen Jennings's blue roan, and I knew Billy had taken Red Gifford's sorrel from the livery. The girl's description of the kidnapper and his horses were too close of a match to deny any longer.

I asked a few more questions, like what did the girl look like and how long had it been since she'd eaten, if she had any special medical needs, and what she'd been wearing when Billy grabbed her. Then I thanked her and started to turn away.

"Sheriff Pratt," she said hesitantly.

"Yes, ma'am?"

" 'Twas one thing more, and I have not told the judge yet, because the young lad what took Missy Susan said I was to tell ye, and that ye should be the one to tell His Honor."

"What's that, ma'am?" I asked with a sudden feeling of apprehension.

"He said." She stopped and her brows wrinkled as she tried to pull her thoughts together, to get Billy's message exactly right. "He said ye was to tell His Honor that now 'twas his turn to buck up. Them was the words he used, too, and said I was to tell ye that for sure and certain. To *buck up.* Do ye know what he means, sir?"

I nodded numbly. "Yeah, I reckon I do," I said, then tipped my hat and walked over to where Tom was waiting with my buckskin. I glanced at the sky, fading toward purple in the east. Under different circumstances it would have been wiser to spend the night at the ranch and get a fresh start at first light, but I couldn't risk that with the judge somewhere ahead of me. I knew how he thought, and I'm guessing that by now, you do, too.

"Are we going on?" Tom asked, although I suspect he already knew what my answer would be.

"Yeah, we'd better." I gathered my reins above the buckskin's withers, then stepped into the saddle.

Buck up.

Do you remember the judge saying that? It was an expression I'd heard often enough over the years, and more than once in the last few days. Lynn had told me to buck up a few days before, when he wanted me to wrap up the investigation into Molly's death as quickly as possible. More importantly, he'd told Billy the same thing just that morning. It had seemed as condescending as hell at the time, but from the lack of emotion on the boy's face, I wasn't sure he'd picked up on it. I guess he had, and that the judge's words had burned as hotly in his belly as they did in mine.

Session Ten

The north-south road connecting the railroad at Echo City with United Lumber's main compound partway up Echo Canyon ran about half a mile east of Judge Lynn's Broken Cinch Ranch. With darkness coming on, there wasn't much use in trying to find Billy's trail along the creek, so Tom and I returned to the main road at an angle, then reined toward the Plateau. I'll admit right up front that I'm not a great tracker, and any notion of our trying to catch up with Billy that way would have been a waste of time. Besides, I figured the odds were good that if he was heading for the Plateau, he'd follow his usual route. At least initially.

"Have you ever been to Jess's place?" Tom asked.

We were keeping our horses to a walk, riding stirrup to stirrup as the last of the light drained out of the sky and the temperature started to drop. I shook my head to his question. "I know about where it is, but I've never been there."

"But you figure that's where Billy is heading?"

"It seems like a good place to start."

We rode on in silence after that, ticking off the miles while the Plateau loomed tall in front of us. Echo City was pretty high up, but I'd guess the Plateau was another twelve to fifteen hundred feet above that. [*Editor's Note:* The San Pedro Plateau averages 9,500 feet in elevation, according to the US Department of Geology (USDG); its highest point is the southeastern tip of Porcupine Ridge, 10,231 feet above sea level.] The sun had long since dropped below the horizon when my buckskin suddenly snorted and threw its head up. Tom's sorrel reacted similarly, and we reined in and put our hands on our revolvers. A few minutes later we spotted a lone individual coming down the pike on foot, a shadowy figure bathed in moonlight. When Tom called out to ask who it was, the man darted into the sage and dropped from sight.

"I'm armed," he shouted. "Don't come any closer."

Tom and I quickly dismounted and led our horses off the road, where they would be less likely to be hit by a stray bullet.

"This is Sheriff Hudson Pratt," I called. "Come out where I can see you."

"Pratt?" The man's head rose slowly above the sage. "Sheriff, is that you?"

"I said it was, didn't I?"

"Hell's fire, Sheriff, don't shoot, I'm coming out."

"Who are you?" Tom demanded.

"Mark Anderson, from the Broken Cinch. I work for Judge Lynn."

I knew him. Not well, but enough to recognize his voice. He stepped out of the sage and approached cautiously, keeping his hands well out from his sides and away from the revolver strapped around his waist. He stopped when we mounted our horses and rode toward him.

"Don't shoot, Sheriff. I ain't huntin' trouble."

Tom guffawed. "Looked to me like you were running from it."

"I reckon that's about the size of it," the cowhand admitted, lowering his hand now that he wasn't as worried about being shot. "I was afraid you were Indians," he added.

"Where'd you get a notion like that?" I asked.

"Ain't you heard about the judge's granddaughter?"

"Yeah, we've heard. What are you doing up here on foot?"

"I was with the judge in that motor buggy of his. We were heading for the turnoff to United Lumber when the judge ran into a rock and busted out half the spokes in one of his front wheels. He sent me back to the ranch to round up some more men, along with extra horses and plenty of supplies. I guess he figures it's going to be a long chase."

"Where's the judge now?" I asked.

"Maybe a quarter mile shy of the turnoff. When he hit that rock, it threw a couple of the boys into the brush, and ol' Herb Finch broke his arm. I'm supposed to get a wagon up there to pick him up, then go into town and find Frank Brady." The cowboy's head wagged sadly. "I ain't never seen the judge so worked up, Sheriff. He's pert near foaming at the mouth with mad."

"What's he saying about Billy Pinto?" Tom asked.

"Said he's going to string the boy up when he catches him. Said it's going to be a whole lot worse if Billy's hurt his granddaughter."

"All right," I said. "Go on back to the ranch and fetch that wagon for Herb, but leave the horses and the extra men behind. Forget the judge ever said anything about Frank Brady, too. The last thing I need is that Indian hater up here tracking for the judge."

"Aw, hell, Sheriff, the judge'd string *me* up if I don't do what he says. You know that."

"You tell the judge that Tom and I are going after Billy, and that we'll bring his granddaughter back. Tell him to keep his men off the Plateau."

"Sheriff, I know you're the law, but so is the judge, and I reckon I'd rather be thrown in jail by you than get the judge riled at me. Especially the way he's feeling now."

"Just do what I said," I replied brusquely, then nodded to Tom and we guided our horses around the stranded cowboy and continued on our way. Mark stared after us for a couple of minutes, then began loping awkwardly toward the ranch in his drover's boots.

"You know he's going to do what the judge told him to, don't you?" Tom remarked.

I nodded grimly. "Best we can do now is catch up with Billy before Lynn does."

"What are you going to tell the judge when we see him?"

I thought about that for a minute, then nodded off to the west, where a long finger of pines had encroached into the sage. "We're not going to see him. There's a trail up there that Red Gifford showed me a few years ago. We were hunting elk, and used it to get above the meadow where they were feeding. If we follow that, we can avoid the judge altogether." I glanced at Tom. "He's got more authority than I do. If he ordered us to give him our horses, we'd be legally obligated to do so."

"Would you?" Tom asked after a couple of minutes.

I didn't have to think about my reply. "No, I wouldn't, but I'd rather avoid the confrontation if we can."

The trail Red had showed me wasn't hard to find. Once we reached the top of the ridge, it was probably as easy to follow as the main road. Tom and I kept climbing until the moon sank, then stopped and made ourselves as comfortable as possible among the ponderosas. It was cold enough that we could see our breath, and the ground was rocky and unforgiving under our butts. We took the bridles off our horses and loosened the cinches, but left the saddles in place. Then we found a little nook where the wind couldn't reach us and made ourselves as comfortable as the circumstances would allow.

We were back in the saddle by first light, and reached the turnoff to United Lumber before the sun came up. We paused in the middle of the road, probably a mile or more above where the judge's automobile had broken down. Up canyon, we could already hear the ripping of timber as the sawmill's heavy blades gnawed into the sappy wood. But what really stopped me was the view. I hadn't been this way in a couple of years, and I was rendered nearly speechless by the progress the company had made in denuding the canyon's steeply sloping walls. I'm not going to bad-mouth United Lumber. This country was built on timber and livestock and raw ore, and the sweat and blood of the men and women who harvested its bounty, but I won't deny a deep sadness as I stared at the rubble United had left behind. Broken and twisted limbs, piles of bark, dying scrub and bare earth, all of it waiting to be washed downstream in next spring's floods.

"It'll grow back," Tom said as if reading my mind.

That was true, too. But it would never be the same, never be virgin again, and I remembered my conversation with Red the day before about how people like Jess Harding and Billy Pinto felt toward the land and the people who labored so hard to change it. It made me wonder if Billy had ever stopped here to stare, as I was, at the scarred earth, and if it had touched him in the same way it did me.

Lifting my reins, I tapped the buckskin's sides with my heels and we left the road, winding carefully through the scrub left by the lumberjacks until we reached the canyon's far ridge. From there on we were back in the tall timber, the air fresh enough to make a man almost forget what he'd witnessed.

It was another two hours before we came in sight of Jess Harding's place. Tom and I came out of the pines single file and hauled up to study the cabin with its small corral and lean-to shed; a neat pile of chopped firewood flanked the front door, handy to reach and an added buffer against winter's winds. The cabin itself was a log structure, maybe thirty feet wide but no more than twenty deep, if the ridgeline of his sod roof could be believed. A couple of deer hides were nailed to the front wall, and there was a small fur press, just a hinged pole above a wooded base, not too far away.

Jess was sitting in a chair out front with a large, thick-haired dog plopped in the shade at his side. A rumbling growl rolled across the broad clearing toward us, although the massive brute remained sitting. Tom and I rode up to within thirty feet of the cabin before we stopped and nodded our howdies.

"Gentlemen," Jess returned politely.

"Mister Harding," I replied.

"Mister? That seems awful formal for the mountains, Sheriff."

"It's your call," I told him.

"How about you call me Jess, and I'll call you Hud." He looked at Tom and grinned. "Mister Schiffer and I have already had this conversation."

Dismounting, Tom said, "How are you, Jess?"

"Fair to middling for an old grizz." Then he placed a calming hand atop the canine's broad shoulders. "I'm afraid Brutus doesn't remember you."

"He will," Tom predicted, although I noticed he wasn't moving away from his horse's side just yet.

Jess Harding was probably in his sixties by then. Although he'd missed the heyday of the fur trade by several decades, what a lot of people don't realize is that the trade itself didn't die out just because the big trapping companies quit the mountains. Established outfits run by men like John Jacob Astor and the Bent brothers went where the money was, and when the beaver trade played out, they started dealing in buffalo robes and Indian-tanned skins. A lot of the old mountaineers, men like Jim Bridger and Joe Meek and those, moved on to other enterprises; they scouted and farmed and settled down; a few even went to work for the Indian Bureau. But others stayed in the high country and continued to trap. Beaver had grown scarce, but there was fox and marten and a lot of other smaller, fur-bearing animals. Even mice would fetch a few pennies apiece if a man wanted to take the time to skin them.

Nobody in the field ever got rich trapping for fur, but if a man was determined to stay in the mountains, he could make enough to support a modest living. A lot of those old-timers would supplement their income from outside sources, too. Jess, for example, sometimes guided Eastern industrialists on hunting trips into the Rockies, taking them up into the high country after elk and grizzly bear and bighorn sheep and mountain goats—whatever struck a hunter's fancy, or might look good with its mounted head hanging on the wall of his study.

People called Jess a mountain man because of his hunting and trapping and the way he lived, but he was a lot more than that. I would have loved to have known where he came from and what brought him to the mountains all those years before. When Tom and I rode up that day, Jess was reclining in a seat made of elk antlers and rawhide. He had a cup of coffee sitting on a chunk of unsplit firewood at his side, and a book laid open on his lap. His long, skinny legs, clad in wool trousers rather than the more romantic notion of fringed buckskins, were crossed to form a rest for whatever it was he was reading, and I remembered Tom telling me after his last visit up here that Jess had shelves inside his cabin filled with books.

"Thirty or forty of 'em," Tom had claimed, "and lithographs on the walls. Pictures of castles and big cities from a long time back. Damnedest thing you ever saw."

I know the cup Jess had at his side was of a blue willow pattern of dinnerware Angie would have given a tooth for. I'd have liked to have seen the inside of Jess's cabin myself, but felt pressed for time.

"Hud, you might as well get down, too," Jess said after a bit. "I've got a stew on the fire and coffee in the kettle, if either of you are interested."

"I reckon I'll pass, but my deputy might like a cup of coffee."

"A cup of coffee sounds good," Tom agreed. "Mind if I fetch it myself?"

Jess's expression turned wary, but he went ahead and tipped his head toward the door. "Go on in and have a look around," he invited.

Tom's face flushed red at having been seen through so easily. Ducking his head, he silently entered the cabin. Brutus started to push off his hindquarters, growling softly, and Jess told him to hush and sit down.

Dropping the buckskin's reins, I approached the cabin without taking my eyes off the dog. "What are you reading?" I asked.

"A book by a man named Jules Verne. Ever hear of him?"

As a matter of fact, I had. Angie belonged to a literary club in Echo City, a group of ten or twelve women and a few men who met regularly at someone's home to exchange books and talk about what they'd been reading. Angie had read Verne's *Twenty Thousand Leagues Under the Sea* several months before, although she hadn't been a fan of the story.

Imaginative, but frightening, was how she'd described it, then added, "I think I would suffocate if I had to go that far under water, I don't care how much air the craft carried with it."

I recall she hadn't been too thrilled with the octopus, either.

I mentioned the novel to Jess, but he said he hadn't read it yet.

"This is *Around the World in Eighty Days.*"

"Heard of it," I replied.

"It's entertaining, although not very realistic."

"That's kind of what Angie said about *Twenty Thousand Leagues.* The unrealistic part. She didn't say it was entertaining."

Jess dropped a dry twig between the pages as a bookmark and set the novel aside. "You didn't come up here to discuss fiction, Hud."

"No, I didn't. We're looking for Billy Pinto. Have you seen him?"

Jess appeared to weigh my question carefully. "I've hunted with Billy. Is that what this is about?"

"No, I don't care about his hunting. It looks like Billy might have killed some men outside of Echo City, and I have witnesses who say he kidnapped Judge Lynn's granddaughter."

"I don't believe that," the trapper replied instantly, and Brutus again started to rise until Jess eased him back with a hand on his collar. "Billy's not a killer, Sheriff, and he sure as hell isn't a kidnapper."

I told him about Early Jennings then, about Molly's death and Judge Lynn's sham of a trial, and you could see the conviction seeping out of Jess's lanky frame. When I finished, he slumped back in his chair with a half-sick expression on his face.

"It would take something like that," he allowed.

"Has he been here?"

"Maybe. Brutus started growling last night, and I got out of bed to take a look. I could hear animals moving through the timber below the cabin like they were trying to sneak around the place, but I didn't think too much of it. Most folks don't like to ride through a man's yard, especially after dark. I went down to have a look this morning and found the tracks of two horses."

I stepped into the cabin's shade on the other side of Jess, away from the dog, and was kind of surprised at how good it felt to be out of the sun. I'd just about froze my butt off the night before, but the days were still warm, even up here. I leaned a shoulder into the cabin's wall and began a cigarette. Tom appeared at the door a moment later with a cup of coffee in one of Jess's old tin cups.

"There's plenty of coffee, if you want some," Tom said to me.

I shook my head and concentrated on shaping the paper for my smoke.

"Molly was a damned fine woman," Jess said reflectively. "It's too bad someone didn't kill that sorry bastard years ago."

He didn't say, but I knew he was talking about Early Jennings. "Red Gifford told me Billy's pa was a trader from the Wind River country. You know anything about that, Jess?"

"Not much. I know there was a man named Bear Williams who used to trade with the Indians up there, the Arapahos and Shoshones. They say he was a fair man who didn't try to cheat the Indians out of their furs. I couldn't say whether or not he's Billy's father."

"Lynn's organizing his own posse," I said, and Jess made a dismissive sound low in his throat. "He's sent for Frank Brady to guide for him," I added.

"Frank Brady couldn't find his ass inside his own britches," Jess replied, although he didn't sound as convinced as he had when I told him about the judge's posse.

You might recall me mentioning Brady earlier, about how he'd lost his wife to a Cheyenne war party and never got over it. What I don't recall telling you was that Frank spent quite a few years after that scouting for the army. I couldn't tell you how good he was, but I doubt if the army would have kept him on if he hadn't been at least halfway competent at the job.

"Brady could get lucky," I said.

"He might," Jess agreed.

I finished rolling my cigarette and struck a match. A thin cloud of smoke sheathed my head as I stared up canyon to where the aspens were starting to turn. On top, probably another seven or eight hundred feet above our heads, they'd likely already be shimmying like fields of gold. I had no way of knowing which direction Billy would run, but I had to guess it would be up. Once he reached the Plateau, there'd be a thousand places for him to hide.

"I've got to find them," I said finally, jetting a stream of tobacco smoke skyward. "I have to bring the girl back, at least."

"It would be the thing to do," Jess said.

I looked at him, studying him in the sharp autumn light that made everything seem so vivid at that time of year. "Tell me how good he is, Jess."

"Billy, or Frank?"

"Billy."

Jess seemed to think about it for a long time before he answered. "I'd say he's pretty good, Hud. It'd take a hell of a tracker to corner him. I couldn't tell you if Frank Brady has that kind of skill." Then he glanced at me and shook his head. "I won't do it. Mind you, I don't condone what Billy did, but I understand *why* he did it. I suspect you do, too."

"The judge has a dozen cowhands he can put into the field, and who knows how many more he could get from Echo City. If he doesn't find Billy soon, he'll put a bounty on his head that'll draw every disillusioned gunman from five hundred miles around, looking to kill an Indian before they go the way of the buffalo. Billy wouldn't stand a chance."

"Billy doesn't stand a chance now," Jess replied with unexpected harshness. He pushed suddenly to his feet and the dog leaped to his side, barking excitedly. "Easy, Brutus," he said, patting the dog's head. "He senses I'm upset." Then he looked at me. "And that you're my enemy."

"I'm not your enemy, Jess. I'm not Billy's enemy, either, but I've got a job to do, and a frightened girl that wants to go home to her family."

Real soft, Jess said, "Goddamnit." I could see the pain and hopelessness in his eyes, and I knew he was right. Billy's odds of coming out of this alive were just about nil.

"What about the girl?" I asked.

"The girl?"

"Judge Lynn's granddaughter. Her name is Susan, but they call her Suzie. She's twelve years old."

"Billy won't hurt her."

"Jess," Tom said almost gently. "Billy's already kidnapped her, and it's almost certain he killed those three men at the Point. Lord knows what'd happen if the judge or some shootist looking to prove his mettle pins him down."

"Help us, Jess," I said, surprising myself with the request. I hadn't come here to ask for Harding's help. I'd only wanted to talk to him, to get a feel for what Billy might do, and which direction he might run. It hadn't occurred to me until that very moment that the old mountain man might well be Billy's only chance—as slim as that might be.

Quietly, Jess said, "I told you I understood why he did it. I'm wondering if you do."

"He did it because he's mad," I replied. "Mad about his mother being killed, and about Judge Lynn letting the men who did it go free. I would be, too."

"There's more to it than that. Have you ever talked to the boy, Hud?"

"No, I can't say that I have."

"Not even once?"

I shook my head.

"But you were in Lynn's court with him, right?"

"A lot of people were, but it was Red Gifford who was speaking for Billy, making sure he understood what was happening."

"Did you know it was Red who brought Billy up here the first time? That was probably . . . what? Four or five years ago, now. He wanted me to teach the boy what I knew of his people, and especially how to get along in the mountains. Billy was a good student, smart, too." He chuckled at some memory. "He'd talk your ears off around the campfire at night."

"I've seen him whispering to Red, but I don't believe I've ever actually heard him talk to anyone," I said.

"No, you wouldn't. Billy's an Indian, no matter who his father was, and that's the way you saw him. I imagine it's the way everyone in Echo City saw him. To the rest of the town, Billy Pinto was just an Indian. Or worse, a half-breed, either one of which would have made him an outcast."

There was a lot of truth to what Jess was saying, and I'll admit I can see it better now than I did then. The trouble is, I was also seeing another side to that argument, one that was a whole lot fresher then than it is today.

"There're too many people in Echo City who remember what it was like in the early years, Jess. They remember losing kin, and friends—men, women, and children—to the wild tribes. People who maybe never did anything to deserve it, other than to be at the wrong place at the wrong time."

"Billy's a Shoshone, and the Shoshone were never wicked-bad. Not like others, but they were all fighting for their land, their way of life. No different than you'd do in the same situation."

"You might make a case for the Shoshones," Tom said from the cabin's door, "but if you tried that argument for the Sioux or Cheyenne, folks will take a pitchfork to your butt."

Jess shook his head. "It's not as different as you think, Tom, although it takes a while to figure it out. It took me damn near thirty years."

I'm not sure what Jess meant by that, nor did I care at the moment, although I'll admit I grew curious about it later on. But right at that moment, I had other things gnawing on my brain. Dropping my cigarette and grinding it out under my heel, I said, "I need an answer, Jess. Will you help me find Billy Pinto, before Judge Lynn does."

"Judge Lynch," Tom added pointedly, and I could see it made a difference.

"All right," Jess said, his expression as hard as a farrier's anvil. "I'll help you find Billy, but only to bring the girl back. I won't betray him, Hud, and I sure as hell won't let you hang that boy from a white man's gallows. I don't care what it takes, I won't let that happen."

Excerpt from:
Inquiry into the Events
Related to the William Pinto Uprising
13 November 1904–16 November 1904
The Honorable Frederick S. Tunstill, Presiding
San Pedro County District Court, 14 November 1904

"Let the record show that Jared Caylin has been duly sworn in before the bench of the San Pedro District Court. Mister Caylin, would you please state your name and occupation on the dates in question?"

"Yes, sir. My name is Jared Caylin, and back in September I was a part-time deputy for San Pedro County. I also worked for Echo City in what they called a joint agreement, where the town and county shared things like the cells in the county jail, or traded off duties when extra hands were needed. I mostly worked for Sheriff [Hudson] Pratt, but if Marshal [Lawrence] McNichol had a prisoner, I'd watch him, too."

"So your primary job was to oversee the jail?"

"I guess you could say that. They called me a turnkey, but I did just about anything and everything that needed doing."

"Would you please tell the court how you became an acting sheriff in the pursuit of William Pinto."

"Well, on the night the judge's granddaughter got kidnapped, the judge went after Billy in his automobile, but then he busted a wheel halfway up the main canyon and had to put together a horse posse. He sent back to town for an officer, but Sheriff Pratt and Tom, that's Tom Schiffer, Pratt's main deputy, had already took off after

Billy, and Marshal McNichol was in Salt Lake City visiting his wife's kin, so I was the only lawman there."

"You were left in charge by Sheriff Pratt?"

"I'm not sure you could say I was in charge of much, but it's true that Sheriff Pratt wanted me to stay in town. It was a Saturday night, and there were a lot of folks come in for the trial that morning—"

"The trial of the Early Jennings gang?"

"Yes, sir, for killing Molly Spotted Horse, who was Billy Pinto's ma."

"So you were summoned by Judge Lynn to join his posse?"

"Yes, sir. Everything was real mixed up at first. The judge had sent for Hud and Tom, but they'd already left, and Carl Hennessy, he's the telephone operator for Echo City, he'd already gone home for the night, so there was no way for the judge to contact the town that way. It was probably the middle of the next morning before I got word the judge wanted to see me."

"Where was that, Mister Caylin?"

"At his ranch. He'd already been back there quite a while by the time I showed up, and he was really faunching. At the time, I didn't know what he wanted me for, which is why I didn't have any gear with me. You know, a good bedroll and such? The judge had to furnish all that for me."

"According to Thomas Schiffer's testimony yesterday, you met the San Pedro County deputy on your way to Judge Lynn's Broken Cinch ranch. Is that correct?"

"Yes, sir. Tom was on his way back to town by then. I

met him on the road north of the judge's ranch."

"The court is curious, Mister Caylin. If Deputy Schiffer was the ranking officer, why didn't you turn the responsibility of meeting with Judge Lynn over to him?"

"Well, you don't know the judge, sir. I mean, maybe you know him, you both being judges and all, but you don't know what he's like when he gets riled. When he says to come, you need to get your hindsights moving real quick."

"I would remind the gallery that interruptions to these proceedings will not be tolerated. Any further outbursts of mirth and I shall clear the room. And Mister Caylin, I would urge that in the future, you choose your words with more care."

"Yes, sir."

"Moving forward, can you tell the court what the mood was at the Broken Cinch Ranch upon your arrival?"

"It was real grim, Your Honor. The judge had been drinking by then, and he was mad as all get-out about me and Frank Brady taking so long to get there, although . . ."

"Brady?"

"Yes, sir. Frank Brady was the town's handyman, but back before things got settled, he scouted for the army all through that country. I reckon Frank was about the best tracker you could find in those parts."

"Let the record show that the Frank Brady Mister Caylin is referring to is the same Franklin Kirk Brady hired by Judge Lynn to guide the San Pedro posse onto the San Pedro Plateau. His name is already on record. You may continue, Mister Caylin."

"Well, the judge's men, those that worked for the Broken Cinch, were all fired up to get after Billy, but the judge said he wanted to keep the posse small, so that it'd be more manageable."

"How small?"

"There was just the eight of us. Me and the judge and Deke Burton. Deke was the Broken Cinch foreman who got his head popped by Billy Pinto's rifle butt when Billy kidnapped Miss Suzie. Deke was still looking a little peaked, but he was determined to go with us. Oscar Larnx and Alfred Hamilton was there, too. They're townsfolk, and good men. The other two were cowhands from the Cinch, Toby Smith and Mark Anderson. Anderson was the one who came into town to fetch me and Frank. Oscar and Al were at the jail when he showed up, and they decided on their own to come along. The judge didn't send for them, but he didn't send them home, either. Anyway, we were all standing around outside the judge's big house, must've been twenty of us, counting all the judge's hands, when Frank and the judge came over and picked out the men he wanted to take with him."

"Excuse me, Mister Caylin. You say Mister Brady and Judge Lynn made the decisions regarding the number and makeup of posse that would accompany you onto the Plateau?"

"Yes, sir."

"And you weren't a part of that conversation?"

"No, sir."

"Why not?"

"Huh?"

"I said, why not? You were acting sheriff, appointed

to the position by Judge Lynn, weren't you?"

"Yes, sir, I was."

"Then shouldn't you also have been involved in the decision making?"

"Well, I guess the judge didn't want me involved."

"Again, Mister Caylin, why not?"

"I guess mostly Judge Lynn wanted me to be a badge, in case he needed one, but everyone knew who was in charge, and it sure as heck wasn't me."

"Then who was in charge, Mister Caylin? Who, in your opinion, was responsible for the deaths that occurred on top of the San Pedro Plateau in September of this year?"

"That was the judge, Your Honor. Judge Lynn. He was in charge when . . . well, when all those killings took place."

SESSION ELEVEN

While Jess saddled a dappled gray gelding next to the lean-to, Tom led his horse over to where I was checking the buckskin's cinch. "Are you sure about this?" he asked as I lowered the near-side stirrup.

"Yeah. Someone has to manage the office. With McNichol in Salt Lake City and you and me up here, that leaves Jared in charge. I'd worry about that after a day or two."

"I would, too," Tom reluctantly admitted. Then he moved back along his horse and pulled a pair of chaps out from under his bedroll. "Maybe you can use these," he said, tossing them over.

I accepted the well-worn leather leggings gratefully. Tom was an inch or two shorter than I was, but otherwise we were roughly the same build. I knew the chaps would fit, and that I'd appreciate them dearly if the weather turned bad. Leather doesn't offer a whole lot of protection against the cold, but it cuts the wind like nobody's business; couple that with a layer or two of wool underneath, next to my skin—longhandles and heavy trousers—and they'd make a huge difference.

"Thanks," I said.

"I've got this, too." He pulled a waxed-paper-wrapped package from his bags and brought it over. "I stopped off at Mae's Café before we left town and had her fix some food to bring along. It's mostly cold roast beef and biscuits and a sack of dried apricot slices. It's short on fancy, but it ought to last you four or five days if you ration it."

"It'll help."

"Anything else?"

"I don't think so. Just keep a lid on things in town until I get back."

He gave me an odd look that I found puzzling at first. Then I recalled our conversation on the night Early Jennings's and his boys had ridden into Echo City. I'd scolded Tom then for not informing me of Jennings's release. He'd gotten pretty indignant about it, and rightfully so, I might add.

"Do what you have to," I told him. "I'll back any decision you make."

"Even if it means arresting one of the county's leading citizens?"

"Even that," I replied. Then we both laughed. I knew he was talking about Judge Lynn, and how impossible that would have been.

Hooking a toe in the stirrup, I stepped fluidly into the saddle. I say fluidly now because I might forget to add later on how much more difficult it became to haul my tiring frame into the cradle as the days wore on.

Jess mounted his dappled gray and rode over. "You coming?" he asked Tom. When the deputy shook his head, Jess looked at me. "Then it's just us?"

"Will that be enough?" It was a rhetorical question. Two was going to have to be enough.

"Let's go," Jess said, reining his horse around.

I nodded a final good-bye to Tom, then tapped the buckskin's ribs with my heels. I didn't look around to see if Tom pulled out immediately. My eyes were already traveling forward, rising toward the crest of the Plateau that, from the trail leading away from Jess's cabin, seemed to tower straight overhead.

There was no road, hadn't been since we passed the canyon

where United Lumber had its sawmill. I didn't know where the judge was at that time, although I suspected he would follow the main canyon to the top. That might not be the case if he had Frank Brady to guide them, but it's what I was hoping for. I felt more confidence in the route Jess Harding was taking, and considered it to my advantage that he knew Billy as well as he did.

Something that was worrying me, though, and would continue to nag at me through the coming days, was how Jess would react when—*if*—we caught up with Billy. I figured he'd support my wanting to rescue the judge's granddaughter, but any effort on my part to arrest Billy for the murders of Early Jennings and his boys might throw a kink in the matter.

Jess's big dog, Brutus, followed along, although it stayed mostly in the trees and out of sight. I had mixed feelings about the brute, especially its loyalty. Take a swing at Jess, and I figured you'd have that monster chewing on your throat before you even knew it was around.

Our route got a lot rougher after we left the cabin. There was a well-worn trail to the top, but it was steep and rocky, and every once in a while it would skinny down until we were traveling along a ledge no more than a few feet wide and maybe two or three hundred feet in length. I've never been especially afraid of heights, but staring down past my boot at the tops of towering pines and jutting granite spires was keeping images of long drops and hard landings prominent in my thoughts.

It was nearly noon when we reached the top. We stopped and dismounted and loosened our cinches to let the horses blow. Brutus plopped down nearby, his pink-and-black tongue lolling. Being able to stand back four or five feet from the edge of the bluff allowed me to better appreciate the view, and I'll admit it was pretty spectacular. The Plateau's northern slopes were scarred with timbered canyons—thousands of acres of ponderosa pine, along with juniper, mountain mahogany, and stands of cottonwood and willow. I could see Echo City way off in the distance, and the flat line that was the Union Pacific tracks cutting across the high desert plain. Farther away, to the northwest, lay the pale blue caps of the Wind River Mountains, with the Laramie Range pushing up closer to the northeast.

The scene was fully as awe inspiring in the other direction, a broad fan sweeping from southeast to southwest, and as far as the eye could see lay glimmering sheets of gold, spotted with groves of dark pines, distant grassy meadows, and gray-blue peaks thrust above timberline. As I'd guessed earlier, the aspens up here were at their peak of color, white-barked trunks striped and pocked, leaves like fresh-churned butter.

Nodding to the south, Jess said, "This is my home, Hud. That cabin we left this morning, that's where I hang my traps and cure my pelts, but this is where my heart is."

"It's a sight to see," I acknowledged.

He gave me a searching look. "Is this your first time up here?"

"It is. I've hunted elk with Red Gifford in the canyons under the rim, but I never made it up this high. Never had to, where we hunted."

He was watching me curiously, and after a drawn-out moment, he said, "I've often wondered why someone like you would want to live in a big city?"

"I'd hardly call Echo City a city."

"It's right there in the name."

"That was some businessman's idea. Call it a city, and the thinking is that people will come and turn it into one, but it's not all that big. As cold as it gets in winter, I doubt if it ever will be."

"How many people live there?"

"Just shy of seven hundred, according to the last census."

"Seven hundred people, all crammed into one place." He

whistled in amazement. "That's a lot of people, Hud." He jutted his chin toward the gilded horizon. "I doubt if there's seven citizens out there altogether, and probably seven hundred square miles to stretch out in."

"Seems lonesome," I replied. "I suspect jobs are scarce, too."

He chuckled. "Jobs don't seem like a solid reason to turn your back on the wilderness. I believe I'd rather make do with less and have this for my backyard, than live somewhere surrounded by other peoples' outhouses."

I had to smile at that. "You make a good argument, but I like my job, and Angie likes living where there are other women to talk to, folks to turn to for help if it's needed." Then my smile faded as I thought of Billy and Suzie, somewhere out there in that dense, yellow land.

"He won't hurt her," Jess said softly, as if reading my mind.

"So you've said."

"I want you to believe it. Billy's a good kid. He deserves a chance."

"That girl's probably scared half out of her wits right now."

"I know, but being scared might make her smarter down the road, too. If nothing else, it'll let her see that life isn't all pampered and safe. At least not for everyone."

"I'm not going to have this argument, Jess. The girl's got to go back to her family, and if you want Billy to get a fair shake, we're going to have to find him before Judge Lynn does."

"Is Billy going to get the same kind of fair shake his mother did?" Jess asked, and there was a sharpness to his words now, like a north wind in winter. My reply was just as bleak.

"He'll get better odds with me than he will from Lynn, and you can bet that sooner or later, Lynn is going to find him."

"It's more likely Billy will find him," Jess replied soberly, then turned to his dappled gray and tightened the cinch.

I stood there a moment, thinking about that and about what

he'd said earlier at the cabin, and I wondered again how far I'd be able to trust Jess Harding. I glanced at Brutus, staring at me as if measuring out a meal, then turned my back on both of them and readied my own rig. Mounted, we rode down a gentle slope toward the belly of the forest, where we'd all soon be lost. Well, not Jess or Brutus, and probably not Billy, either, but as the trees swallowed me and my horse, I knew I wouldn't have stood much of a chance of finding Billy and the girl up here by myself.

It didn't take long to pick up Billy's trail. Jess pointed out where the tracks crossed in front of us. "Two of them," he said.

I studied the narrow trace of trampled grass winding into the forest. "It looks like one horse is following the other?"

"Billy's leading the second horse. He's probably riding Jennings's mount. What did you say it was?"

"A blue roan."

"Gelding or mare?"

"Gelding."

"A good horse?"

I nodded. "Better than you'd expect for a man recently set free."

"Then Billy's riding that. I know Red's sorrel, and it's getting old. It wouldn't catch a young man's eye like something younger and flashier-colored."

"Would that make a difference?" I asked.

Jess eyed me quietly for a moment. "You don't know him very well, do you?"

"No, but there're a lot of people in Echo City I don't know very well." His question annoyed me, probably because Red had asked something similar the day before. Hell, I'd just told Jess there were close to seven hundred people living at Echo City. What did he expect, that I'd have time to sit down and chat with every one of them?

We moved on into the trees with Jess up front and me right behind him. If you've never ridden with a posse, I'll tell you it isn't as exciting as you might imagine. Especially if the person you're chasing is out of sight, or the trail is more than a day or so old. Sometimes, if you have a sense of where a fugitive might be headed, you can cut around in front of him. Head 'em off at the pass, like they say in the picture shows. But with Billy having such a lead and the Plateau so big, our only option at that point was to find his trail and stick to it. If you were tenacious and didn't lose the track, you could often catch up, although any lawman will tell you there's been more than one bad man slip through a noose, no matter how tight you think you have it drawn.

We kept our horses to a walk and never left the trees all day. I've already mentioned how the forest on top of the Plateau had turned to gold, but fortunately the leaves hadn't started dropping yet. As dry as it was, a bed of fallen leaves would have made our little two-man posse sound like a herd of buffalo tromping through the timber.

Around sundown, we came to a stream no more than a couple of paces across. You could tell from the prints in the soft soil along its banks that Billy had stopped there. Jess handed me his reins and went in first, kneeling at the stream's edge to examine the tracks. He poked along both banks for a few minutes, then waved me forward.

"They've got a good start on us," he said.

"How much of a start?"

"I'd say twelve hours, at least. He must've ridden all night."

"He'll wear his horses out if he keeps up that pace."

"He will if he doesn't steal fresh mounts along the way."

I gave the old mountain man a hard look. "Just how much did you teach that boy, Jess?"

"As much as I could, law dog," he replied flatly, then took his reins and led his horse downstream to drink.

"What about the girl?" I called after him.

"She's still with him."

I kept my mouth shut as he walked away, then began my own search of the stream's moist bank. It took only moments to pick out the smaller prints of Susan Stokes's shoes, pressed into the gravelly mud at the water's edge. From the deeper impressions at the toes, I figured she must have been leaning forward over the creek, presumably to drink. It made me wonder how she was holding up after nearly twenty-four hours as a captive, and most of that time spent on the back of a horse. She'd likely be worn out. A kid, especially one who grew up soft, like the judge's offspring, probably wouldn't have much stamina to draw from, I reflected. I remembered Lynn telling me about a tenth birthday party for one of his grandkids—it might have even been Suzie's—and how they'd rented ponies for the children to ride and brought a big cake in from the local bakery, and how the *Denver News* had sent a reporter up to cover the event like it was a damned political convention. Thinking about it there along that stream irritated the hell out of me for some reason. Then my horse pulled impatiently at the reins, and I loosened my grip to let him drink.

We made a cold camp that night, picketing our horses on short leads so they wouldn't get their ropes tangled in the trees. There wasn't much conversation, and I was tired enough after the last few days that I dropped off not too long after crawling into my blankets. We were in the saddle again as soon as it was light enough to begin tracking the next morning. Jess kept the lead, with Brutus staying close to the dappled gray's side. I brought up the rear and kept my mouth shut and my eyes open. So far the trail had been fairly easy to follow, but I knew Jess's eyes, while older and maybe not as sharp as mine, would be far more attuned to reading sign; he'd pick up on things I might be more likely see, but to also dismiss, like a broken limb or the way a blade of grass was turned.

It was about ten o'clock that morning when we heard a rifle's distant echo off to the west. Jess drew up, staring. Then he glanced over his shoulder at me. I shook my head. "It could've been anyone," I said. "A hunter, even a cowboy looking for strays."

"Yeah, could've."

I chewed thoughtfully at my lower lip. The shot had come from several miles away. If it was a hunter, or someone unaware that a girl had been kidnapped and that a killer had taken flight across the Plateau, we'd lose valuable time tracking him down, only to find out he didn't know anything. On the other hand, what if it was Billy? What if, hungry and needing to feed himself and the girl, he'd risked a shot to bring down some kind of game for food? If that was the case, we could potentially cut hours off his lead.

"Shit," I said softly, then looked at Jess. "All right, let's go see who it is."

He nodded agreement and reined away from the trail we'd been following steadily southward ever since reaching the Plateau. My gut said we were on a fool's errand, but logic held a different view; it was telling me to leave no stone unturned, to check out every possibility.

It was early afternoon when Brutus veered away from our westerly course and led us to a small spike mule deer, lying dead at the edge of a grassy clearing. It had been winter fat and sleek when shot—you could tell that much from what was left—but he'd also been partially skinned, the hide thrown back and both haunches and back straps taken, along with some of the shoulder and neck meat. It was a fair job for the field, though hurried. Jess called his dog away from the carcass, then dismounted and handed me his reins. He circled the deer with his eyes cast to the ground, moving here and there through the tall grass. At one point he stopped to pick something up off the ground, then came over to where I was sitting my buckskin.

"I figure seven or eight men," he said.

"A hunting party?"

"I don't think so. It looks to me like just one man did the butchering, while the others sat back and watched." He handed me the thumb-sized object he'd plucked from the grass. "Recognize it?"

He wasn't asking for an identification, but if I knew who smoked good Cubans. I took note of the rich brown color of the outer leaves, the shape of the tooth-frayed butt, then tossed it back in the grass.

"Lynn?" Jess asked.

"Be my guess. I wonder how he got up here so fast."

"Probably came straight up the big canyon, rather than take the long way past my cabin. We're lucky Billy took the long way, too."

"Do you think Lynn knows where Billy is?"

"No one knows where Billy is," Jess replied. "The question the judge has to ask himself is, which direction is Billy likely to head. If he guesses that, it'll only be a matter of time before he cuts the boy's trail. If not . . ." He shrugged, then walked back to grab the small buck by its rear leg and haul it over on its other side. Drawing a knife from a simple leather sheath on his belt, he stooped and quickly cut away what neck and shoulder meat hadn't already been taken. He tossed a few scraps to Brutus, then sliced off a square of hide at the flank, where it was thinner and more pliable, and wrapped the meat inside. Then he brought the bundle back to his horse and tied it behind the saddle.

My buckskin spooked a little at the smell of blood, but Jess's dappled gray stood patiently, like a hunter's horse would. When he had the meat secured and was wiping his hands and blade clean on wads of grass, I asked something I'd been thinking about ever since we made camp the night before. "What about you, Jess? Do you know where Billy's headed?"

"I told you yesterday, there's a thousand directions he could take off in."

"That was yesterday, on the rim. We've been following him ever since, and he's still headed in the same direction."

Jess was quiet a moment, thinking. Then he sheathed his knife and led his horse out to the middle of the clearing. I followed along on my buckskin. Jess was looking a little west of due south, toward a line of pale blue mountaintops.

"You see those two tall peaks to the left of that bare ridge?" he asked, pointing; when I said that I did, he went on. "Those are called the Mule Ears. There's a trail between them, real narrow and dangerous, but it'll take you into one of the prettiest little basins I've ever seen. Billy and I went in there once to hunt, and he was taken with it. Said a man could live there his entire life and never have to look at another white-eye." He glanced at me to see if I knew what he meant, and I nodded that I did.

"They look a long way off," I remarked.

"They are. If that's where he's headed, it's at least a two-day ride, as rough as the country is between here and there. Three might be closer to the truth. He's wrong about living up so high, though. The snow probably gets twenty feet deep in that basin by January, and won't fully melt off until June or July. That's too much snow to keep horses in, and the wildlife will move out with the first hard frost."

Even though Jess's words brought a chill to my gut, I hesitated before broaching a subject we'd already discussed. I guess I was kind of like a dog with a fresh bone, though. I couldn't let it go. "What about the girl?"

He waited a long time before answering. "What do you mean?"

"You know what I mean. What does he intend to do with her?"

Jess kind of sighed, then gathered his reins above the dappled gray's withers. He started to mount, then paused with one hand gripping the narrow horn, the other holding lightly to the saddle's fender. After another long pause, he said, "I don't know, Sheriff. If you'd asked me two days ago if I thought Billy Pinto was capable of kidnapping a girl and taking her into the mountains, I'd have called you a damned fool." He turned halfway around to look at me, and I'll swear there was pain in his eyes. Not for himself, or even for Susan Stokes, but for the boy he'd taught the ways of the wilderness. "A white girl," he added softly, and we both knew that if it came to a trial, that would make all the difference. Then, muttering a curse, he stepped into his saddle and we took off toward the Mule Ears.

Excerpt from:
Inquiry into the Events
Related to the William Pinto Uprising
13 November 1904–16 November 1904
The Honorable Frederick S. Tunstill, Presiding
San Pedro County District Court, 14 November 1904

"Let the record show that the inquiry into the William Pinto Uprising has reconvened after a brief recess for dinner. Jared Caylin has the stand. Mister Caylin, I will remind you that you were duly sworn in before the bench of the San Pedro District Court at nine a.m., and that your oath remains valid."

"Yes, sir."

"You testified this morning regarding your summons from Judge Henry Lynn to accompany his posse onto the San Pedro Plateau in pursuit of the fugitive, William Pinto. We stopped as you were about to relate your experiences with the Ute Indians known as Albert Bull, Clarence Broken Foot, Old Man With His Horses, Raven's Call, and Floyd Packs His Meat."

"And the women, Your Honor."

"I am well aware of the women, Mister Caylin. I don't need you to remind me of that."

"Yes, sir. Sorry."

"For the record, the name of the women are Bernice White Earth, Tall Water, Bird's Flight, and Tail of a Doe. Now, Mister Caylin, in your own words, tell us of the posse's encounter with these aborigines. Please be specific, as well as succinct."

"All right. Well, it was our second day on the Plateau, and we'd just killed a nice little mule deer. It was Frank Brady shot it. The judge didn't like it. Said we had enough grub on the packhorses, but Frank did it anyway. Said we'd need more than beans and biscuits, and the judge didn't say anything after that. We rode on south with Frank leading the way and the judge and Deke Burton right behind him. I came next with Oscar Larnx and Al Hamilton, and those two Broken Cinch cowboys brought up the rear with packhorses and supplies.

"After a time, we came to a big meadow, probably fifteen or twenty acres, all told, and saw a wagon and one of those old-time tepees made out of skins instead of canvas, and Frank said here was luck. Those were his words, too: *Here's luck, boys,* and we rode on over.

"I know you said earlier not to add too much to the story, and to keep to the facts as much as I can, but the fact is, I never seen the judge look so eager. Frank, too. Like little kids at Christmas. I guess they figured they'd found Billy, but he wasn't nowhere around when we got there. It was just Old Man With His Horses and Raven's Call and the women.

"Old Man was old, like his name says, all hunched over and shriveled up like a prune. Raven's Call was pretty old, too, although not as wilted. The women were a mixed lot, and I only found out yesterday, when you was talking to that Indian Agent, that Bird's Flight and Tail of a Doe were Old Man With His Horses' wives, and that the two younger women were their daughters. It was a family bunch, you see, with Raven's Call being Old Man's younger brother. We didn't know about the others, though,

Albert Bull and Clarence Broken Foot and Floyd Packs His Meat. They'd already taken off for the day.

"Anyway, it was a hunting trip for winter meat, like Agent Sullivan mentioned, and they'd had some pretty decent luck so far. There was half a dozen mule deer and a couple of elk already hung up, and the women were cutting the meat and jerking it on racks made out of willow limbs.

"Old Man and Raven's Call came out with the passes and a letter that Agent Sullivan had given them to be off the reservation. They spoke pretty good English, so they were quick to tell us they weren't doing anything wrong. I guess Judge Lynn had other notions. Old Man must've seen my badge, because he was coming over to show me their documents when the judge rode his horse in front of him and snatched the papers out of his hand. He glanced at them, but didn't really give them much notice. Then he tossed them back into Old Man's face.

"The judge asked them where Billy Pinto was, and naturally Old Man didn't have no idea what he was talking about. I say naturally now, but we didn't know what those Indians knew at the time. Heck, Billy could have been hiding in their tepee right at that minute with his rifle trained on all of us.

"Anyway, it went on like that for a while, Frank and the judge both demanding to know something that redskin wasn't never going to be able to answer, and all the time Raven's Call was kind of hanging back, and you could tell he was wishing he was armed—"

"Mister Caylin, I'll ask again that you confine your remarks to facts. I only want to hear what you

witnessed firsthand, not what you thought, unless those thoughts were a cause for action."

"Yes, sir, but I reckon the way Raven's Call was starting to act is what got me to thinking the way I started thinking, and it's kind of why things got so out of hand."

"Very well, but I warn you to proceed with caution, sir."

"I will, Your Honor. Anyway, after about twenty minutes of going back and forth with Old Man With His Horses, Frank turns to the judge and tells him he didn't think Billy was around, but the judge wouldn't swallow it. He said they were Indians, and that all Indians lie. Those were his words, too: *They're Indians, Frank. One'll lie and the others'll swear to it.*

"Frank kind of laughed and agreed, but I was starting to get nervous. So were the others, except for Deke and Oscar. I guess I didn't know Oscar as well as I thought I did, because he wasn't acting the same out there as he did in town. He was getting strutty and acting big and tougher than I knew he really was. Anyway, it was right in there somewhere that the judge told Frank and Oscar to search the camp. Old Man With His Horses tried to stop them, but Deke just about rode that old man over. Raven's Call jumped in front of them, too, waving his arms and trying to spook their horses, and that's when Oscar pulled his pistol and shot him. Just shot him down, then rode on by.

"Those Indian gals started crying and hollering, but they took off real quick when Frank and Oscar spurred their horses forward. I thought at first Raven's Call had been killed, but he got right back up, although his side was bloody as all get-out from where Oscar's bullet had cut him deep across his ribs. The judge said something to Deke and Deke loosened his rope and dropped a loop over Raven's neck and pulled it tight, then half dragged him over to a cottonwood tree at the edge of the meadow. The judge and the rest of us followed along, and so did Old Man With His Horses, shouting about his papers and how Agent Sullivan had told them they could hunt there, but the judge said he didn't give a hoot what Agent Sullivan had told the old fella.

"Deke got his rope over a limb before Raven's Call could get the noose off and took a turn on the saddle horn with the free end of his lariat. Then he backed his horse off and Raven's Call was lifted right off his feet. While he was dangling there, the judge got down and told Old Man he'd better start spilling beans, or he'd let that other redskin hang until the crows plucked out his eyes, but Old Man wouldn't budge. I have to give him credit for that. If it was my brother dangling and kicking with his face turning black as thunder, I believe I would have told the judge anything he wanted to hear.

"I thought Raven's Call was a goner for sure, but then Deke kicked his horse forward and Raven's Call hit the dirt. That was when the judge turned his attention on him. Kept asking about Billy and Miss Suzie, but heck, Raven's Call didn't know anything more than Old Man. Old Man got around in front of the judge and was demanding they be let go, and the judge hit that old boy square in the face with his gloved fist. There was blood everywhere, and I felt about half sick at the sight of it. It's one thing to handcuff a troublemaker, then whup him good back in the cells, but

I don't hold with punching old men in the face. Not even Indians.

"Old Man With His Horses was still sitting on the ground squirting blood when Frank and Oscar came back with one of the old women. Frank said that if we started cutting little pieces off of her, he'd bet Old Man would start talking. To his credit, the judge wouldn't let them do that, but he did order Deke to haul Raven's Call back up into the limbs and let him swing a couple more minutes. While all that was going on, Old Man With His Horses must have slipped back to his tepee, although I didn't see him do it. All I know is he came out a minute later with one of those old Winchester rifles with the brass frame, the kind they used to call the Yellow Boy. [*Editor's Note:* Caylin is probably referring to the Winchester Model of 1866, in .44 Henry caliber; testimony from Agent Sullivan also mentions a Winchester, but not the model or caliber.]

"It was one of Judge Lynn's cowboys who spotted Old Man first. [*Editor's Note:* Alfred Hamilton states it was Toby Smith who informed the posse members that Old Man With His Horses was returning with a rifle.] He sings out and we all turn, and Old Man throws that rifle to his shoulder and lets fly. He missed Deke by not much, and later on Deke showed us his saddle, which had a bullet scar across the top of the cantle. Most of us, and I'm not ashamed to say I was one of them, took off like scared kids. Frank didn't, though, and in camp that night, he told us he was glad the old buzzard had come back armed. Frank already had his pistol drawn, and he raised it up and fired before Old Man could get off a second shot.

"Old Man With His Horses went down like a rug had been pulled out from under him, and the old woman yanked free and ran to him. That's when the judge pulled his pistol and shot her in the back."

"That will be enough of that. If the gallery cannot control its emotions and maintain a silent decorum, I'll clear this room of anyone not directly related to the proceedings. Go on, Mister Caylin."

"Yes, sir. Anyway, like I said, Frank Brady shot Old Man and Judge Lynn shot the woman, and we could hear those other women out in the brush howling like coyotes when they saw their folks go down. The judge ordered us after them and everyone went except for me and Deke and the judge. Raven's Call was still hanging from that branch, but he wasn't kicking anymore. When Deke let him down, it turned out he was dead, too. I guess we kept him up there too long that last time. Deke did, I mean.

"After Deke got his rope free, him and me did another search of the tepee and around the wagon, but there wasn't any sign that Billy Pinto or the judge's granddaughter had ever been near the place. We heard several shots out in the trees, and not too long later our boys came back. They said they'd found the women and shot them, but I found out afterward that Bernice White Earth and Tall Water got away. It was Toby who told me he and Mark had found them hiding in the roots of a tall cottonwood tree. Toby shot into the limbs overhead, then told the women to stay out of sight until they were gone. Frank and Oscar said they'd found Old Man's wife, Tail of a Doe, and shot her. I reckon they did, since Agent Sullivan said she didn't come back.

"Alfred Hamilton was probably the most sensible one in the bunch. As soon as he got out of sight of the judge, he took off for home. We didn't see him again, but Judge Lynn said his leaving was of no consequence. That's what he said, too: *The loss of Hamilton is of no consequence, the dirty coward.* He called him a few other choice words, as well, but after that it was as if Al hadn't ever been there.

"Judge Lynn ordered us to burn down the teepee and knock the stakes out from under the meat so that it all fell in the dirt. He told us to toss the meat onto the fire, but by the time we got that far along, the fire was near about out. Frank wanted to burn the wagon, too, but the judge was getting antsy and said we needed to get back after Billy Pinto, so that's what we did. Like I said before, we didn't know about the others, those younger bucks who were out hunting. I reckon if we had, the judge might have handled things differently with Old Man and them. I kind of wish he had. It would have saved us a lot of grief and bloodshed later on."

Session Twelve

I'm sorry this keeps happening. Angie's not feeling well today or I'd have her take Humphrey out when he asks. He's really her dog, anyway, although I guess Humph feels like he belongs to both of us. Or vice versa. You can never tell with that mutt. He's a good ol' boy, though. But . . . getting back to what I was saying.

Jess Harding and I were on our way to the Mule Ears, but it seemed like the sun dropped out of sight before we'd covered more than five or six miles. The air began to turn really cold, and in the west I can still remember the way the clouds were hovering low over the horizon, turning into a kaleidoscope of reds and golds and purples—more shades of color than I reckon even a smart man could count. In the soft twilight we came to a narrow meadow with a stream running down its middle, and there was a pretty little beaver pond at the far end. Jess stopped his horse and sat there a moment, just staring until I heeled my buckskin up alongside his dappled gray.

"What do you see?" I asked, thinking it must be sign telling us Billy Pinto had passed that way, but it wasn't.

"Better times," Jess replied wistfully, and I realized then that he was looking at the pond, at those fresh-cut trees and sturdy beaver lodges, and reliving a past he'd probably never recapture. It kind of irritated me, to tell you the truth.

"We'd best keep riding," I said, but Jess shook his head.

"It's late enough. We'll stay here tonight. There's water and good graze for the horses, and we'll build a fire before it gets dark enough that someone might spot its light."

"We've got another hour before true nightfall," I replied stubbornly. "I say we keep riding."

Jess gave me that studying look, like he had before. Like he was trying to read something more into my words, or to see if there was more to them than what appeared on the surface. Then he shook his head a second time. "No, it's dark enough under the trees now that we'd risk missing Billy's trail, even if we did come to it."

"Well, we'd better find that trail soon," I said, frustrated with our slow progress and general lack of success so far.

"We'll find it," Jess assured me, then stepped to the ground and began unsaddling his horse.

I stewed for another minute or so, then got down and slid my rig from the buckskin's back. We led our horses to water and let them drink, then picketed them on that lush meadow grass. As aggravated as I was with our early stop, I knew it was best for the horses. They needed the rest, and that grass was better than any I'd seen all day.

Jess set about cutting some green willow limbs about as big around as my pinky finger, while I gathered several armloads of dry stuff and dumped them close to our saddles. While I got a fire started, Jess began slicing off pieces of venison that he skewered onto the greens limbs. He handed me one and I started to hold it over the flames like a basket of popcorn until I saw how Jess was drilling the larger end of his stick into the dirt so that it sloped over the fire. Brutus sat off to one side, eyeing our every move with keen interest.

While the meat roasted, Jess dug a small tin kettle from his saddlebags and headed for the stream above the pond to fill it. When he came back, he dumped a cotton sack no bigger than a packet of sewing needles inside, then set the container close to the fire. By the time he got all that accomplished, it was dark.

"Did you bring any coffee?" Jess asked.

I told him no, that I hadn't seen the need for that kind of luxury.

"Folks think they have to have a mule to pack along enough food and gear to stay out for any length of time, but they don't." He was staring into the flames as if his thoughts were a thousand miles away, or forty years in the past. "Not if they pack tight and learn how best to use their equipment," he went on. "I've had this old kettle since the late seventies, and it's served me well without taking up much more room in my saddlebags than a can of beans. I've used it for stews and rice and beans. I've warmed water to dress bullet wounds and soak leather, and tonight it's going to fix me a fine cup of coffee—pot and cup in one."

"Sounds like greasy coffee to me," I replied. I'd slipped into my sheepskin coat after working up a light sweat gathering firewood, but I was still chilled. A hot cup of coffee would have tasted mighty fine that evening, but the mood I was in, I believe I'd have preferred watching my toes freeze and break off before I said anything.

Jess chuckled and settled back against his saddle, his supper dribbling grease into the flames. "I can carry enough food and supplies in my saddlebags to last a month if I need to. Longer if I take time to hunt along the way."

I didn't respond, and after a while he seemed content to let it drop. Our supper was still dripping and sizzling when we pulled it away from the fire. I downed mine like a starving rat, and Jess wasn't far behind. Brutus watched intently, but Jess didn't offer him anything. A short while later, the big canine disappeared into the trees. When he returned, he had blood smeared along one side of his jaw and a tuft of fur clinging his chin. Rabbit, I thought, and realized the dog could fend for itself just fine.

After eating, I rolled a cigarette while Jess sipped contentedly at his coffee. Full dark had settled over the little meadow by then, with crystal skies and a light breeze teasing the coals as they faded under the ash. Despite my earlier attitude, I was starting to relax when a beaver loudly slapped its tail atop the pond's calm surface. I half rose in alarm, dropping my cigarette into the coals and reaching for my rifle, not so much frightened by the splash as concerned for what might have startled the animal in the first place, but Jess made a motion for me to sit back.

"He's just complaining," he said quietly.

"About what?"

"More than likely that we're still here, disturbing his evening constitutional."

"You sure of that?"

"I'm sure. Critters have a larger vocabulary than most people realize. Even beavers. It just takes a while to learn it."

"Some of us have jobs and families to take care of," I reminded him.

"I know, and I don't begrudge a man the security he thinks he gets from that. I was only commenting on beaver talk. They're an interesting animal, when you think about it." He made a motion toward the meadow, spread before us in the crisp starshine. "Take a look out there, Hud, and tell me what you see."

"I ain't in the mood to try and guess what you're talking about," I replied, edging closer to the fire and holding my hands out to its warmth. "If you've got to talk, Harding, get it started and finished."

"All right, I'll tell you what I see. I see an animal that comes onto a good piece of ground and starts to claim it for his own. They'll chew down old trees along the bank to dam a stream, and it's not long before a beaver ponds grows behind it. Once they've got deep enough water, they'll build their lodge, chewing down more trees and building more lodges as the community grows. Meanwhile, the grass takes hold where the trees have been gnawed out and the land turns soft and marshy. And that attracts other kinds of wildlife, like deer and elk and bighorn sheep. The wolves and cougars come for the meat, and what's left behind brings in smaller prey and smaller predators, like badgers and wolverines eating gophers and ground squirrels and snakes. But it's not only the meat eaters and grass eaters that benefit. You'll see more birds around a beaver pond. They're there for the insects that the water and the dung attracts, and pretty soon the whole world has changed around that first tree a solitary beaver chewed to the ground." He chuckled. "At least their world," he added. [*Editor's Note:* Like the black-tailed prairie dog (*Cynomys ludovicianus*) and the timber wolf (*Canis lupus*), the beaver (*Castor canadensis*) is classified as a *keystone species,* meaning its impact on a given area is usually great enough to ecologically alter the environment for a noticeable distance around it.]

"Is it true beavers are related to the rats I've got chewing burlap in my barn?" I asked.

"Damned if you're not in a snippy mood tonight, Hud."

He hadn't been paying much attention if he was just then picking up on my disposition. I'd been feeling surly ever since we left the clearing where we'd found the partially butchered mule deer. To my way of thinking, we'd given up a solid lead by abandoning Billy Pinto's trail, then replaced it with a half-assed supposition—that the boy was headed for the basin beyond the Mule Ears—based on no more than an offhand remark made to Jess who knew how long before. But Jess was wrong about one thing. I wasn't just snippy, I was scared.

"I want to know something, Jess. Something you've been dancing around ever since we got up here. Is that boy going to hurt Susan Stokes?"

"You mean kill her?"

"Kill her, rape her, try to make her his wife, so that he can live happily ever after, like they do in those fairy tales Angie reads to my daughter."

Jess's face turned to stone for a moment, like he was going to shut down and not reply. Then he looked away and almost angrily snapped his wrist to shake the coffee dredges from his kettle.

"I'm waiting for an answer," I said quietly.

He turned back, his expression briefly furious, then it shifted to uncertainty. "I don't know, Hud. Goddamnit, I don't know."

Well, it wasn't the answer I'd wanted, but I sensed it was more genuine than the assurances he'd been feeding me. "Yesterday, you about guaranteed he wouldn't harm her," I reminded him.

"Then why the hell did you ask me again tonight?"

"Because you weren't convincing enough yesterday."

"How about now?" he asked bitterly. "Are you convinced now?"

I waited and didn't reply, and after a minute, Jess said in a low voice: "I don't know what Billy will do, Sheriff. I wish I did, and that I could guarantee that girl's safety. I don't think he'd hurt her, but if the judge's posse corners him, or it pushes him too hard . . ."

Exhaling loudly, I sank back against my saddle; this time, I believed him.

We continued south toward the Mule Ears the next day, traveling in as straight of a line as the terrain would allow. We'd been slowly climbing toward a high ridge ever since leaving the Plateau's rim above Jess's cabin, the country through there cob-rough with canyons and rocky hogbacks trailing down off its sides. [*Editor's Note:* From Pratt's description here and elsewhere in these transcripts, it seems likely he is referring to Porcupine Ridge, a short mountain range bordering the San Pedro Plateau on the west and running roughly north to south; the Mule Ears are located southeast of this range.]

I think we traveled more up and down than we did forward that day, and would stop every four or five miles to rest our horses. Finally, late in the afternoon, we halted long enough to pull our saddles and give our mounts a chance to rest. I used my gloves to wipe down the buckskin's sweaty back and flank; I was especially vigorous behind his front legs, where the cinch clung tightest. The gelding seemed to enjoy the attention, and walked off afterward to pull lazily at the summer cured grass.

Jess and Brutus were already lounging in the shade of a nearby boulder, and I walked over to join them. Brutus gave a warning growl as I made myself comfortable, probably because I was sitting closer to his master than I normally did. Jess told him to shut up without even opening his eyes.

"He's gentle as a lamb," Jess said, "though a bit overprotective at times."

"I believe he'd take my hand off if I tried to pet him."

"He's not a petting kind of dog, for a fact. He likes me well enough, and tolerates your deputy and Red Gifford better than most. He likes Billy, too, but I think he senses you and I aren't friendly." Jess opened his eyes and looked at me. "Why is that, Hud?"

"Maybe he ain't as smart as you think he is."

"Oh, I'm not saying he's smart. I've played checkers with him, and he hardly ever wins. I'm just wondering why you're so distrustful of me."

I pulled the makings out of an inside pocket of my vest and began a cigarette. "It goes with the job, I guess."

"Was that part of the oath you took as sheriff? I solemnly swear not to trust anyone?"

"There are people I trust."

"But not many?"

After a moment's consideration, I had to nod. "Like I said, it goes with the job." I tore a thin sheet of paper from my little bible and shaped it with a forefinger. I was smoking Dukes tobacco in those days, and after spilling a nice pinch into the trough, I pulled the string closed with my teeth and dropped it back in my pocket. Then I ran my tongue lightly along the paper's gummed rim and rolled it closed. I struck a match with a thumbnail and drew in a deep lungful, then tipped my head back to savor the smoke for as long as I could hold it. At my side, Jess laughed softly.

"I've seen that same look on the faces of men laying with a woman."

"I never bothered to peek," I said, exhaling gently toward the clouds.

"That's because you grew up too civilized. You should have been out here before the Bible-thumpers and wives showed up."

It was an opening I'd been waiting for, and I glanced curiously at the old mountaineer. "What brought you out here, Jess?"

"Me? I came looking for beaver to trap and hell to raise."

"That comes off as sly," I remarked, and Jess smiled and shook his head.

"Maybe, but it wasn't anything illegal or immoral that brought me West." He was silent a moment, idly stroking his dog's massive head. "I don't suppose I really have one single answer for you, Hud. I know I didn't want to go into law, which is what my father was hoping for. I didn't want to go into manufacturing, either, which is what his family did." His expression seemed to relax as his thoughts wandered backward. "My father and uncles were in the shirt business. Harding shirts, fine ties, and collars. Maybe you've heard of them?"

I shook my head.

"Well, it doesn't matter. They sold mostly along the East Coast, but never any farther inland than Pittsburgh that I know of. I thought maybe they'd expanded by now, and I hadn't heard about it."

"Sounds like there was room to grow for a young man getting into the business."

"Oh, there was plenty of room to grow, and plenty of brothers and cousins wanting their share of the company. It was shaping up to be a quite a fight. Not the shooting kind, but the lawyer and courtroom kind, which I figure is why my father wanted me to become an attorney. It wasn't what I wanted, though. I liked to hunt and fish, and I'd read magazine articles about the old trappers and plainsmen. The West sounded mighty fine to me, and I decided I had to see it for myself. I suppose I was born a little too late for its heyday, but I've never regretted my decision to come out here."

"And you've never gone back home?"

"No, I haven't, and I should have. Or at least I should have written and told my mother and father where I was and what I was up to. I guess I knew if I did, Father would send someone out to bring me home. I wouldn't have gone, but I didn't want the battle, either. And I know Mother would have been disappointed with my choices.

"So I stayed and did the best I could to educate myself in the ways of the wilderness. I lived with the Assiniboine up in Canada for several years, then with the Flathead over in what's western Montana now. I had a Flathead wife for close to twenty years. We had a couple of sons, but they died young of some disease I never did learn the name of. Maybe that's why I took to Billy so much, after Red brought him up that first time. I guess he reminded me of how my own sons might have turned out, if they'd lived." He paused, and his brows furrowed in memory. "I guess he reminded me a lot of the orphans I knew among the Flatheads, too. Kids whose fathers had been killed in war or from some sickness. Looking at Billy, you could tell he was lost, like those Flatheads. Lost and lonely, and I suppose I saw in him an opportunity to do something good. Maybe pay back a little of what I've taken from this ol' world. So I told Red that Billy was welcome at my place anytime, and that I'd show him what I could of the things I'd learned."

"What was he like?"

"Billy? He's a good kid, Hud. Angry underneath, like a lot of younger Indians are, but he was real eager to learn. I think he already knew he'd never fit into the white man's world, and I doubt if he could have gone back to the Shoshone, no matter how much his father might have been respected. In this day and age, with white blood in his veins, he never would have been trusted." He shook his head with what might have been remorse. "We didn't think much about what we were doing in those days, about what we'd leave behind for others to deal with. Hell, who would have ever believed there'd be things like telephones and electric lights in a place like Echo City?"

I believe I might have actually smiled for a moment. Then I turned away to stare out over the distance. An elk bugled way off, a kind of choky whistle that flows like honey over the mountains. Then I heard a shot, and my first thought was: *Damn,* thinking that someone had harvested himself a few hundred pounds of prime meat for the coming winter. Before I could comment on it, though, a flurry of gunfire broke out to the west, coming quick and hot as a forest fire, and I threw my cigarette down and ground it out under my heel even as I rose.

"Maybe three or four miles away," Jess said tautly, standing next to me with Brutus leaning against his leg, trembling. Then he cursed. "They caught him, Hud," he said, and I didn't have to ask who he meant.

Excerpt from:
Inquiry into the Events
Related to the William Pinto Uprising
13 November 1904–16 November 1904
The Honorable Frederick S. Tunstill, Presiding
San Pedro County District Court, 14 November 1904

"Let the record show that the inquiry into the William Pinto Uprising has reconvened after a thirty-minute recess. Jared Caylin still has the stand, and remains duly sworn in before the bench of the San Pedro District Court. To clarify, Mister Caylin, your oath before the bench this morning remains valid."

"Yes, sir, I understand."

"You were about to relate your experiences on the third day of your pursuit of William Pinto. Please continue."

"Well, it was the day after what we'd done to them Indians back in the big meadow. We'd moved on and were still looking for Billy, and Frank Brady got it in his mind that we ought to head for the highest point of land around, which was a long mountain with a sharp drop to the south called Porcupine Ridge. [*Editor's Note:* As stated earlier, the highest peak on the San Pedro Plateau is the summit of Porcupine Ridge, at 10,231 feet.] Frank said getting above timberline would give us a better view of the country, and we might be able to spot Billy's campfire, or at least its smoke.

"That country through there is really rough, and I'm not sure where we were, but Frank and the judge didn't act like they were lost, so the rest of us just followed along and didn't ask any questions. I reckon it was the middle of the afternoon when we came to a narrow canyon and Frank turned into it. He said it would take us to the base of the Porcupine, and that we'd be on top before noon the next day.

"That canyon was narrow and winding, and the sides were steep enough that it would have been hard to get a horse out of it without dismounting. There were pine trees along the south wall, but the sunny side was mostly open."

"The sunny side? Could you elaborate, please, for the record."

"Yes, sir. What I mean by sunny side is the canyon's north slope, which faces south and catches the sun most of the year. The south wall faced north, and was usually in shadow. That's where the pines generally grow thickest."

"Very well, thank you, Mister Caylin. Continue with your account."

"Like I was saying, the north wall, the one facing south, was mostly bare, but we could see aspens on top and there were groves of aspens along the canyon's floor, too. I don't know what the name of that creek is, or if it even had a name, but it was running a good little stream of water for so late in the season. Maybe five or six feet across and a foot deep. Cold as a hound dog's nose, too, which was nice, because even though it was September and we were pretty high up, it got warm during the afternoons, and stopping ever once in a while to take a long drink eased our mood considerably.

"That's what we were doing when the wheels came off the buggy, as the saying goes. The judge and Frank and Deke were already in their saddles, and I was about to grab a handful of horn to climb onto my own horse when somebody shot Frank right out of his seat. First off, I figured it was Billy by himself, but then shots started coming from all directions, bullets smacking into trees and horses screaming and men hollering, and that's when I knew we were facing a war party."

"You knew immediately that your attackers were Indians?"

"That's what I figured, and you said it was okay to say what I was thinking if it affected how I reacted."

"Yes, I recall that. Very well, continue."

"Well, it was Indians, and that was later confirmed. I just want to make that clear. Anyway, when they opened up on us, my horse spooked real bad and jumped sideways with my left foot still in the stirrup, and that yanked me off my feet. I saw other horses doing the same, and Oscar Larnx's bay was hit in the side and fell with its front hooves not ten inches from where I was still laying on my back with the wind knocked out of me. That right there was enough to tell me to skedaddle, and I rolled over on my hands and knees and crawled down into the streambed and got down behind the bank. My rifle was still on my saddle, but I had my Colt and I hauled that out and started shooting.

"Those red devils had us pinned down with old-timey rifles using old-timey gunpowder, so every time they took a shot, a big ol' cloud of powder smoke would come spurting out of the pines. That made it easier to sort of tell where they were hiding, but not exactly where, since the pines were so thick up there."

"If I might interrupt for one minute, Mister Caylin. Could you tell the court from which direction

these individuals were firing? I ask because you said the south side of the canyon's slope was bare. Is that correct?"

"Yes, sir, it was. Well, mostly bare. There were shallow coulees coming down off the top, and sage and other kinds of brush and rocks, but the thing is, there wasn't anyone on that side of the canyon. All the shooting was coming from the north-facing slope."

"From the pines?"

"Yes, sir, and I was down behind that bank with guns going off every which way and bullets kicking up dirt and tearing into those aspens around us. I fired several times, real fast and kind of wild, then a bullet struck the bank right in front of me and kicked up a bunch of dirt, some of which hit me right in my face. I reckon I cussed some. I know my right eye was tearing up real bad, and I was spitting out dirt and grass, but at least it settled my aim. I emptied my revolver after that, but I was shooting slow and had a target picked out, instead of shooting like a blind goat. I still couldn't see who I was firing at, but I was aiming at the rear of those spurts of gun smoke, and I must have been putting my bullets pretty close, because whoever was there soon quit shooting. I didn't know then if I'd hit anyone, or if they just moved. I found out later they'd moved to another tree."

"At this point, sir, did you have an idea how many individuals were firing at you?"

"No, I didn't, but judging from all the smoke pouring out of those trees, I figured it had to be at least half a dozen."

"You make that statement in spite of differing

testimony that claims there were only three ambushers?"

"Yes, sir, I do. What I think, even if no one believes me, is that there were more men up there, and the others got away. I know what people are saying, but I was there, Your Honor, and I don't believe there were only three men shooting at us."

"Then what happened, Mister Caylin?"

"After emptying my Colt, I ducked back down behind the stream bank and punched out the empties and reloaded. Then I crawled back into the trees, where I figured I'd have better cover. I got down behind an aspen with a rock beside it, maybe a foot high, and started shooting back from between that and the tree. None of us were shooting fast anymore. I know I was taking time to aim, and I could see Anderson and the bull boss nearby, and they were doing the same.

"The bull boss?"

"Deke Burton, Your Honor. That's what the Broken Cinch hands called him. I guess I picked that up from Anderson and Smith."

"Mark Anderson and Toby Smith?"

"Yes, sir."

"Go on."

"Well, it kept on that way for a good long time. I'll bet it was forty-five minutes or more of us shooting at them and they were shooting back at us. I saw Burton get hit, and later on I saw Oscar Larnx go down, too. Another of the horses was shot and it fell and started screaming that throaty way they do when they're hurting real bad. It was unnerving with all the guns popping off around me.

Nobody tried to put the horse down, though, and nobody crawled out to check on Oscar, although I know he was alive because I could hear him begging for help. I'd have gone if not for those Indians keeping us pinned down.

"By and by, I ran out of bullets, so I crawled over to where Oscar's bay horse had fallen when the fighting broke out. Oscar had a good Marlin rifle in his scabbard, and I slid that out and got behind his horse and started firing from there. Then, out of the blue, the shooting just stopped. For a while, no one knew what to think. Most of us were worried it was a trick, but then Burton told Anderson to go drag Oscar back into the trees where there was more cover. Anderson looked kind of walleyed about it, but Deke told him to get his tail end out there. Ass is what he actually said, if you don't mind me repeating it. *Get your ass out there, Anderson,* is Deke's exact words, and Anderson did it, too. When no one took a shot at him, we one by one started coming out of our holes and taking stock of what had happened."

"Meaning?"

"Meaning who got shot and who didn't and how bad and all that. I went over and put the wounded horse out of its misery, but when I was coming back into the trees I started to feel kind of funny. That's when I noticed I'd been shot, too, and that I was bleeding real bad."

Session Thirteen

Although Jess and I made our way toward the sounds of the battle as fast as our horses could carry us, our progress was slow. From the edge of the Plateau's rim, right after we'd made it to the top, I'd looked out over the land to the south and marveled at how beautiful it appeared. Gently rolling swells blanketed in gold, clear skies and scattered meadows. Three days in, and I felt lost within a demon's maze of hidden canyons and rocky gorges, the trees so dense in places it was next to impossible to worm our way through them.

We were moving laterally to the mostly northwest-to-southeast direction of the canyons, so that we were constantly climbing out of one and into another. In places, the slopes were so steep I had to lean back until my shoulders were nearly touching my mount's croup, my feet jammed into their stirrups and the stirrups poking out like spars to either side of the buckskin's shoulders as we wove a dangerous course through the trees. Climbing the other side had both horses digging in with their front hooves, their hindquarters kicking loose little avalanches of earth and stones that would rattle all the way down behind us.

At first the shooting was hot and lively, but it gradually tapered off to erratic pops, like firecrackers set off on a hot Fourth of July afternoon. I recall it being that way in some of the smaller skirmishes we'd had in Cuba, too, as if once the surprise and excitement of the initial attack had worn off, the participants on both sides were content to settle in for the long haul. The shooting was still going on when we topped out on the rim above the canyon where the fighting was. I heard a shout from the opposite rim, and soon afterward the shooting stopped altogether. An unnatural silence drifted over the land, as if even the birds and insects were waiting to see what happened next.

Jess trotted his horse up close to where I'd drawn the buckskin to a halt—for once, he'd been following me, instead of the other way around—and nodded toward the far ridge. "There," he said tersely.

I looked up in time to see a woman astride a black-and-white paint lead a pair of saddled horses into the pines. "An Indian," I said in surprise.

"So I noticed."

Brutus was standing between us, leaning eagerly forward and growling low in his throat. He looked ready to take off, but Jess told him to stay. The dog whined as if disappointed, then eased back a half a step and sat down.

"What do you want to do, Hud?"

"I'm going down to see what all the shooting was about," I replied, sliding the Krag-Jørgensen from its scabbard.

"If you don't need me, I think I'll ease over to the other side and see what I can find."

"Watch yourself," I told him, then heeled the buckskin toward the canyon's steep slope.

I kept a tight rein on the way down, my feet light in the stirrups in case I had to bail out real quick. I could hear the crackle of broken limbs in the ponderosas across the canyon, and knew there were men and horses on the move over there. I didn't see anything, though. Not even a flash of color. Then after a while, even those sounds disappeared, and the silence returned. Moving steadily toward the canyon's floor, I began to see men stumbling around in the trees below me like they were lost or drunk. At first I couldn't make out who they were. Then I caught a glimpse of Jared Caylin, walking out of the aspens to stare up canyon like he was waiting for someone to tell him what to do. I swore and straightened and thumbed the rotating lever on the Krag's lock to safety.

The posse was bunkered in behind saddles and packs and chunks of dead wood they'd dug out of the sod and thrown up before them. Their horses were tied back in the trees, all but two of them that were lying dead in the sun. Even from a couple of hundred feet away, I could tell they'd been hit hard. I saw Jared sitting on a rock and rode over. I didn't think he recognized me at first, then he stuck out his left hand, wrapped in a bloody rag, and blurted, "They shot my fingers off, Hud."

I dismounted without speaking and took his wrist and gently unwrapped the crude bandage—a piece of his own shirt, torn from its tail—and nodded agreement. "Looks like they took two of them," I said.

He was acting stunned and not altogether there. "Am I going to die?"

"Not today." I returned the bloody shirttail, having to shove it into his unmaimed paw. "Wrap that around your fingers until I come back. Keep it tight, and don't wander off or move around too much. It's pretty much quit bleeding already, but you don't want it to start again."

Jared was still looking at his bloodied hand when I walked away, as if not quite comprehending the empty space where his pinky and ring fingers had been only a short time before. I went into the trees and Mark Anderson, the cowboy Tom and I met riding out of Echo City the night Billy kidnapped the judge's granddaughter, came over with the same kind of distracted expression that I'd seen so often in Cuba.

"Are you hurt?" I asked him.

"No, sir, but the judge is."

"How bad?"

"I think it's pretty bad. His horse was shot out from under him and he took a bullet in his belly at some point, but it's his head I'm worried about. When he came down with his horse, he must have cracked it on a rock. He's been sort of conscious, but not making a whole lot of sense."

"What about the others?"

"Frank Brady and Oscar Larnx are dead. Deke's been shot, too. Toby caught a bullet in his leg, but I believe he'll be all right. It's the judge that scares me most."

"Let's go have a look," I said.

Mark led me to where the judge lay on his bedroll under an aspen. The old man's face look like fresh-rolled dough, and his breath was coming quick and shallow. I knelt at his side and pulled the blanket back. Someone had cut his shirt away, then wrapped a clean cloth around his midsection, but it was soaked with far too much blood for me to feel hopeful.

"Has he said anything?" I asked.

"Nothing I could make out."

I considered pulling the bandage away to see how badly he'd been shot, then decided I didn't care. Pushing to my feet, I stared down at the old man for probably a full minute. "You son of a bitch," I finally said.

"Hey!" Mark cried in alarm. "You hadn't ought to talk to him like that, Sheriff. He can't help the way things turned out."

"The hell he couldn't have," I retorted, my ears like torches. I waved a hand in an arc that encompassed the tiny grove. "This is all his fault, Anderson, no one else's. No one's." Then I walked over to where Deke Burton was sitting with his back to a tree, leaving the cowhand to stare uncertainly after me.

"How bad are you hurt?" I asked the foreman.

He gave me a hard stare. "Go to hell, Pratt."

"Burton, I'm short on time and long out of patience." I nodded at the bindings around his chest. "Do you want me to take a look at that, or not?"

"Take care of the judge. I can look after this myself."

"The judge is going to die, Deke, and there's not a damned thing you or I can do about it."

"By God, you save that man, Pratt, or I'll sic the federal authorities on you."

"You can go all the way to the governor's office if that's what you want, but the judge is going to die. Do you know why?"

"Yeah, I know why. Damned Indians bushwhacked the shit out of us."

"It wasn't Indians who killed him. It was his own damned arrogance that got him in the end. Got a couple of others killed with him, too." I thrust my chin toward the foreman's torso. "What about it, Burton? Do you want me to take a look at that?"

Deke Burton was as stubborn as sin, but I think my news that the judge was about to cash in his chips took some of the starch out of him. He moved his hand away from his chest and let it fall to his lap. Then he looked away as if embarrassed, not for his lack of strength, I suspect, but for his need to let someone else take charge.

"Doubt if there's much you can do for me, either," he said. "Bullet went in my left side. It didn't come out. Was spitting blood for a while. Ain't now, but I'm pretty sure I'm still bleeding on the inside."

I carefully unwrapped the old cattleman's bandages. Deke stiffened and grunted, but didn't cry out as I peeled the blood-gummed fabric away from the pale flesh of his chest. What I saw wasn't encouraging.

"How bad's the pain?"

"Ain't too bad," he replied. I didn't argue with him, although judging from his expression and the way his body twitched every time I touched him, I'd say he was hurting like hell. "What's the verdict, lawman?" he asked after a while.

I rocked back on my heels. "I think you're right," I said bluntly, staring at the puckered wound below his nipple, the swollen flesh under his ribs. "You're swelling up like a tick, Deke, and I don't know what to do about it."

"Ain't nothing can be done. That old sawbones from Echo City likely couldn't fix this."

I stared a moment longer, then shook my head.

"No point pondering it," Deke growled. "What's done is done."

"If we try to move you, you'll probably die."

"I'm going to die anyway, Pratt. Wasn't sure until you pulled these rags off my chest, but hell, look at me. I'm bleeding out like a butchered steer. I just ain't being messy about it as some."

I placed the wad of bandages back on the cattleman's chest and rose. "Let me take a look at the others first, then I'll let you know what I decide."

"Don't stop the chase because of me," Deke said. "Go get those sons of bitches that bushwhacked us."

"Did you see who it was?"

"Didn't Caylin or Anderson tell you?"

I shook my head and Deke guffawed, then grew rigid with pain. When the spasm passed, he said, "It was Billy Pinto and his boys."

That brought a scowl to my face. "What boys?"

"Indians, probably off the reservation. Didn't get a good count, but figure there was a half dozen, at least."

"And Billy was with them?"

The cowman's face grew grim. "I saw him, didn't I?"

"I don't know, Deke. Did you?"

"Right out front, lawman. Probably had Miss Suzie hid out

in the pines, all tied up and scared shitless."

"But you didn't see her?"

"Nope, half-breed son of a bitch kept her out of sight."

I nodded and turned away, unconvinced by the foreman's words, wary of the anger behind them.

Toby Smith was sitting about twenty paces away. He had his back to a tree, and perspiration was streaming down his face. Mark had already described the injury, a bullet through the meaty part of his left thigh. It was bloody and swollen and hot to the touch, but I didn't think there would be any permanent damage if he took care of himself and allowed the wound to heal properly. Mark and Jared came over as I was retying Toby's bandage. Mark spoke first.

"What do you think, Sheriff?"

"I think you boys are in a hell of a bind."

"What should we do?" Jared asked.

I thought about that for a minute, my gaze shuttling from Deke with his swollen midsection to the judge and his addled brain, and came to a decision that was going to make me mighty unpopular with a lot of men, not the least of which were those right there in front of me. "That's going to be your decision, Caylin," I said brusquely. "It's your posse."

Jared's mouth fell open; even Mark looked surprised. "It's the judge's posse, Hud," Jared said in a soft whine.

"You rode with him, didn't you? After I told you to stay in town."

"The judge sent word for me to come. What was I supposed to do?"

"You were supposed to stay in town, like I told you."

Jared started to swear and protest, all in the same breath. He had his ass buried too deep in the coals for his own comfort, and wanted somebody to bail it out for him. I couldn't entirely fault him for his frustration. I'd gone, too, when the judge summoned me, but I also had other priorities at the moment, not the least of which was finding Suzie Stokes.

Mark took a more levelheaded approach to their predicament, and I have to say I admired him for it. "If you were in our shoes, Sheriff, what would you do?" he asked.

"Anderson, I'm glad I'm not in your shoes, but if I was, I guess I'd have to weigh whether to try to get my wounded back to town, or keep them here and send for help."

"Doc Freeman is too old to come this far by horseback," Mark said after a pause. "We'd have to send to Rawlins, or maybe even Cheyenne, for a younger doctor. That could take days."

"It sure could."

Mark glanced at Jared, and I could tell the gravity of their situation was starting to sink in. All Jared did was shake his head in helplessness, and I knew then that the posse was no longer his. Hell, it likely never had been. The judge had put it together, then no doubt commanded it in his usual heavy-handed fashion. At least until that morning. Now no one was in charge, at least not yet, but I figured if they were going to make it back, it would be because of Mark Anderson, not Jared Caylin.

"If you decide to take your wounded to Echo City, you might try rigging up some kind of litter for Deke and the judge," I suggested.

"What kind of litter?" Jared asked, but it was plain that Mark knew what I was talking about.

"Come with me," I told Jared, and we walked over to where I'd left my horse. When we were alone, I said, "What happened here?"

"We were bushwhacked."

"Why?"

He looked puzzled. "What do you mean?"

"Why'd they bushwhack you, Jared?"

Shrugging, he said, "Deke thinks it was Billy Pinto's bunch. He figures they knew we were after him, and wanted to stop us."

"Billy doesn't have a bunch, and I don't believe he was here with these men. So that leaves me wondering. Why'd they jump you?" Jared looked away, and I knew I was on the right track. "Tell me, damnit."

"Aw, hell, Hud. It might've been some others we ran into yesterday." He stopped there, but I waited without speaking until he continued. He told me about the posse's encounter with a hunting party of Utes, about the people they might have killed and the property they'd definitely destroyed. I won't repeat it here because I wasn't along at the time, and I'd probably get something wrong if I tried. I do know there's an official record of the affair somewhere, if you want to take the time to look for it. [*Editor's Note:* Excerpts from a San Pedro County Court of Inquiry are located elsewhere within these papers.]

With growing disgust, I finally cut him off. "I've got one important question, Jared. Did you see Billy Pinto today? I mean, personally see him?"

"No, not with my own eyes, but someone must have. I heard them hollering his name when the shooting started."

"Who was hollering?"

He glanced back into the trees, as if whoever it was might raise his hand. After a moment, he said, "I ain't sure, Hud, it was all happening so fast, but I think it might've been Judge Lynn."

"It wasn't Deke?"

He was quiet a moment, thinking, then shook his head. "Nope, it was the judge, right after everything busted loose. I remember Frank was already down, but the rest of us were still on our feet and reaching for our pistols, and that's when I heard the judge shouting that it was Billy. He didn't want us to harm his granddaughter, but said we was to kill Billy if we got a clear shot at him."

"But you never saw him or the girl?"

"No, neither one, but my horse dumped me about that time. I could've missed him."

"Could've? But *did* you?"

After another long pause, Jared shook his head. "I don't think so."

I nodded curtly and headed back into the aspens. Deke Burton was still conscious, but you could tell he was starting to fade. He looked up as I approached.

"Going after her, lawman?" he asked, his voice already weaker.

"You said you saw Billy Pinto?"

"I did."

"With your own eyes?"

"Calling me a liar, Sheriff?"

"I want to be damn sure he was here, Deke, because I don't want to chase after a bunch of angry Utes while Billy's heading off in a different direction with the girl."

That gave him pause, and he glanced briefly at the judge.

"The truth, Deke."

"I'm telling you as best I can. Judge said he was there. I thought I saw him, but . . . maybe it wasn't. A glimpse was all I caught, and things were pretty hectic at the time."

"So you can't say for sure that Billy was with them?"

"I can't say for sure he wasn't, either."

I stared firmly down at the man, but his return gaze never faltered. "All right," I said. "I'll take a look."

"Get her back, lawman. That's all that matters."

That might have been the only time in all the years I knew Deke Burton that he and I agreed completely with one another.

I left the aspens and gathered the buckskin's reins and

stepped into the saddle. Jared stood watching morosely from the shadows, but Mark was already roaming through the grove looking for trees straight enough, light enough, and strong enough to get his wounded back to Echo City. I figured it was largely a waste of effort. The men who needed medical attention the most weren't likely to live long enough to see the inside of a doctor's office, and the others—Jared and Toby—would probably survive whether they saw a physician or not. Excuse me.

Session Fourteen

I apologize for leaving the table so abruptly. Humphrey gets thirsty, and sometimes he gets lost looking for his water bowl. I don't care. That old mutt saw us through some mighty difficult times, and I don't begrudge a minute of looking after him now. I do regret leaving you alone so often, though. I'll try not to do it any more than I have to.

I was telling you about Judge Lynn's posse down there in that canyon near Porcupine Ridge, after they'd been waylaid by what was at that time parties unknown. Of course, we found out later who they were, but as I rode away from the aspens, I wasn't really sure what to think.

I went back to where Jess and I had parted company earlier and set my horse to the steep slope of the canyon's south wall. There were a lot of pines growing all the way from the bottom to the top, but with gaps in the trees that made it easier to climb out of than some of the other canyons we'd crossed. I paused on top to get my bearings, and not two minutes later saw Jess come out from the next canyon over. He saw me and pulled up, so I knew we'd soon be going back the way he'd come.

Jess got down to rest his horse, and was standing there rubbing Brutus's head when I rode up. I looked out over the direction he'd come from, but there were only more trees—aspens and pines—sundered by canyon and gorge. We were pretty high up. I could see the bare blue of timberline not too far away, and to the south the Mule Ears were jutting toward the sky like . . . well, hell, like what you'd expect of a couple of peaks named after a mule's ears.

Jess asked what I'd found out in the aspens, and I told him what I'd heard. He started shaking his head as soon as I reached the point where Jared said Judge Lynn had shouted that it was Billy Pinto leading the attack.

"Who was it?" I asked.

"Probably those Utes your deputy mentioned."

"From the way he talked, they were too old to follow," I replied, still thinking at that point that the judge's posse only "might have" killed someone, as Jared had put it.

"I've seen the prints Billy's horse makes, Hud. They aren't with this bunch."

"Maybe he changed horses."

"Maybe," Jess replied, although it was pretty obvious he didn't think so.

I stared out over the rolling country, thinking about where we were and what we still had to accomplish. The sun was getting low; full dark was only a couple of hours away. Under the trees it would soon be too dim to track. Frankly, I was wishing we'd never abandoned Billy's trail after picking it up on the Plateau's rim, but we had, and the responsibility for leaving it was my own. I'd thought then that the odds were more than fair that we could cut him off, if he was indeed making a run for the Mule Ears. Now I wasn't so sure.

I doubt if Jess was, either, but the decision wasn't his to make. He stood by quietly, giving his dog some affection while I pondered our next move. At last, with a soft curse, I said, "We're going after them."

"The Utes?" He sounded surprised by my decision.

"Are you even sure they are Utes?"

"No, I'm not. I'm just assuming they are, based on what your deputy said."

"So am I," I replied, pulling the buckskin's head out of a clump of grass. "Let's go."

Jess mounted and led the way. At the bottom, we turned southeast with the canyon. The trail of five unshod horses lay plain before us, and when we came to where they'd stopped long enough to water their mounts, I counted five sets of moccasined footprints to go with them. Jess got down to examine the tracks as best he could in the waning light. He ran his fingers along the lines of the moccasin prints as if trying to feel whatever story they might tell. After a while he leaned back and pointed out two smaller sets of prints toward the middle of the group. "I'm thinking those belong to women, or girls."

"Suzie Stokes?"

"I don't know. If it is, they've got her wearing mocs and riding her own horse."

"How far ahead are they?"

"No more than a couple of hours. Trouble is, they could easily keep on riding after the sun sets. We won't be able to do that."

"Any idea which direction they might take?"

"No." He stood and brushed the damp sand from his fingers. "Unless you want to do some more gambling."

"I'm already cussing myself for leaving Billy's trail after we found that butchered deer."

"I know, and I wouldn't blame you for not wanting to try it again."

"Not without a solid reason," I agreed hesitantly.

"Well, it's not much, but do you remember that long ridge we saw from the top of the canyon?"

"Porcupine Ridge? Why would they want to go up there?"

"Because they're Utes, and once they get on the other side of that, it's going to be pretty much downhill all the way to Utah.

I'm thinking after what they've been through, they'll want to go home as quick as they can."

If they were Utes, I thought. Yet there was a certain logic to Jess's argument, and despite some doubt on my part, I did want to be sure Susan Stokes wasn't with them before they left the state. "All right," I said reluctantly. "Let's chance it. Can you get us there in the dark?"

"I can get us partway." He climbed into his saddle, then called his dog over. "Brutus, stay close." He spoke firmly and distinctly, and the dog stared back with its ears perked alertly forward. "Stay close," Jess repeated, and the brute whined in response, before falling in behind Jess's dappled gray as we crossed the creek and plunged into the pines on the other side. As far as I could tell, the dog never strayed from his master's side all night.

A horse ain't a motor bug. You can't add oil and gas, or even hay and grain, and expect it to run all day and half the night. Not without it taking a heavy toll on the animal. We tackled that slope before us with the light fading rapidly, and the land grew steeper the higher we climbed. It was hard going, and for a while I was afraid we might have to give up and return to the bottom of the canyon. Then we came to a game trail heading in more or less the same direction we wanted to go, and that made our horses' work a little easier. Even so, their weariness after the past three days was beginning to catch up. Around midnight I called for Jess to find a place to stop, and not long after we came to a flat spot among the pines. There wasn't much graze, so we kept the horses tied close and sat with our backs to nearby trees to await the dawn.

Not to complain, but so that you can fully understand the situation, I'll mention that Jess and I were feeling pretty wrung out ourselves. We'd had very little sleep since reaching the Plateau, and had eaten as many meals in our saddle as we had on the ground. Nevertheless, we were up again at first light, and on the trail soon after. It was shortly before sunup when we came to a large clearing on the side of the mountain and spotted our destination a few miles away. We stopped immediately and dismounted. Our horses were puffing heavily because of the altitude, and it was cold enough—hell, the frost on the grass that morning was longer than the stubble on my chin—that our breaths were fogging the air in front of us every time we exhaled. I was damn glad I had my sheepskin coat and gloves, along with those leather chaps Tom had loaned me.

Jess and I spent thirty minutes sitting and watching, but other than some small birds flitting through the scrub, the land between us and the ridge seemed deserted. After a while we crawled back in our saddles and started paralleling the ridge, though careful to stay in the trees where we weren't as likely to be seen, in case those Utes had already reached the top.

We were skirting timberline, and if you've never been above it, I should probably explain how that's kind of an ambiguous term. Although basically timberline is where the tall trees stop growing, the reality is that there are always a few tracts of spindly pines in the sheltered vales above it, along with lots of scrub and patches of low, wind-twisted conifers that we called knee timber. The wind that morning was blowing hard, but it always does at those elevations.

It didn't take long to cover the final few miles. Halting under the tall peak at the southernmost point of the ridge, we briefly discussed our options. In the end, fearing that there wouldn't be any place to hide our mounts on top, we decided to leave our horses tied back out of sight and go the rest of the way on foot. I dug a pair of binoculars out of my saddlebags and the three of us—me and Jess and Brutus—made our way toward the rocky crest.

That land along the top of the ridge was dense with boulders that had broken off over the ages. Some of them had rolled on down the slope, but most hadn't traveled more than a few rods before stopping. In places the mass of stones looked damn near impenetrable, but when you got close you'd find winding paths that would take you in nearly any direction you wanted to go. Occasionally you might have to duck under a leaning slab of granite, or squeeze through a place so tight you'd scrape your butt and belly button at the same time, but there were also a lot of holes to hide in. Jess and I found a likely spot that offered a decent view of the country we'd recently vacated and settled down where we wouldn't be seen. Brutus scrambled in behind us, ears up, eyes bright with anticipation. For a while we just sat and looked, then after about ten minutes, Jess said, "I want to take a look along the top of the ridge, see if I can find some tracks."

"Go on and do it," I agreed.

Jess turned to his dog. "Brutus, stay here. Understand, *stay!*" Then he slipped out between a couple of boulders and started toward that high peak, a few hundred yards away. Brutus wanted to go with him, but Jess had done a good job training the dog, and he finally sat down on the far side of the pocket where he could keep an eye on his master until Jess disappeared among the rocks.

Meanwhile, I stretched out against the boulder I was crouched behind to glass the mountainside below. I did a quick sweep first, looking for color or movement, then began a slower, more systematic search. After thirty minutes of not spotting anything out of the norm, I rose with my binoculars in one hand and the Krag in the other and started toward another position. As soon as I did, Brutus jumped to his feet, his lips peeling back in the kind of snarl that can turn a man's blood to ice. He took a menacing step forward, and I knew our time of reckoning had come. That damned dog had been eyeing me like a piece of raw meat ever since Tom and I first approached Jess's cabin, but Jess wasn't around now, and Brutus was going to test my mettle. I guess I should have been frightened. Instead, I got mad as hell. I dropped my glasses and snapped the Krag to my shoulder, rolling the safety off with my thumb and, smooth as gravy and quicker than snot, had that rifle pointed right between the dog's eyes. "Shut the hell up, you son of a bitch," I told him. "Shut your damned mouth, or I'm going to blow your head off."

He looked at me and the fire in his eyes seemed to flare brighter, but a dog ain't dumb, and this one had been around hunters long enough to know what a rifle could do. He growled once more, and I said in a grating voice: "Sit down . . . *now.*"

Brutus huffed a little, but then he sat and the blaze that had flared bright in his eyes a moment before died.

"You ain't as thick-skulled as I was afraid you might be," I said, and I'll admit I was feeling a little shaky as I stooped to pick up my binoculars. "Stay here," I told the canine, then turned my back on him. You might think I was a foolish to do so, and you're probably right, but I was still mad as hell. I swear if I'd heard that dog so much as wag its tail, I would have shot him. I suspect Brutus sensed that, too.

I made my way through the rocks to where I could run my glasses over the slope on the opposite side of that ridge. The land there wasn't as thickly timbered as where Jess and I had come up that morning, and the view was awe-inspiring—mountains rolling away to the west as far as the eye could see, with a sky so blue it nearly hurt your eyes to stare into it. But after another thirty minutes of scanning the ridge's western slope, I still hadn't spotted anything to arouse my curiosity. There'd been a herd of bighorn sheep way off in the distance, and some crows cawing from the trees below me. Not too far away a marmot was lying out in the sun, occasionally trilling its shrill, almost bird-like call, although there was never any answer; I guess it was doing it just to hear itself make a noise.

Finally, I lowered my binoculars. I was starting to fear that we'd guessed wrong, and that the Utes had taken another direction, when I heard a shout from the far side of the ridge, followed by a rifle shot. Several more shots came on the heels of that first one, along with a lot more shouting, and I dropped my glasses and started racing toward the top of the ridge, maybe fifty yards away. I hadn't covered quite half that distance when I noticed movement near the crest, and quickly ducked behind a lichen-covered boulder poking up out of the grass. As I did a big man on a paint horse came barreling over the top. He was pounding his heels against the pony's ribs while waving a rifle above his head. He was yelling wildly, too, although I couldn't make out what he was saying. Even though there was a lot of gunfire still coming from the far side of the ridge, I figured this was the man I needed to concentrate on first.

I was still thirty yards from the top and at least seventy-five from where the man on the paint—an Indian, I realized almost immediately—would pass. I waited until he got as close as he was going to, then popped out from behind the rock with my rifle shouldered. He saw me instantly and started slamming his rifle against the paint's hip, but the horse was already giving him everything it had. I yelled for him to stop, but it was plain he wasn't going to. Then two more Indians came over the top of the ridge riding nearly side by side, and I swore and started to swing my rifle toward them. As I did, the Indian on the paint abruptly wheeled toward me and started firing. I don't know where his first bullet went, but the second plowed into the dirt close enough to kick a few pieces of sod against my legs. I swore again, and swung back to face him.

He was a big man with a broad chest, and my bullet caught him square in the middle of it, flipping him off the back of his horse while still sixty yards away. It was a good shot, and I'll confess there was more than a little luck in my making it, what with that Indian being on the move and those other two racing their ponies down the slope toward us. But when I turned back, the two riders broke apart. One headed north along the ridgeline, while the other veered toward the man I'd sent flying off his mount. It was only then that I noticed the rider was a woman. A second glance confirmed that the other one was a woman, too. She was getting away, and I started to raise my rifle, then lowered it uncertainly. I'd never shot at a woman or child in my life, and I didn't want to start then. On the other hand, I knew it was likely she'd been actively involved in the ambush on Judge Lynn's posse. Somehow or the other, I was going to have to stop her. Then it dawned on me, and I shouted, *"Brutus!"*

The dog appeared out of the rocks like he was catapulted and instinctively took off after the second rider. I had to smile as the woman began frantically pounding her moccasined heels into the horse's ribs. Then a bullet tore through the lining of my sheepskin coat and I whirled back in surprise to see the first woman on her knees beside the man I'd shot. She was levering a fresh round into the rifle's chamber, and there I was facing the same dilemma I had earlier. Only this time I didn't have any qualms about firing, and snapped off a shot just as she was taking aim. I knew she was hit hard by the way she was flung away from the man on the ground, her cloth skirt twirling up past her brown knees as she rolled twice, then lay still.

Even with everything that was going on around me, I felt remorse for having taken the shot, and anger for being forced to take it. Then I heard a scream and turned as the second woman's horse pivoted away from Brutus's charge. The horse's rear legs skidded out from under it and the animal nearly fell. The woman screamed again as she lost her hold on the saddle.

She spilled to the ground like a load of firewood off a dump-wagon. It had to have hurt like hell, but she was up in an instant and quickly scurried away. Brutus immediately abandoned the horse and turned on the woman. For a minute, I thought he was going to attack her. Then she fell back and rolled onto her side, curling into a fetal position with her arms over her head, her knees drawn up to her chest. Brutus came to a slinking stop, then began circling warily to keep her pinned to the ground, no doubt treating her to the same throaty growl he'd used earlier to curdle my blood. Wisely, I think, the woman stayed where she was, and I marked her down as good as cuffed as long as Brutus stayed on the job. Figuring he would until released, I grimly turned back to deal with the man and woman I'd shot.

Session Fifteen

As I was making my way toward the pair on the ground, a fresh flurry of gunfire came rolling over the top of the ridge. I hesitated only a second, then changed course. With Jess needing help, I was going to have to postpone examining the two I'd shot until I had more time.

I started racing toward the ridge as fast as my lungs and legs could carry me, but I didn't burst over the top like a damned fool. I slowed before reaching the crest, and kept my head down as I picked my way through the labyrinth of rocks. It didn't take long to spot Jess holed up behind a boulder about the size of a small buggy. He was trading shots with an Indian in tan canvas trousers and a red blanket coat, his black hair wrapped in two long braids. The Indian didn't see me and I had a clear shot, but I wasn't going to kill him if I didn't have to. Instead I put a bullet into the rocks a foot or so above his head, showering him with pieces of lead and granite and scaring the hell out of him. He jumped and looked around just in time to see me throwing the Krag's bolt on another round, and he must have realized I had him dead to rights.

"Put your rifle down and your hands up," I shouted, and he hesitated but a second before complying. "Jess, are you all right?"

"I'm all right," he replied, although I thought his voice sounded unusually taut.

"He's surrendering, but keep your gun on him."

"I've got him."

It was hard to know back in those days whether or not an Indian understood you. Most of the younger ones had picked up enough English by then that you could hold a conversation with them, but it was always hit or miss with the older ones, and no way to tell if they honestly couldn't understand what you were saying, or were only acting like they couldn't. This Indian in the red blanket coat looked young enough to know where things stood, but to be sure, I gave the Krag's muzzle a couple of quick, upward jerks.

"On your feet," I barked in my best lawman's voice, and the Indian rose slowly with his hands above his head. "Come on out here."

He picked his way carefully through the rocks, limping badly on his left leg. When he got out in the clear, I saw blood staining the front of his trousers just below the knee, as vibrant in that high country sun as a cardinal's crown. There was a long clear stretch between where he stood and where Jess was hunkered down, and I waited until he reached the middle of it before I told him to stop.

"Watch it, Hud," Jess called. "There's another one out there somewhere, and three that made it over the top."

"I've got those three stopped. Where's the other one?"

"He spilled off his horse when the shooting started and ducked into the rocks south of me. He was heading for that peak yonder, the last time I saw him." Jess pointed toward the ridge's highest peak, less than half a mile away. "I haven't seen him since."

The Indian got a kind of smirk on his face, and if I hadn't been completely sure of his comprehension of English before, I was then.

"Where's your friend?" I called to him, and he looked away as if neither Jess nor I existed. It was about what you'd expect, and I didn't take any offense from it. What did puzzle me was that Jess hadn't moved out of his place in the rocks yet. I asked again if he was okay, and his reply seemed almost perturbed.

"Yeah, I twisted my ankle moving from one place to another. The damned thing might be broke, Hud."

Well, there was a fine fix, and when I looked at the Indian again, his sly smile had grown by nearly an inch.

"Stay where you are," I called to Jess, then began easing down through the rocks until I was close enough not to have to shout. Making another motion toward the Indian with my rifle, I said, "Get over here."

He came slowly, hobbling on his bad leg. When he was close, he said, "What are you going to do now, white man?"

"I'm going to take you back to Echo City for murder."

"Who did I kill?"

I gave him the names I had for sure, then tacked the judge and Deke to the list, because I figured it was only a matter of time for them. The Indian's expression didn't change.

"They sound like stupid men who probably did something foolish to earn the wrath of their enemies."

"Likely so," I agreed. "Then you and your pards did something equally stupid."

He shrugged and looked out over the tall timber to the east. Keeping the Krag's muzzle leveled on his chest, I backed over to where Jess was leaning against the boulder he'd been hiding behind, its near side pocked and chipped from all the lead that had been thrown at him.

"Can you keep an eye on this one?" I asked.

"Sure, you do what you have to. Me and this buck'll be right here when you get back."

"If he gives you any trouble, shoot him." I looked at the Indian. "We can bury him with the others, if we have to."

"He's pretty skinny," Jess observed. "We probably wouldn't

even have to dig the grave any deeper. Just tamp him down with our feet. You'd be surprised how many men you can cram into a single hole with a little effort."

You might think our words were cruel, and you'd be right under different circumstances. But out there in the middle of nowhere, with Indians on every side and Jess so gimped up he could barely haul himself around, I wanted that Indian to think we meant business. We did, for that matter. I just wanted to be sure he knew it, so that we wouldn't have to shoot him, too. Jess and I did what we had to that day, and some of it was dirty work, but I'll guarantee you that neither of us took any pleasure from it.

I was still wearing my sheepskin coat and chaps, and had a glove on my left hand, although I'd shed the right one when the shooting started, leaving it on the ground somewhere on the other side of the ridge. Now I removed the remaining glove and shoved it into my pocket, then took off the coat, wanting mobility more than I did warmth. I still had to go after that Indian who'd gotten away, but first I wanted to check on the three I'd left west of the ridge.

"Sit down," Jess told the Indian, and when he did—awkwardly, because of his wound—I told Jess what I was going to do. "I'll wait for you here," he replied dryly, then eased down on his own butt to take the weight off his leg.

I hoofed it back across the ridge and found things pretty much as I'd left them. The man and woman hadn't moved, and the second woman was still curled up on the ground like a pill bug, Brutus standing alertly over her. I walked over to where the man and woman lay first and rolled the man onto his back. He was a big one, with a broad, square jaw and large forehead. He was wearing a buckskin shirt under a wool coat, and there was a small hole in the very center of it, but not much blood. A body—man or animal—doesn't bleed much after it's dead; judging from the location of the wound, I figured I must have shot this one near the heart.

The woman was alive and seemed unharmed save for a bump above the bridge of her nose that reminded me of a hen's egg. I glanced around and spotted her rifle nearby. There was a deep gouge in the wood along the forearm, and I thought that must have been what hit her. Had it been the Krag's bullet, she'd have been stone dead.

She looked a lot younger than I expected, slim and attractive, with long hair the color of a crow's wing and a soft, dusky complexion. She was dressed like the others in a mishmash of white and Indian clothing. Kneeling at her side, I gave her a couple of small slaps on her cheek. Nothing hard, but enough to start drawing her back toward consciousness. After a few more gentle pats, her eyes fluttered, then opened. She appeared confused at first. Then she saw me looming above her and gasped in terror. Rolling onto her hands and knees, she tried to scramble away, but I snagged a moccasined foot and pulled her back. Standing, I dropped her ankle and pointed the Krag at her midsection.

"On your feet," I ordered.

She gave me an uncomprehending look, and I thought for a minute that perhaps she didn't speak English. Then she brushed the hair out of her eyes and stood, her expression defiant. I tipped my head toward where the other woman was huddled beneath Brutus's jaws and told her to start walking. She hesitated and almost looked toward the dead Indian at her side, then determinedly pulled her gaze away and moved toward the woman and dog.

Brutus snarled as we came up, and there was slobber on his jaws. I could sense the fear in the woman beside me, and didn't think there was any doubt about what the woman on the ground was experiencing.

"Brutus," I said. "Step back." The dog just looked at me, and I wondered if we were going to have another little tussle of wills. "Step back," I repeated, low but firm, "or you and I are going to tangle."

This time the dog did as commanded, backing up several paces and sitting down, although he remained vigilantly on guard, and there wasn't a doubt in my mind he could be on any one of us before I could swing my rifle to stop him. If you weren't Jess Harding, that was one damned, dangerous dog.

I nudged the woman's hip with my toe and told her to get up. She didn't respond at first. Then the woman beside me spoke in a language I didn't understand, and the woman on the ground looked up.

"On your feet," I said, and she rose slowly, her eyes fixed on Brutus. "What's your names?" I asked.

Neither answered, but with another man loose and Jess on the far side of the ridge with a bum leg, I was feeling short on patience.

"I want your names," I said in that voice I sometimes use with unruly lumberjacks and cowboys on a Saturday-night spree that's gotten out of hand.

The women exchanged glances, then the one who had been stopped by Brutus said, "I am Tall Water."

"And I am Bernice White Earth."

I nodded toward the dead Indian.

"My brother," Bernice said in an eerily calm tone.

"What's his name?"

She gave me a startled look, then shook her head. It was Tall Water who spoke. "It is best not to mention the names of those who no longer ride this land."

I remembered hearing how some Indians felt that way. Not having anything to prove, I let it drop. "Let's go," I said, motioning with my rifle, and the four of us, counting Brutus, hiked back to where Jess and the other Indian were awaiting my return.

"Have any trouble?" Jess asked.

I shook my head, then introduced the two woman. Jess nodded toward his prisoner. "That's Clarence Broken Foot. Kind of ironic, isn't it?" he said, indicating the warrior's bloody shin. "He says the one who got away is Albert Bull, and that the man who went over the ridge is Floyd Packs His Meat."

Bernice White Earth jerked her head away, and Tall Water spoke softly to her in their native tongue. Clarence's lips thinned, and he also looked away.

"Got him, huh?" Jess asked quietly.

"You speak their language?"

"It's Ute. I spent a couple of winters with them, probably before these cubs were even born. I can get along in it, and they speak English when they aren't being stubborn about it."

"I've got to go after Albert Bull," I said.

"It might be too late if he kept running."

"You said he was on foot?"

Jess nodded. "I can see his horse from here, so I'd guess he still is."

I stared silently toward the high point of Porcupine Ridge. I didn't want to do it, didn't want to take the time I figured could be better spent pursuing Billy Pinto and Susan Stokes, but as I've mentioned before, I was wearing a badge, and that always added weight to any decision I had to make.

"I'm going after him, Jess, but first I want to gather up all the loose stock. I don't want him catching a stray and getting away on horseback." I glanced at the old mountain man's ankle, swollen large enough to draw the leather of his boot tight around the calf.

I've mentioned more than once how in a situation like that, it seems as if there are a hundred things that need to be done immediately. That day on Porcupine Ridge was no exception. But since there wouldn't be anything gained by going into a lot of detail, I'll keep it brief. I rounded up the Indian ponies first, then brought my buckskin and Jess's dappled gray up from where we'd left them in the pines. After that, I helped Jess pry the boot off his injured foot.

The ankle was swollen and bruised, but I didn't think it was busted. Not all the way, at least. I wrapped it as best I could with cloth torn from a spare shirt in Jess's saddlebags, counting on Brutus to keep a sharper eye on our prisoners than I could. I've got to admit that, despite our differences—mine and Brutus's—I was glad to have him along that day.

It seemed like hours before I got everything taken care of, but when I finally looked up, it was barely noon. I had all afternoon to track down Albert Bull. I'd probably need it, too.

The three prisoners were sitting on the cold ground with blankets taken from their own saddles wrapped around their shoulders. I'd brought along a pair of handcuffs with the hopes of taking Billy Pinto in alive. Now I had them fastened to the wrists of Clarence and Tall Water. I'd also tied a six-foot lead rope around Bernice White Earth's waist, before hitching the free end to the chain between Clarence and Tall Water. It wasn't ideal, but it was the best I could manage under the circumstances.

I put my sheepskin coat back on as I prepared to leave, but left my gloves—both of them, having retrieved the one I'd shaken loose earlier—in the large side pockets. The binoculars hung from a strap around my neck, tucked inside my coat for protection. Although I'd briefly considered riding, I'd dismissed the idea as too risky. I was going to be wasting a lot of time going after Albert Bull on foot if he'd continued to run, as Jess speculated he might, but if he was holed up somewhere above me, I wanted to stay in among the rocks where I wouldn't make such an easy target.

It's always pretty chilly above timberline, even in summer. With early autumn already upon us and nothing to block the wind, it was edging toward miserable, even at midday. My nose was still dripping, and it wasn't long before my fingers started to go numb around the Krag's stock. I didn't let the cold prod me into hurrying, though. That high point where Jess had seen Albert Bull heading wasn't quite half a mile away, but it took me the better part of an hour to reach it. I was still a couple of hundred feet from the top when I settled down among the boulders to glass the stony promontory.

I scanned that peak for twenty minutes, but if Bull was up there, he wasn't showing himself. Still, I couldn't shake an uneasiness stirring in my gut, and felt hesitant to leave my shelter. I kept waiting and watching, but after another thirty minutes, I figured I was either going to have to move forward and check it out, or freeze to death waiting for something that might never occur.

I was starting to rise when a marmot whistled its shrill warning from somewhere to my left. I knew they were up there; hell, I'd seen one earlier and commented on it to you, but this one surprised me so much I actually flinched and ducked back a little. The minute I did, a shot rang out from the base of the peak, and a bullet struck the curled brim of my hat with an irritating flick. I swore and dropped flat to my stomach. My heart was pounding. I hadn't had a bullet come that close since Cuba, and it instantly brought back the familiar, brassy taste of fear I remembered so well from that hot island jungle.

I flipped the Krag's safety off, then real cautious-like rose to my knees. Although I hadn't seen exactly where the bullet came from, it had been pushed out of the bore by one of those older cartridges that creates enough smoke to choke a bobcat. Peering around the side of my rock, I saw a few tendrils still lazily swirling over the ground between a pair of boulders. Dropping back out of sight, I quickly scuttled sideways to a new position before risking another look. As I did, a second round came clipping through the air above my head. I dropped instinctively, then popped back up and slid my rifle over the top of the boulder. Snagging the gap with my sights, I squeezed off a round before my ambusher could chamber a fresh cartridge.

Dust and shards of granite exploded from where my bullet struck just to the side of the gap, and I knew whoever was back there was going to be spitting grit and wiping his eyes for a few seconds. Putting that time to good use, I darted out from where I'd taken refuge while glassing the peak and sprinted toward another large chunk of stone about fifteen feet away. I got down behind it without being shot at, but still had to wonder if I'd been spotted. From time to time I'd peek around the boulder's edge, but there was nothing to see. Either I'd gotten luckier with my shot than I had a right to expect, or Albert Bull was up to something.

Concluding that my luck wasn't that reliable, I decided to wait for him to make the next move. It seemed like a good idea at first, but after forty-five minutes or so, I began to run out of patience. I kept scanning the rocky landscape around me, thinking maybe Bull was trying to put the sneak on me, and although I listened as best I could, that damned wind wouldn't quit blowing; it rattled the knee timber to my left and hummed among the rocks from every other direction. As cold as it was, I swear my palms were starting to sweat. Then I heard a clattering of small stones and jerked rigid with concentration. I hadn't been able to tell which direction the noise had come from, but it wasn't thirty seconds later that I heard another sharp, short bark of a marmot, and rolled quickly to my left as a rifle blasted from the top of a tall boulder behind me.

The bullet slammed into the gravelly soil where I'd been laying even as I brought the Krag's muzzle to bear. Bull stood less than twenty yards away. Close, but not so close a man couldn't miss with a hurried shot. There wasn't going to be time to aim, but I still took a fraction of a second to make sure my barrel was pointed straight before pulling the trigger. The Krag slammed hard into my armpit, and that Indian made a sound like none I'd ever heard before. Then his body went limp and he tumbled backward off the boulder. I jumped up and darted through the rocks, but there was no need to hurry. By the time I got to where he'd fallen, Albert Bull was already dead.

Excerpt from:
Inquiry into the Events
Related to the William Pinto Uprising
13 November 1904–16 November 1904
The Honorable Frederick S. Tunstill, Presiding
San Pedro County District Court, 14 November 1904

"Let the record show that the witness, Jared Caylin, in accompaniment to his statement that he had been wounded in the ambush on top of the San Pedro Plateau, has visually displayed his left hand, and that said appendage is indeed missing its small and ring fingers. Proceed with your account, Mister Caylin."

"Well, Your Honor, like I said, I got to feeling real funny after that, and soon after I had to sit down. Then pretty soon, not more than thirty-five or forty minutes later, Sheriff Pratt showed up and took over. He looked to the wounded and told me what he wanted me to do, and he let [Mark] Anderson know he was supposed to help, which was a good thing, because I was feeling pretty weak by then. After ticking off four or five orders, Hud . . . Sheriff Pratt . . . took off again."

"Abandoned you?"

"No, sir, not exactly. I guess he was just more worried about the judge's granddaughter than a shot-up posse. Jess Harding, who we talked about earlier, had already started tracking the Indians that attacked us, and Sheriff Pratt went after him."

"What happened in the canyon after Sheriff Pratt left?"

"We did pretty much what Hud told us to do. Anderson was the only one among us that wasn't bleeding from some hole or gouge, so he cut some sturdy branches to make litters. We rigged those up as best we could, using canvas off our bedrolls and damn near every saddle string we had to make them secure. We had to bury Frank Brady and Oscar Larnx there in those aspens, but as soon as that was done, we got Judge Lynn and Deke Burton on their litters.

"I know the army has used litters, probably been using them for hundreds of years, but what we had didn't work very well. The horses in back kept spooking from the load that was right above their heads. They just about tossed the judge and Deke out of their beds a time or two. We knew we were doing something wrong, but we kept on doing it because we didn't know what else to do, and figured it was more important to get the wounded back to Echo City. Deke was in real bad shape by then. His gut was swollen before we left, but it got even worse as the day went on. By the time we made camp that first night, he wasn't talking anymore, and sweat was running off his face in rivers. The judge wasn't much better, but at least he was unconscious. If he was hurting, he wasn't showing it.

"Ain't none of the rest of us were feeling very well. Not even Anderson, who looked like he was about to fall over from being so tired. To look at us around the fire that night, you'd think we'd all ate bad meat for breakfast, then had a second helping for lunch. I thought more than once I was going to keel over myself, but knew I couldn't. It wouldn't have been fair to leave Anderson to run the whole outfit by himself.

"I ain't lying when I say I was surprised as all get-out

the next morning when I realized nobody'd died overnight. I figured we'd be digging at least one more grave before sunup, and maybe two, but Deke and the judge, they hung on. It wasn't until the second night after the ambush that Deke finally cashed in his chips. I'd say it was the Lord's own mercy that took him, him being in so much hurt it just about made your skin crawl to look at him. We buried him up there and marked his grave with a wooden cross, although I'm saddened to admit I'm not sure I could locate the site again.

"That second day, on our way back to Echo City, we ran into Curly Dunn and his boys. Curly worked for United Lumber, and his bosses had sent him up there with a sizable posse to hunt down Billy Pinto and rescue the judge's granddaughter. That's what he called it, too: *A by-God, get-the-job-done posse.* He said it real boastful-like, although we all commented later on how none of them had been wearing badges. Curly claimed folks were tired of waiting for Sheriff Pratt to handle things, and that Nathan Mosby, who ran United's operations in San Pete County, had put up a five-hundred-dollar reward for Billy's capture. He said he had fifty men scattered across the Plateau, but as far as I know, none of them ever got within a country mile of Billy and Miss Suzie. [*Editor's Note:* Records from the Rawlins (Wyoming) Historical Association quote sources with access to United Lumber's financial accounts as stating only nineteen men received wages for the *"pursuit of the fugitive, Billy Pinto."* Those records do not indicate if these were regular employees of United Lumber, or if others were deployed in the search for Pinto and Stokes.]

"We got back to the Broken Cinch late the following day and immediately sent a rider in to fetch Doc Freeman. The doc was there before dawn, but said there wasn't anything he could do. Those were his words, too: *Boys, there's nothing I can do for the man.*

"Miss Henrietta [(Lynn) Stokes] was beside herself after hearing that. She was already half out of her wits about having her girl taken. When the doc told her that her daddy was going to die, she had to take to her bed to keep from fainting right there in the parlor. The judge lived two more days, which was four more than I'd expected. Not just me, either. A lot of folks were saying they were surprised he hung on for so long."

"Yes, the court is aware of that from earlier testimony, Mister Caylin. I am now going to consider your contribution complete, unless you have anything further to add."

"Not so much. I guess you know Miss Henrietta made Mark Anderson manager of the Broken Cinch after the judge passed on, and that Anderson gave the job of foreman to Toby Smith, after Tobe's leg healed? I tried to get on at the Cinch myself, but Anderson wouldn't hire me. He said they had enough hands. I don't know if that was a dig at my injury, or if he was dealing square. I never could read that ol' boy."

"Am I to understand that you no longer work in law enforcement, Mister Caylin?"

"No, sir, I don't. After what happened to Judge Lynn and the others, I think folks needed someone to blame, and I was it. The county fired me first. Then the city council fired me. Even Hud fired me, after he got back. I've never been so fired in my life. I work for United Lumber now, stacking planks as they come off the belt at the sawmill, and to be real honest, after what happened on the Plateau last September, I don't think I'd even want to wear a badge anymore."

Session Sixteen

I buried Albert Bull and Floyd Packs His Meat up near the top of Porcupine Ridge. Not having a shovel, I had to improvise with what was available, then make sure the single grave was covered with stones to keep the scavengers away. Bernice White Earth and Tall Water wailed the way Indian women do when they're mourning their dead, and Clarence Broken Foot sang some kind of low chant. They didn't help with the interment, and I didn't ask if they wanted to.

You might be wondering about their Christian names—Bernice and Clarence and Albert and Floyd. I can pretty well assure you their parents never used those labels. It was reservation policy in a lot of places back then to modify a native name with an Anglo-Saxon addition, the reasoning being that it would help make the transition into the white man's world easier. I never saw any evidence that it did, but then, I never hung around reservations much, either. I've heard they tried to do the same thing with some of the older tribal members, those who had been born before the reserves were established, but that they'd never had any luck with it. I don't doubt it, and now that I'm older, I don't blame them, either.

After I finished, Jess and I hunkered down out of earshot of the prisoners to talk.

"What are you going to do, Hud?"

"I've got to go after Billy. If it wasn't for Susan, I'd let him go, but I can't give up as long as he's got her."

"And them?" He nodded toward the Utes, huddled together with the women still softly keening their grief toward the heavens. It was, according to Jess, a part of their religion, to help the deceased move on into the next world, and who the hell was I to argue against it?

"What do you want me to do?" Jess asked.

"How's your ankle?"

"Sore."

"Can you walk?"

"I can hobble. I'll cut a sapling and make myself a walking staff as soon as we get off this damned mountain"

"Jess, you've got to tell me honest. Can you get these prisoners to Echo City?"

"By myself?"

"You and your dog."

"I guess I can . . . if you'll deputize Brutus."

That brought a smile to my lips, and not many things had since the Jennings bunch rode into town. "Consider it done," I said.

"One thing, though, Hud. I won't take them to Echo City. With what happened to Judge Lynn and the others, these Utes would be lynched before they ever got to trial. I'll take them to Utah, to Fort Duchesne, and turn them over to the agent there, but if that doesn't suit you, then you're on your own with them."

I never did like ultimatums, but figured Jess was probably right about this. It galled me, though. Not his refusal to take them into Echo City, but to be reminded of the self-righteousness of those I knew who would probably be first in line with a rope. Good, solid citizens, too. In their minds, at least.

"All right," I said grudgingly. "Do what you think is best."

Jess nodded and grinned, and we shook hands. I made the suggestion that they stay where they were until morning, but

Jess was as anxious to get off that mountain as I was. Leaving him and Brutus to watch the prisoners, I went to get things ready. I kept Clarence and Tall Water handcuffed together, after first running the manacles' chain under the high gullet of the woman's saddle. I also made sure it was Clarence riding behind her, and not the other way around. He protested that it wasn't a fitting position for a man, but I reminded him of his own bum limb—a deep, ripping gouge across the calf of his left leg that still hadn't completely stopped bleeding—and told him if he gave Jess any trouble, they could both walk. Then I tied Bernice White Earth to her saddle—waist to horn, then ankle to ankle under her mount's belly. When I was finished, I walked over to where Jess was sitting his dappled gray.

"Listen, don't risk your neck with this bunch. If you can't handle them, either shoot them or turn them loose."

"I'm not going to have any trouble," he said. Then we shook hands again, and Jess told Tall Water to lead out. He had his rifle balanced across his saddlebows, and Brutus stood nearby, watching vigilantly. No one looked back as they rode over the top of the ridge and started downhill toward Utah. Not even Jess.

It might interest you to know that I never saw Jess Harding again, although I've wondered about him, about all of them, for a long time afterward. I even wrote to one of the agents at Duchesne, a man named Randolph Sullivan, but beyond acknowledging that all four of them had arrived safely, his reply was vague. I was still curious, and not at all certain I trusted Agent Sullivan's response. Then one day in late October, Red Gifford came into my office with a letter he'd received from Jess, asking him to go to his cabin and bring down all his stuff. Red said Jess wasn't wanting much for himself, just a couple of rifles he'd left behind and a good double-barreled shotgun that had been a gift from his family at some event in his distant past.

"I wanted you to know what I'm doing before I go up there," Red said, handing me Jess's letter. It was short and to the point, and it gave Red permission to do whatever he desired with the rest of the items in and around the cabin. "Have you got any problems with this, Hud?"

I told him that I didn't, and a few days later he took a string of packhorses up to the cabin to retrieve what had been left behind. Tom went with him to help wrap up the lithographs and books and the blue willow china and a nice herringbone suit that didn't look like it had ever been worn. There were other items as well, but except for Jess's traps, well-oiled but long unused, Tom said there wasn't much of value. Red shipped the guns to an address in Utah and gave the books to the Echo Literary Society, which I mentioned earlier. It was the same reading group Angie was a part of, and Jess's books became the seed for a small public library in the courthouse basement.

Not too long after Red brought Jess's stuff down, I received notice that the prisoners delivered to the agency at Fort Duchesne had been released through the efforts of Agent Sullivan. The notice claimed Sullivan had argued that since there'd been no charges filed against the three Utes, there was no legal reason to hold them. Eventually, the San Pedro county attorney's office, at Roy Sandler's edict, did file charges, but the Utes were never brought in, and Roy never made any effort to have them extradited. This is just my speculation, because I didn't push it, either, but what I think happened is that, even though the law required Sandler to issue some kind of charge against the three, a lot of people didn't want word to get out about what Judge Lynn and his posse did to Old Man With His Horses, Raven's Call, and those two women, Bird's Flight and Tail of a Doe. Around Echo City, it became one of those dirty little secrets common to a lot of small towns, something known but never discussed, especially not with outsiders.

I don't know if you were interested in hearing that. If you ain't, I guess you can have it struck out when you transcribe these recordings to paper. Frankly, I'm glad they weren't charged, and I hope they lived a good, long life after they got home. [*Editor's Note:* Records indicate that Clarence Broken Foot recovered from his wound and took jobs on various cattle ranches throughout northeastern Utah until his death in 1947; his age was listed as sixty-two years. Tall Water married an Arapaho from the Wind River Reservation in Wyoming, and went there to live; no record of her death could be found. Bernice White Earth moved to Salt Lake City in 1909, where she resided until her death in 1971; her age was listed as eighty-seven; she was preceded in death by her husband, Willis Jones, and survived by six children and seven grandchildren.]

I stood on top of Porcupine Ridge for a good long time that day, watching Jess lead his prisoners into the heart of a wilderness few men had ever seen, and I doubt if many still have. Then I went back and checked the cinch on my buckskin before swinging a leg over the cantle. I reined east, down off the ridge the way we'd come. The Mule Ears lay maybe twenty miles farther south, but looking at the country in between, I didn't anticipate reaching them until late the next day.

Travel became easier the farther I got from Porcupine Ridge. The steep-sided canyons and rocky gorges gradually gave way to gentler terrain, and I soon left the brooding ponderosa forests for rolling swells of golden aspens. The land appeared more open and inviting, and I began to see more game; deer flitted through the shadows like ghosts, and at one point I stopped to watch what must have been a herd of fifty cow elk walking almost silently through the white-barked aspens. Hawks soared overhead, and jays and magpies darted from branch to branch as if following my progress. The air turned warm again as I dropped in elevation, and I was able to shed my heavy coat and chaps before noon on the day following Jess's departure. I could have felt almost chipper if not for the gut-nagging fear that I was on a fool's errand, that when I arrived at the Mule Ears there would be no sign of Billy or the girl, and that all my gambles would leaving me standing there empty-handed and without hope.

The twin peaks of the Ears grew larger as the day progressed. Towering pillars of some kind of dark stone, their nearly vertical sides furrowed as if by giant claws. [*Editor's Note:* Although geologists disagree about what caused the two formations to stand so dramatically close to one another—the eastern column rises 516 feet above the surrounding landscape, while the western "ear" stands a mere 479 feet; base to base measurements are 291 feet—the generally accepted belief is that they are the twin cores of two "spouts" of the same volcano, probably from the Paleogene Period, approximately 50 to 60 million years ago.]

It was early afternoon when I came to a yard-wide trail leading toward the low pass between the ears. Hauling up, I stared in near disbelief at the sign before me—two well-defined sets of horse prints, clearly evident among the multitude of elk and deer tracks. Dismounting, I knelt beside the trail to run a forefinger lightly along the ridge of the nearest print. My excitement grew as the track of the shod horse crumbled easily beneath my slight pressure. Hell, even as poor of a tracker as I was, I knew these prints couldn't have been more than a day or two old; otherwise the wind would have already rounded off the sharper edges.

My pulse surged with grateful excitement as I rose and stared south along the well-traveled path. Although wider than most game trails, saplings and clinging brush prevented me from describing it as perfectly clear. Still, to be so well-used, it must have been a fairly common route to some location where other entrances and exits were rare. Like maybe that basin on the other side of the Mule Ears that Jess had told me about.

I mounted and turned onto the trail. It was easy to follow even from the saddle, and after a while the lawman in me got to thinking that maybe it was a little *too* easy. With images of Early Jennings and his boys lying dead at the Point floating through my mind, I slid the Krag from its scabbard and butted it to my thigh. I kept my thumb on the safety and the buckskin to a walk, and my eyes never stopped moving. If I rode into an ambush, it wasn't going to be because I wasn't being watchful.

The twin monoliths loomed taller as the afternoon wore on, the trail continuing steadily toward the low saddle between them. I was making decent time in spite of my cautiousness, but the day still gave out before I reached the base of the pass. I hauled up in frustration as twilight closed in around me. The woods grew silent and the shadows under the trees turned to ink. A part of me wanted to go on, but a larger, wiser part knew I'd be risking the girl's life if I somehow blundered along the way. As much as I hated to do it, I guided my horse off the trail. We wound through the close-growth forest for a quarter of a mile before coming to a small beaver pond with an open park beside it. Satisfied that we'd traveled far enough, I pulled my saddle from the buckskin's back, then rubbed the gelding's back and legs down briskly with my gloves before picketing him on grass alongside the shallow pool.

Although I wouldn't kindle a fire this close to the Mule Ears, I still had plenty of grub to chew on. With my horse secured, I slid into my sheepskin coat, then sat down with my back to a log, saddlebags and bedroll already loosened and resting in the tall grass at my side. As I leaned forward to rustle a meal from the bottom of the saddlebags, I pushed my hat back on my forehead. When I did, my fingers brushed the ruffled felt of its brim. I stopped and frowned and touched it again. I guess in all the hullabaloo of getting Jess on his way and taking up Billy's trail again, I'd forgotten some of the details of the gunfight from the day before. Like that bullet Albert Bull had sent my way, flipping the brim of my hat like an annoying child's finger. I pulled the Manhattan Hat Company's version of a Stetson—a narrower brim and a fancy "M" branded lightly into the side of the crown—off to study the damage.

Albert's bullet had missed my ear by less than three inches. I've heard the expression, and you probably have too, that a miss is as good as a mile, but as I studied the ragged piece of felt, I experienced a sobering realization of how close I'd actually come to having my brains splattered across the top of Porcupine Ridge. Staring at the hat reminded me of something else, and I pulled my coat's hem around until I found a thumb-sized hole punched through the mottled sheepskin, halfway between my hip and backbone. It looked like I'd come even closer to taking a slug in the side from Bernice White Earth.

My supper forgotten, I let go of my coat and put my hat back on my head. For a long time I sat there thinking about my life and what I'd done with it so far. More important, I started pondering what I wanted to do with it in the future. I had an election coming up in less than two months if I wanted to keep my job as sheriff, and two opponents who'd already tossed their hats into the ring.

My biggest competitor was probably going to be Curly Dunn, who was United Lumber's head of security, which in those troubling times meant he was the company's chief skull buster, in case anyone on the payroll got the idea that talking to a union rep might be a good idea. Rumor had it that United's bigwigs wanted more autonomy on the Echo City end of their operation, and they figured having their own man in the sheriff's office would be a good place to start. Curly lived at United's compound along the Plateau's base, where the company kept a barracks, mess hall, company store, saloon, and billiards hall; they also employed a number of laundresses who, according to those same rumormongers, made a lot more money on their backs in the evenings than they did splashing suds during the day.

I wasn't too worried about Curly. He was loud and arrogant, and had rubbed too many people the wrong way before he found out his masters wanted him to run for public office. The only thing he really had on his side was the amount of money United Lumber could pour into his campaign, assuming the company's officials decided to really back him.

My other opponent had almost no financial backing at all, other than what a small collective of Echo City businessmen had decided to throw his way, on the offhand chance he'd strike a spark and start to surge in popularity. His name was Harold Davis, and he'd been practicing law in San Pete County for five or six years by then. Had I not already decided to re-seek the office myself, I would have thrown my support behind Davis without hesitation. He was young and something of an idealist, but I felt certain he had the county's best interests at heart. The problem was that those very same characteristics—youth and idealism—were going to play against him when the election drew close. There were still too many men like Early Jennings and his crew roaming the Western trails, and the citizens around San Pete knew it. The question a lot of those folks were going to be asking as the election drew near was: How would a man like Davis fare against Jennings's kind? I knew it was something I'd want to know.

The fact is that, despite the competition, I felt fairly confident of winning a second term. Except now, sitting there alone in the growing cold while the night turned to soup around me, I started reflecting on those two bullets that had come so close to snuffing my candle. It made me wonder if I even wanted the job. I had a wife and two kids and a third one on the way. I had a home, small but paid for, and the respect of most of the county, at least as far as I knew. What would happen if I was killed in the line of duty? Where would that leave Angie and the children? Hell, it wasn't like I didn't have other options. I was young enough to cast my rope in just about any direction I wanted to, and likely wouldn't have too much trouble finding employment elsewhere. For that matter, I could even leave the county, maybe go back to Greeley where my folks and Angie's still lived. [*Editor's Note:* Pratt is referring to his hometown of Greeley, Colorado, approximately forty-five miles north of Denver.] Or we could move somewhere warm, like Southern California, where the snowdrifts didn't rise so high every winter they nearly blocked the view out the windows. It was a troubling subject to ponder, but a damn fine place to do it in, and it was probably ten o'clock before I unfurled my bedroll and crawled inside.

I was still fairly ambivalent about my future when I awoke the next morning, but quickly put those thoughts out of my head. It wasn't just that I had a job to do in the here and now, it was that it was the kind of job that could get me killed in a hurry if I didn't give it my full attention.

With a breakfast of cold roast beef and a crumbling biscuit behind my belt buckle, I saddled my horse and rode back to the trail I'd abandoned the night before. It was another crystal-clear day, although it seemed colder than on other mornings. The frost was thicker, and a breeze rattled limbs and sent leaves swirling to the ground. There'd been a dime-thick shelf of ice along the edge of the pond that morning, too. I had to break it loose with the side of my fist before I could drink.

Reining toward the pass, I hauled the Krag from its scabbard and rested it across the saddle in front of me. I was feeling real uneasy that day, and kept glancing to the sides and behind me.

I could put some of it down to the noise the wind was making in the trees—enough to mask my approach, but equally capable of covering someone else's advance—but I knew there was more to it than that. The chase was coming to its conclusion; I sensed its ending like a storm brewing beyond the horizon. I'd been on prolonged manhunts before and never felt this way. In fact, it was often a surprise when we did catch up with whoever we were pursuing. But like I said, this time it was different, and my nerves were feeling jangly.

The land began to tilt upward, the Ears towering dizzily overhead. The trail narrowed as it approached a gorge with sides that weren't entirely vertical, but were close enough to it that my heart started creeping toward my tonsils. The distant image of a low saddle connecting the two monoliths had been misleading.

A creek filled the bottom of the gorge, waist deep and loud enough to muffle the sounds of the wind. The trail followed the chasm's east flank, rising for a while, then narrowing until it was barely a foot wide. On my left, the ground was close enough that I could lean out of my saddle and brush the short bunch grass that grew there with my fingers. It still wasn't a sheer drop on my right, but I knew if my horse lost his footing, we wouldn't be stopping until we reached the rocky bottom, and that kept growing farther away the deeper we penetrated the pass. My only consolation was that the tracks of the two horses, along with those of countless elk, deer, and other game, were still in front of me.

At its worst, I'll bet that buckskin and I were two hundred feet above the canyon's floor, with the wall on my left—rough granite, now—close enough to scrape my shoulder. The grade was so steep that my horse had to dig for footing, and it really made me wonder why anything—elk, deer, or human—would want to risk such a route in the first place, without knowing what was on the other side. Then, finally, the grade tapered off and the trail became less treacherous. I spotted trees down below, scattered pines and small groves of aspens, rather than the dense stuff we'd been traveling through. It wasn't long until the trail started edging downward, and I began to breathe easier.

The Mule Ears were mostly behind us now, although the ground higher up the sides of the pass was still rocky; solitary pines stood like sentries atop jutting crags, and there were a lot of prickly bushes and what looked like shallow caves peeking out from beneath some of the massive stone slabs that had flaked off over time.

As soon as we reached level ground, I pulled up and got off, grateful for the solid feel of the earth beneath my feet. The creek flowed nearby, its waters so cold it damn near hurt my teeth to drink it. Then I stood and pulled the buckskin around and was stretching for the near-side stirrup with my toe when movement on the far bank caught my eye. I froze for a moment, then slowly lowered my foot. My gaze darted among the trees, but all I could see was the hindquarters of Early Jennings's blue roan, grazing unaware on the hillside above me.

I led my horse in the opposite direction and tied it to an aspen, then shucked my heavy coat and hung it off the saddle horn. I already had a round chambered in the Krag—had ever since that first day on the Plateau—and as I made my slow way toward the roan, I gently rolled the safety over with my thumb, making the rifle ready to fire. I still had five rounds in the magazine and six in my Colt. I was hoping I wouldn't need any of them.

Crossing that narrow creek was like sticking bare feet in a bucket of crushed ice. The water was deep enough to spill a little inside my boots, causing my toes to curl under the sturdy leather. Truth be told, the way I was feeling, I hardly noticed the discomfort. I climbed slowly and the grade began to steepen.

As my gaze traveled ever upward, I noticed a shelf of land about two hundred feet above me, with what looked like the arch of a cave's entrance just beyond its lip. I stopped and stared, and as I did a figured suddenly appeared at the edge of the shelf, black hair loose and flying in the wind, chest bare and dusky as old saddle leather. He screamed a warrior's cry and fired twice, and I threw the Krag to my shoulder and fired once.

Session Seventeen

That was a bad time for me to stop, wasn't it? It must be frustrating for you to have me jumping up every little whipstitch to let that dog in or out, or to lift him into bed with Angie. I guess with all my talk about Billy Pinto and Suzie Stokes and everything that happened up there on the San Pedro Plateau in aught-four, I never did get around to telling you how Humphrey came into our lives.

You might recall me mentioning that Angie was pregnant when all this was going on. In a family way was how we referred to it in those years. She gave birth to a girl we named Jenny in late February of aught-five, following a pretty hard snow that kept the Union Pacific tracks blocked for almost forty-eight hours, so we were glad it was an easy delivery, and that we didn't have to rush to the hospital in Rawlins or Cheyenne.

She was a sweet girl, our Jenny, and sharp as a tack. Angie and I are proud of all our kids, but there was something different about our third child. I don't know, maybe it's that way no matter who you lose. They become something more than what they were when they were alive. Or maybe it's because you only remember the good times, and not the rough spots.

Jenny was fifteen when she died. Cory had already joined the army and was stationed at Fort Bliss, down in Texas, and Lily had only recently moved to Sacramento and to take a job as a clerk with an engineering firm. She'd been dating a geologist who worked there at the time, and unbeknown to us, he'd already proposed marriage. With the tragedy, Lily didn't mention it until some weeks later. Poor kid. What should have been a happy time for her turned out so horrible.

We weren't living here in Stockton then. We had a little place outside of town where we raised some sheep and cultivated a small cherry orchard that we'd harvest a couple of times a year, then sell the fruit to area grocers. I was also working security for the railyard, so we were doing all right. Keeping busy and making ends meet.

It had been a blazing hot August that year, and Jenny and some of her friends decided to go down along the Calaveras River to wade and cool off. There'd been some heavy rains earlier in the day—you could see the clouds above the Sierras in the east, as black as the bottom of a cast-iron skillet—but we were so far away from the mountains that no one gave them much thought. It was a flash flood that took her, shortly after two o'clock that afternoon.

I wasn't there, but witnesses said the water started rising really fast. Most of the others climbed out immediately, but Jenny and two of her friends moved to a sandbar to watch it pass. Everyone was so intent on the main channel that no one noticed the river spreading around the back side of the sandbar until the waters had cut off their retreat. They said the girls didn't look worried, even then. The water was barely a foot deep, and even though it was moving along at a pretty good clip, they felt like they could still walk out. But flash floods . . . well, you can't predict them. The waters took a surge, and things got dangerous real fast. The sandbar was nearly covered and their footing was getting soft, so they decided to get out.

Two of the girls made it. Jenny very nearly did. She was already on the bank, though still on her knees, when the earth caved out from under her. She went in headfirst, and they say she never came up. Not even once. The flood just swept her away. We found her two days later, five miles downstream. [*Editor's Note:* Jennifer Allison Pratt died on August 15, 1919, in a brief and otherwise uneventful flood that probably wouldn't even have made the newspapers if not for that single casualty; no one else was injured, and there was no reported property damage.]

Cory and Lily came home for the funeral, but they couldn't stay. After they were gone, it was just Angie and me, but that final emptiness was too sudden. We'd had time with our older children, and even though we still fretted they may not have made the best decisions—especially Cory, what with the war in Europe barely ended and all the unrest still going on in Mexico—we could accept that their leaving was a part of life. But Jenny was taken without warning, without even a good-bye, and the pain damn near destroyed us.

Humphrey didn't replace her. Nothing can ever replace a child who's been taken too soon, but that old basset and whatever the hell else is in there helped fill a mighty big hole in our lives. I'm not sure what would have happened if he hadn't shown up one afternoon, half-starved and thick with fleas, but he did, and I owe him. I owe him more than I can ever repay, so hoisting him onto the sofa or taking him for a walk every morning and evening is a small price to pay for what he's done for us.

I think it only fair for you to know that, so that you understand why I get up every little bit to give him some more water, or let him out to do his business, and in when he's ready. Normally, Angie would do that, so you and I could talk uninterrupted, but she's been feeling poorly herself lately, so . . . well . . . anyway, we were talking about Billy Pinto.

There's no doubt Billy startled the hell out of me, popping up off that shelf so sudden and yelling like those old-time warriors used to do when they wanted to strike fear into your heart.

Billy did that in spades, but I didn't freeze up the way some might. Cuba had taught me more about fighting than wearing a badge ever did, and instinct took over real quick. Billy got off two quick rounds, but I fired back before he could get off a third. I never did know where his bullets went, and I never cared. I was just glad to be alive.

My shot hit the boy in the chest, and he spun halfway around before falling backward off the ledge. He must have slid six or seven yards down the side of the mountain before coming to a stop with his arms splayed above his head, which was downhill from his feet. Dirt and small stones continued to roll past and below him for another minute or so, and dust rose like tiny sprites around his bare shoulders. In the crisp autumn sunlight, his skinny breast glistened red.

With the slope as steep as it was, I'd automatically dropped to one knee as soon as Billy appeared. I remained that way a moment longer, my rifle still shouldered, my pulse thundering; that damn war cry was still coursing through my body like rippling jolts of electricity. Then, remembering Suzie, I scrambled up the base of that tower as fast as I could.

If Billy had been looking for a good place to defend, he couldn't have found much better than right there. Had he stayed inside, he probably could have easily picked me off. With the judge laid up and likely dead, it might have put an end to his pursuit for a while, too. But Billy was young, and hadn't yet learned how important it is to keep your head and your ass down when there are bullets in the air.

I found Susan Stokes inside, unharmed save for trail dirt and fright. She was hunched up at the far end of the shallow cave with her arms clasped around her knees, her eyes looking as big around as baseballs in the shady light. There was gear scattered all over the cavern's floor, and meat draped over an aspen-wood frame just inside the entrance, where it would catch the full rays of the morning sun; a hide I recognized as being from a bighorn sheep lay on a rock behind the drying rack, flesh side up. I asked Suzie if she was all right and she nodded that she was, but she didn't start to relax until I pulled my vest back to show her my badge.

"I'm Sheriff Hudson Pratt, of San Pedro County," I told her. "Your grandfather sent me up here to bring you home."

It was kind of a lie, but I figured it would help me as much as her if she thought her grandpa was behind my being there. I sure as hell wasn't going to tell her the old fool had gotten himself shot, and was probably dead by then.

"Wait right there," I told her, then skidded down to where Billy lay on his back in the sun. The blood on his chest had already started drawing flies. I wanted to be sure he was dead, and he was. After that, I crawled back up to the shelf and had a another look around. The lawman in me wanted to be sure it was just Billy I was dealing with, and that there wasn't anyone else involved.

Satisfied that there had only been the two of them, I knelt close to the girl and tried to get her to talking, mostly to reassure myself that she was okay. I didn't ask about her captivity, and she didn't volunteer anything. When I felt confident she was all right, just dead tired and still scared, I led her down off the side of the Ear and over to where my buckskin was tied. Telling her to wait for me there, I returned to the cave, gathered up all the loose stuff I could find, and lugged it down to where Billy had picketed Jennings's blue roan and Red Gifford's sorrel. I saddled both horses and strapped the gear in place, then climbed back up to the cave a final time and dragged Billy's body inside.

I think I probably mentioned in our first session that Billy was as slim as a beanpole, but he'd gaunted down even more after his run across the Plateau. I doubt if he weighed more than a hundred and thirty pounds that day, all ribs and knotted muscles. He sure looked small, lying there on the floor of that cave. Small and way the hell too young for the hole that my rifle had put in his chest.

It hadn't bothered me one bit when I killed Whitey Bowen outside of Molly Spotted Horse's house, and although I'll always regret having to shoot Floyd Packs His Meat and Albert Bull, I still consider it a part of my job as sheriff. But Billy was different, and his death has haunted my dreams a lot over the years. What he did was wrong—I'm not saying it ain't—but what happened to him was just as wrong in my opinion, and maybe even more so.

After hollowing out a place at the back of the cavern, I placed the boy in it and covered his body with a blanket. Then I carried rocks inside until I had him entombed. When I was finished, I came down and got our horses and got Susan Stokes astride Red's sorrel, and we came on home.

Session Eighteen

So what do you think? Was it a war? It sure as hell wasn't an Indian uprising, like some people wanted to make it out to be. And I'll tell you this, too, no matter what people say, it wasn't *Billy Pinto's* war. It might have been Judge Lynn's war. It might have even been his uprising, but Billy didn't have anything to do with what happened between the judge's posse and those Utes. That was all Lynn's doing.

I suppose you already know Lynn died of the wounds he received on the Plateau. I didn't find out for sure until I got back to the Broken Cinch with Susan Stokes, but he and Deke Burton both passed away from their injuries. I don't feel bad about either one of them, but I did feel bad for Susan. I don't think that girl said more than a couple dozen words the whole time she was with me. Not that I encouraged her any. Back then, I figured it best that we didn't talk about what had happened, although Angie informed me later that I was dead wrong on the matter. I didn't argue with her. I just chalked it up to another dumb mistake on my part, and looked forward to when I'd be old enough and wise enough not to keep making them. I don't guess it comes as any kind of surprise that I'm still waiting.

I left Susan at the Broken Cinch with her mother, and came on in by myself, even though it was after midnight by the time I got home. Angie was still up. She was sitting at the kitchen table with a cup of tea when I walked in, her eyes red and puffy from crying, and she nearly threw herself into my arms. The last word she'd had was that Jess and I had gone off alone after an Indian war party of upward of two dozen bloodthirsty savages—rumors rising faster than warm dough in those days.

At first, based on what the surviving posse members said, people believed it was Billy leading the war party. A lot of folks continued to believe that even after I tried to set the story straight. Maybe it was the way the news was spread. We had reporters there from all over the country—Chicago, San Francisco, even New York—all of them wanting to know about the Billy Pinto War. I kept telling them it wasn't an uprising, but nobody seemed to listen. Even after all the reporters went home, the story continued to grow.

I decided to run for a second full term after all, even though, if you recall, I was giving serious consideration on the Plateau to quitting the race and finding a job where I could take care of my family without risking my neck to drunks and thugs. What changed my mind was finding out upon my return that United Lumber was making a big push to get their own candidate, Curly Dunn, into office, even going so far as to take out a full-page ad in the Echo City *Echo* accusing me of cowardice and incompetency. Somehow they'd gotten wind of my not going into the Yellowstone Saloon the night Early Jennings and his crew rode into town, and I'll give you one guess as to where they got that lie. [*Editor's Note:* Although no record could be located regarding Pratt's veiled accusation, one assumes he was referring to Carl Hennessy, based on comments made in Session Two.]

Well, you can bet I wasn't going to let that go unchallenged, so the gloves came off and I started campaigning in earnest. It got pretty ugly in the weeks leading up to the election, culminating with a late-October summons from Curly himself to meet me on the street in front of the Yellowstone . . . if I had the grit.

Tom wanted to go with me, but I told him no. It was after dark on a Saturday night, and Curly was already there when I arrived, along with a good portion of the population that didn't have families or business to better occupy their time. Dave Elder, from the *Echo,* and a man named Savage, from the *Denver News,* showed up to cover the contest. It was my good fortune that Curly had been drinking heavily before the slated deadline of six o'clock. He even had a bottle in hand when I got there, which strengthened my position. Curly immediately ordered me to drop my gun and meet him in what he called a *manly manner,* but I didn't have any intention of playing that kind of a game. I told him he was drunk and under arrest for public intoxication, and when he came swaggering toward me making bold threats, I used my pistol to coldcock the son of a bitch. I didn't knock him out all the way, but I had to get a couple of boys to help hold him up for the walk back to the jail.

United made all kinds of accusations about the cowardly way I'd conducted myself. They even took out another ad in the *Echo*—although it was only a two-column spread this time—but the damage to Curly's campaign had been done. Ten days later, I won the election with sixty-four percent of the vote. Harold Davis received eleven percent, with Curly getting the rest. His high numbers didn't surprise me. The grapevine claimed United Lumber was paying a silver dollar to every man who could prove he voted for their candidate; of course, being a closed election, nobody could, so United's management made out like bandits, while the damned fools who voted for Curly didn't get anything.

Angie and I stayed in Echo City until the spring of 1909. I didn't run for office in aught-eight, and after selling our home the following year, we moved to California, where Angie's brother, Mike, got me on with the railroad. We've been here ever since. Now, if you'll excuse me, I hear Humphrey wanting up on the sofa with Angie.

End Transcript

Susan (Stokes) Gibson Interview (Addendum to Hudson Pratt Interview)
Bozeman, Montana
9 March 1936
Begin Gibson Transcript

Thank you so much for coming. You don't know how excited I was when I received your letter last month, informing me of your interview with Sheriff Pratt. I'll confess to some hesitation with your interest in my time with Billy, but after thinking about it, I decided I wanted to clarify parts of the story that I don't believe even Mister Pratt is aware of.

In our telephone conversation last week, we discussed Billy's last hours at the Mule Ears, and how Sheriff Pratt felt he was forced to return Billy's fire, which, as we know, cost the younger man his life. It's that part of the story that I want you to record with your Dictaphone. Hopefully, it will resolve the question of Billy's motives in my abduction, as well as his flight across the Plateau.

I'm sure you recall Sheriff Pratt's encounter with Billy under the westernmost Ear, and how Billy appeared so suddenly at the cavern's entrance. I've wondered since we spoke if Mister Pratt was able to articulate his feelings at that moment. Was he startled? Or was he petrified with fear, as I was? As an observer of the incident, I can assure you that he would have been justified in either emotion. Unfortunately for both the sheriff and Billy, neither was necessary. Let me tell you why.

It's true that Billy Pinto abducted me from my grandfather's ranch. We were not, and never had been, lovers, as some of the more lurid accounts have hinted at. I was still a child, although approaching womanhood, when Billy entered my life and changed it forever. [*Editor's Note:* Susan (Stokes) Gibson returned to her home in Cheyenne after her rescue in 1904. Eight years later, she joined the Bureau of Indian Affairs as a stenographer, then quit the organization in 1914 to attend Smith College, with an emphasis on Cultural Rights. After graduation, she and several classmates founded the Friends of Tribes Society, providing legal and social services to families and individuals on reservations throughout the United States. Stokes married attorney Wilbur Gibson in 1924; they divorced two years later. Susan Gibson remained single afterward, and devoted to her cause throughout her life. She passed away peacefully in her sleep in 1971.]

We—meaning my siblings and myself—were wandering the creek bank behind Grandfather's barn when Billy appeared out of the willows. He frightened each of us, but Molly most of all. Molly O'Brien was our *au pair,* a delightful girl from Ireland, although I suspect, now that I'm an adult, that she felt somewhat overwhelmed by her responsibilities. Nevertheless, she was devoted to us children, and as soon as Billy appeared, she stepped in front of us with her arms spread wide, instructing us to stay behind her and remain calm. [*Editor's Note:* Molly O'Brien was fired by Henry Lynn within twelve hours of Susan Stokes's abduction. Without family and nearly broke, she found employment in Echo City as a waitress at Mae's Café. In 1905 she married San Pedro County Deputy Sheriff Thomas Schiffer; the couple had three children between 1906 and 1911. Thomas Schiffer continued as deputy under Hudson Pratt through the latter's second full term as sheriff, then ran for the office himself in 1908. After a resounding win, Schiffer held the office until San Pedro County was dissolved through redistricting in 1918. Afterward, the couple and their children moved to Casper, Wyoming, where Thomas and Molly resided until their deaths in the 1960s.]

I remember how Billy seemed as surprised to see us as we were to see him, and how he was starting to ride wide around us until Molly ordered him to leave that very instant, else risk incurring the judge's wrath. That was when Billy stopped and turned toward us. I very clearly remember him asking Molly to repeat her demand. When she did, he asked if she was speaking about Judge Henry Lynn, and Molly said she was.

I'll confess to quite a chill running through me when Billy looked at me. I wanted to curl up and hide under a rock, but of course that was impossible. By this time Molly was shouting for help, and we could hear Mister Burton hollering that he was on his way. Unfortunately, the ranch foreman wasn't overly cautious in his approach. Billy saw him coming through the trees and quickly dismounted with his rifle. When Mister Burton came through the brush, very much like a rushing bear, Billy struck him a frightful blow to the head.

It was then that Billy grabbed me by an arm and forced me into his saddle. He crawled up behind me and put his arm around my stomach to prevent me from attempting to escape, although I was so terrified by then that flight never even occurred to me. Billy forced his horse close to where Molly stood and spoke to her in very earnest terms. He told her to tell Sheriff Pratt that grandfather was to *"buck up,"* and take my abduction like a man. Of course, it wasn't until much later that I learned the significance of those words, and what they must have meant to Billy.

We fled then, Billy and I, and to all those whose thoughts seek the very lowest denominator, no, I was not molested by Billy Pinto, nor anyone else. In fact, I don't believe Billy was even aware that there were other Indians on the Plateau. I do know I never felt truly threatened by him. Certainly I was afraid, but Billy was never anything but kind and thoughtful to my well-being—for instance, did Sheriff Pratt tell you how Billy fashioned a sort of poncho dress for me to wear when the weather turned cold? He made it out of a blanket, and it was very comfortable.

I think Billy realized early on that taking me hostage was a mistake. My abduction clearly wasn't planned. It was simply a crime of opportunity, created largely from a chance remark from our governess. But with my kidnapping, Billy understood there would never be any escape for him. The murder of the three men who had killed his mother might have been ignored had he continued his own flight, and he later confessed to me that had been his original intent. It was why he took Mister Gifford's horse, and why he kept Jennings's mount when he got the opportunity to seize it. Two saddled horses to aid in his flight, but it was all for naught, wasn't it?

I won't waste space on your recording disks with mindless prattle about our route across the Plateau. The truth is, I remember very little of it. What stands out is the incredible vastness of the forests, how cold it got at night, and the anxious way Billy kept looking back over his shoulder.

We reached the cavern the night before Billy's rendezvous with Sheriff Pratt, but we were already aware of some kind of altercation on top of Porcupine Ridge. Billy's mood changed drastically after listening to those distant gunshots. They seemed to convince him that pursuit was not only inevitable, it was also a lot closer than he'd anticipated.

It was his decision to stop at the pass between the Mule Ears. When he spotted Sheriff Pratt guiding his horse along that treacherous route into the basin, something seemed to just flow out of him. It was as if his spirit somehow deflated, right there before my eyes. I didn't ask what troubled him. Although he'd speak to me from time to time, and I would reply when I felt a response was appropriate, I never initiated a conversation.

When Billy saw the sheriff approaching, he came back into

the cavern and sat there for the longest time. It was as if he was considering his options, and found them wanting. Then, with his every move an act of reluctance, he stripped off his shirt and loosened his hair. He brought out the rifle he'd taken from Jennings and removed all but two of the cartridges from its magazine.

It was puzzling at the time, but significant in hindsight. Gathering the ejected cartridges, Billy threw them into the trees south of the cavern's entrance. Then he returned and sat on the ground with his back to me. I thought at first he was speaking to himself, but I soon realized he was chanting. It was his Death Chant, you see, and those words should be capitalized, as it was a very special element to his religion.

Then, without even a backward glance, Billy moved to the mouth of the cave. He waited there until Sheriff Pratt was well advanced along the side of the Ear. That was when he jumped to his feet and shouted his war cry, as chilling a sound as any I've ever heard. It still sends goosebumps down both my arms when I hear it in my mind, usually at night, right before I fall asleep. I recall whimpering at the time, and scooting farther back into the cavern. Billy fired his rifle twice—twice, and only that. It was all the bullets he'd left in his rifle, but he didn't fire them at the sheriff. He fired into the trees, well above Mister Pratt's head. He did so deliberately, you see? A means of bringing to a conclusion what he must have felt could only end one way. Sheriff Pratt reacted as any responsible lawman would, and Billy's ordeal . . . his ordeal, sir, not his war, was brought to a close.

That's the part of Billy Pinto's story that I suspect Sheriff Pratt isn't aware of. I've debated for years whether it's information I should share with him. Would he want to know he killed a man—a boy, in reality—when death wasn't necessary? My instinct has always told me he wouldn't, yet I've always felt the knowledge of that final conflict was too important to be lost forever. Someone, somewhere, needs to know what really happened in those final few minutes. So perhaps now you can see why I was so happy when you contacted me. This knowledge should be shared, and with its telling, hopefully, the fable of Billy Pinto's War will finally be laid to rest.

End Gibson Transcript

Obituary from: Calaveras City *Recorder* May 12, 1956 Hudson James Pratt May 6, 1874–May 10, 1956

Hudson "Hud" Pratt, of this city, passed away at the home of his daughter on Sunday afternoon. He was eighty-two.

Pratt was a thirty-five-year resident of Calaveras City, having moved here with his family in 1921. Although described by friends and neighbors as an "unassuming fellow," the *Recorder* has learned that he was a veteran of the Cuban-American War, and was with former President Theodore "Teddy" Roosevelt's Rough Riders on their gallant charge up San Juan Hill. Pratt later enjoyed a distinguished career as a lawman during our country's Frontier Era, and was a key figure in the infamous Billy Pinto War, during the early years of this century.

Despite his fame as a soldier and Indian fighter, in his later years Pratt was active in numerous activities promoting American Indian causes. He was considered an honored friend of several local tribes, and often asked to speak on their behalf at city and state levels.

Pratt is survived by his daughter, Lillian Ann (Pratt) Applegate, of Calaveras City; a son, Colonel Cory James Pratt (US Army, retired), of Sacramento; five grandchildren; and thirteen great-grandchildren. Mister Pratt was preceded in death by a daughter, Jennifer Allison Pratt; his wife of forty-seven years, Angela (Angie) Pratt; and a "giant-hearted" basset hound named Humphrey.

Services will be held at the Calaveras City Mortuary at nine a.m. on the fifteenth; interment will follow at ten a.m. The family asks that in lieu of flowers, a donation be made to the Jennifer Pratt Scholarship Fund for American Indians, located at the Calaveras Indian School, where Mister and Missus Pratt often volunteered as teaching assistants.

R.I.P., Old Friend

ABOUT THE AUTHOR

Michael Zimmer is the author of sixteen previous novels. His work has been praised by *Library Journal, Publishers Weekly, Booklist, Historical Novel Society,* and others. *The Poacher's Daughter* (Five Star, 2014) was the recipient of the 2015 Wrangler Award for Outstanding Western Novel from the National Cowboy and Western Heritage Museum; it received a Starred Review from *Booklist,* was included in True West Magazine's *Best of the West* (January 2015), and was a Spur Finalist from the Western Writers of America. *City of Rocks* (Five Star, 2012) was chosen by *Booklist* as one of the top ten Western novels of 2012. *Rio Tinto* and *Leaving Yuma* have also won awards. Zimmer resides in Utah with his wife Vanessa, and two dogs. His Web site is www.michael-zimmer.com.

The employees of Five Star Publishing hope you have enjoyed this book.

Our Five Star novels explore little-known chapters from America's history, stories told from unique perspectives that will entertain a broad range of readers.

Other Five Star books are available at your local library, bookstore, all major book distributors, and directly from Five Star/Gale.

Connect with Five Star Publishing

Visit us on Facebook:
https://www.facebook.com/FiveStarCengage

Email:
FiveStar@cengage.com

For information about titles and placing orders:
(800) 223-1244
gale.orders@cengage.com

To share your comments, write to us:
Five Star Publishing
Attn: Publisher
10 Water St., Suite 310
Waterville, ME 04901